D1063291

THE GOBLIN WARS
WARS

PART ONE
Siege of Talonrend

an epic fantasy adventure by

Stuart Thaman

All rights reserved. No part of this publication may be reproduced, distributed or transmitted in any form or by any means, including photocopying, recording, or other electronic or mechanical methods, without the prior written permission of the publisher, except in the case of brief quotations embodied in critical reviews and certain other noncommercial uses permitted by copyright law. For permission requests, write to the publisher, addressed "Attention: Permissions Coordinator," at the email address below:

Nef House Publishing
stuartthaman@gmail.com

Publisher's Note: This is a work of fiction. Names, characters, places, and incidents are a product of the author's imagination. Locales and public names are sometimes used for atmospheric purposes. Any resemblance to actual people, living or dead, or to businesses, companies, events, institutions, or locales is completely coincidental.

Ordering Information:
Quantity sales. Special discounts are available on quantity purchases by corporations, associations, and others. For details, contact the "Special Sales Department" at the email address above.

Copyright © 2013, 2016 by Stuart Thaman

Cover design by J. Caleb Clark
www.jcalebdesign.com

The Goblin Wars Series, Part One: Siege of Talonrend /
Stuart Thaman – 1st ed.
ISBN-13: 978-0615935751 | ISBN-10: 0615935753

For Darling, my muse.

THE
GOBLIN
WARS

PART ONE

Siege of Talonrend

I N THE SHADOWY depths at the center of Kanebullar Mountain, Lady Scrapple writhed with excitement. She was queen of the goblin race, Mistress of the Mountain, and had worked for centuries to bring her greatest plan to fruition.

Utilizing the hive mind she had magically constructed among her kin, she peered through the eyes of a goblin several miles from her mountain lair. The goblin was nameless, an expendable drone created specifically by Lady Scrapple to serve a singular purpose as one of her many scouts.

The goblin crouched low on a rooftop in the center of a village which the humans called Cobblestreet. It watched, its eyes only moving when

Lady Scrapple commanded them. The humans moved about their lives in complete ignorance.

Even if her scout was seen, it would not matter. Surely, the humans would kill any goblin on sight, but the Mistress of the Mountain was not concerned. Hundreds of new goblins were born every week, growing from huge tentacles that spread out through the ground from Lady Scrapple's massive body.

Each goblin began as a tiny bud, an outgrowth of flesh from the queen's own body, and rose up through the bedrock of Kanebullar Mountain like some sort of grotesque flower. After only a few weeks of gestation, the budding goblin cocoon would split open, revealing a fully formed offspring ready to serve the hive.

Though her mind was vast, Lady Scrapple did not possess the strength or will to directly control every action of every goblin in her mountain. Instead, she created a semblance of free will to occupy their minds, and that imitation of autonomy had led to the development of society within the mountain.

Lady Scrapple turned her attention back to her scout in Cobblestreet. *They don't suspect a thing,* she mused. For nothing but her own amusement, she made the goblin jump down from the rooftop to reveal itself.

Humans shrieked and ran into their buildings out of fear, but not all of them. Only the women and children feared a single goblin enough to run. Several nearby human males rushed at the goblin. One of them had a sword, but the others only balled their fists. She could have commanded her scout to run or to fight back, but Lady Scrapple's concern for a single individual was nonexistent.

In a moment, the humans had knocked her goblin to the ground and slit its throat. Fearfully, they remained on their guard and searched the nearby buildings for other goblins. Lady Scrapple relished their response. The humans considered goblins to be so easy to kill that they would not even alert their city guard. She knew she could send an entire score of goblins to the village without humanity understanding the severity of the actual threat against them.

That disrespect fueled her plan.

When the real war began, humanity would not be ready. They would see goblins moving on the horizon, but they would not prepare their army. They would send soldiers to kill the goblins, but they would never send enough.

Humanity would not be ready.

III

One

G RAVLOX MADE HIS way slowly through the tight quarters of a dark mineshaft. His goblin eyes were well-adjusted to the lightless bowels of the mountain, but he still had trouble identifying the goblin standing before him.

"Have you found the vein?" the miner asked. Even by goblin standards, his voice was thin and high-pitched. Gravlox recognized him as Blabar, one of the other foremen.

Gravlox rubbed his calloused hands together. "Not yet," he replied. "Perhaps we will find it tomorrow."

"I heard a rumor that might interest you," Blabar continued, lowering his voice despite the two of them being alone.

1

"Oh?" Gravlox prompted. He had never particularly enjoyed the deception and treachery so loved by his kin, but he understood the value of secrets.

Blabar snickered. "One of the miners in the eastern tunnel found a pool of mercury this morning. You know what that means," he let his voice trail off, allowing Gravlox to make his own conclusion.

"Where there is mercury, there is gold," Gravlox finished. Though the maxim did not always hold true, Gravlox was becoming desperate. The section of tunnels he oversaw had not struck a gold vein in months.

"I know the name of the goblin who found the mercury," Blabar whispered, a sinister smile plastered to his pale face.

Gravlox let out a heavy sigh. "I don't want to hurt anyone," he said. "It shouldn't have to come to that."

Blabar ran a dirty hand through his already greasy, dust-filled hair. "I've also heard he hasn't reported the location of the vein to his foreman. He might be waiting to entertain offers. Let me kill him before he gets the chance."

Gravlox mulled the idea over in his head. In all his years as a foreman, he had never taken another goblin life with his own hands, though he had ordered several assassinations to be carried out. "You know what it means if the miner's death is tied to our coterie?"

"Of course, Gravlox," Blabar reassured him. "We can use a different poison, one that will point to a different mine."

"Misdirection?" Gravlox wondered aloud. "It could work. If we only had the resources to buy him off and take the vein for ourselves," he murmured to himself. "Killing is risky."

"But you have me," Blabar cooed. "And I have never been caught."

Gravlox knew he was right, but the notion didn't bring him any comfort. How easy would it be for Blabar to remove him and take control of the mining operation himself? Perhaps it was that very fear which made him acquiesce.

"So," Gravlox replied with a nod. "Which poison do you have in mind?"

"The north tunnel already has a reputation for using Heart-Stopper, but the ingredients are extremely rare. We could use something more mundane, but the risk would be higher." Blabar knew how Gravlox would respond.

"We will use the Heart-Stopper," he said at once. "We do it perfectly or we don't do it at all."

Blabar nodded his head in excitement. "Once we poison him, we can send our own miners into his tunnel to find the mercury for ourselves."

"Of course," Gravlox said. He was filled with trepidation, but didn't see any other choice before him. If he appeared weak to a subordinate, especially one so apt in the art of murder, he would not survive long. On the other hand, if his mine continued to fail, he would be replaced by his own superiors before long.

Blabar handed him a rolled piece of paper which Gravlox quickly deposited in one of his many pockets. "Bring me the ingredients when you can," he said.

Gravlox shook the goblin's hand and departed, ready to begin work on his new task before he could change his mind.

An hour or so later, Gravlox arrived in the cave he called home.

"If only I had magic," he lamented, looking over the ingredients list. The goblin race was not known to frequently possess magic, but powerful shaman were occasionally born who could bend the elements to their will. Such power would make a poisoning like the one Gravlox planned obsolete.

"Yes, this poison will be very hard to acquire," Gravlox said.

Pulling a small clump of cave moss from a jar to eat as he went, Gravlox left his cave and started back toward the center of the mountain.

The center of Kanebullar Mountain contained a system of storehouses and businesses cut into the stone, a vast area full of goblins going about their day. Gravlox ducked into one of the first cave openings, a general store he frequented often.

Behind the counter, a female goblin waved to Gravlox as he entered. "Hi, Grav," she said with a smile.

"Hello, Vorst," Gravlox responded. She was smaller than him, if only by a couple inches, and she possessed a melodious voice full of life which Gravlox found intoxicating.

"How's it going?" she asked, moving from behind the counter to stand next to him.

"Pretty well," Gravlox responded, smiling. "I only need a few things," he said, not wanting to give away his intention. He drew the list out of his pocket and slowly unfolded it, treating the object like some revered artifact. "Do you have any spotted lizards?" he asked, looking around the cluttered shop.

"I think so, what do you need them for?" Vorst responded, pointing to a small cage filled with lizards at the back of the cave.

"Oh, just a new recipe I want to try," he lied. He felt bad deceiving his friend, but he couldn't be too careful. "What kind of lizards do you sell?" As much as he tried, he couldn't keep the nervousness from his voice.

"We have the ones with yellow spots and the ones with orange spots. Here, let me get you a bag." Vorst grabbed a burlap sack from behind the counter and moved to the cage, reaching in to grab a few lizards. "What kind of recipe is this for? Most people don't like the taste of lizard."

"I need the ones with orange spots, two of them, please," Gravlox said, trying hard to think of a recipe that might call for lizards. He was never known as a good cook and he didn't know many recipes off the top of his head. "I'm making… a soup. Yes, of course, it's a new recipe that one of the miner's wives taught me today. Soup with bits of ground up lizard, among other things."

"You know that the lizards with the orange spots are poisonous, right?" she questioned. "You can only eat their eyes and heads. Their bellies will make you sick." Gravlox panicked in his mind, thinking that his plot was discovered.

"Yes, well…" The foreman stumbled over his words, trying to avoid Vorst's gaze. "If you prepare them right and heat them high enough, it should boil the toxins out, so the recipe says." It was a pretty convincing lie, Gravlox told himself. Luckily, it seemed to work.

"Oh, that sounds pretty interesting, Grav, you'll have to let me come over and try it when it's done," Vorst said with a warm smile. Gravlox hated it when she called him Grav. It felt so personal. It wasn't that Gravlox didn't want Vorst to think of him that way, he just wasn't used to it.

"Sure thing," he replied casually, picking a few other things off of the shelves in the store and taking them to the counter. He was able to find almost everything for his poison in her shop and also bought himself a leg of mutton to eat that night.

"I should have asked her to come eat dinner at my cave tonight," Gravlox mumbled to himself as he exited the store. He had never found the courage to ask Vorst to do anything with him. He always did all of his shopping in her store, but that was about as far as the relationship went.

Gravlox's cave felt lonely that night. He spread out the ingredients for his poison on the small wooden table in the center of the damp cavern. He had two lizards with orange spots, a bushel of hibiscus leaves, some odd looking cave mushrooms, and little pouch containing a fine brown powder that supposedly came from bats that had been ground between rocks.

He sat on a three-legged stool and looked over the ingredients. "Only one thing left," he whispered over his shaking hands.

He contemplated his decision for a long moment, questioning his bravery and resolve. Gravlox was startled out of his sullen thoughts by a quick knock on the door. Panicking, he looked around the small hovel for something to use to cover the ingredients on his table. Frantically searching for a solution, Gravlox knocked over a jar of mead from a shelf and sent it shattering to the floor.

The door to his cave opened behind the scrambling goblin which set his heart to racing. Gravlox feared that his chest would explode from the adrenaline in his veins.

"Hey Grav!" came the beautiful voice from the doorway. Gravlox slowly stood, turned around, and tried to hide his embarrassment.

"Hey Vorst, what are you doing here?" he sputtered, trying hard to use his body to block the table of poison ingredients. "I mean, it's nice to see you here…" Gravlox managed to say. His eyes intently scanned the floor.

"Is everything alright?" Vorst asked with concern in her voice. "I heard something shatter, what is going on in here?" She peered behind Gravlox to the table and inspected the mess on the floor. "What are you doing, Grav?"

"Oh, nothing," Gravlox said past a growing lump in his throat. "Just getting ready to test out that recipe, you know." Even as he said it, he knew he wasn't very convincing.

"Um, Gravlox, I hate to pry, but who are you planning on killing? I work at a shop that sells reagents for poisons, you know. I can tell a would-be assassin when I see one." She grinned from ear to ear, moving around the stunned goblin to look closer at the table. "I hope it isn't me," she whispered to Gravlox jokingly.

"How do you even know where I live?" the foreman sputtered, confused and taken aback. The cool demeanor with which Vorst spoke about his plan was unnerving.

"I followed you, silly. After you left my shop, I just walked behind you. You were so nervous, you never saw me. I'm curious; tell me who you plan on killing!" Gravlox was so entranced by Vorst's beautiful voice that he barely understood the words she spoke.

Gravlox unrolled the paper Blabar had given him and showed it to her.

Vorst took a moment to go over the list and found all the ingredients except for one already assembled on the table. "This poison is pretty intricate," she said, looking Gravlox in the eyes as she spoke. "Are you sure you know what you are doing?"

Slowly, Gravlox began to nod. "Yes. It needs to be done. If the mine is to survive, we must take things into our own hands. I'm ready." It was as confident as the foreman had ever sounded in his life, and his own words terrified him.

"Well then," Vorst said, putting a hand on the male goblin's shoulder, "let's go get that last ingredient together. What is it…" her finger traced down the list, looking for the final item. "Necrotic dust? I'm not even sure what that means!" The look of surprise on Vorst's face was almost as profound as that of Gravlox.

"I think we have to get that from a necromancer," Gravlox replied, not sure what to say.

"Let's go find ourselves a necromancer and get some dust. We leave in the morning. I'll meet you here." With that, Vorst bounded from the cave and left Gravlox standing in front of his table with a baffled expression plastered to his face.

"What have I done?" he questioned. His plan had been revealed so easily. He trusted Vorst not to sell him out, but where would they find the dust they needed? In all his years, he had never even left Kanebullar Mountain.

Two

*Y*OU WILL NEVER *be king. You will never sit upon your brother's throne. Your fate is not in this kingdom. Your destiny has been written elsewhere. You will never be king.* The dreams were always the same. He shifted and rolled in the over-sized bed, always restless, with the voice of his god echoing in his skull. Herod Firesbane had endured the same dream for nearly thirty years, every single night. *You will never be king. You will never sit upon your brother's throne. Your fate is not in this kingdom. Your destiny has been written elsewhere. You will never be king.*

When Herod was born, he was taken to the Oracle of Vrysinoch to have his destiny foretold. Like his older brother before him, Herod had received a favorable prophecy. The wrinkled and decrepit oracle told his parents that Herod would grow to be tall, strong, handsome, intelligent, and brave, just like his brother. The Oracle of Vrysinoch proclaimed that Herod would one day inherit his brother's kingdom. King Lucius Firesbane, Herod's older brother, had been destined to die in combat before producing any heirs, according to the oracle.

As long as Herod could remember, he had haunting dreams of the moment the oracle spoke over him. He was just an infant, barely a month old, but he saw the moment vividly in his mind. His parents, the former king and queen of Talonrend, held him before the oracle, deep within the castle that was their home. Castle Talon, the seat of the monarchy, was built over an extensive system of caves and underground rivers. In the deepest cave, miles beneath the surface, stood the most holy place in the entire kingdom: the Temple of Vrysinoch. Other than the oracle, no one was allowed to enter the temple at any moment. The prophecy of a new-born prince was one of the few exceptions.

The king and queen stood underneath a great marble statue of their god, the winged Vrysinoch, and placed the newborn prince into the stone bowl at the statue's feet. Vrysinoch's likeness stood forty feet tall in the dark cavern, his four angelic wings spread out to encircle the entire temple with their jagged ends forming the doorway. The deity held a sword in one hand with half of the blade buried deep in the stone at the statue's feet. His other hand grasped an emerald the size of a boulder, raising it up toward the ceiling of the cavern as if presenting the sacred relic to the world. The emerald shimmered in the palm of Vrysinoch's hand and bathed the cavern in an eerie green light.

The oracle had spoken his prophecy, much to the delight of the king and queen, but a different prophecy had been spoken directly to Herod. *You will never be king. You will never sit upon your brother's throne. Your fate is not in this kingdom. Your destiny has been written elsewhere. You will never be king.* It was the voice of his god, Vrysinoch, sounding in the mind of the young prince. Herod heard the voice every single night for his entire life, always the same, always calmly telling him that he will never reign.

The restless prince of Talonrend awoke in his bed with beads of sweat staining his pillow. He looked up, gazing from his sheets to the white canopy that hung on the ceiling of his bedchamber. The unrelenting gaze of Vrysinoch met the pained eyes of Herod, causing the prince to turn away. A white tapestry displaying the visage of Talonrend's winged god was a common adornment above almost every bed in the kingdom. The canopies were meant to bring good luck, and the overly zealous priests in every village and hamlet made sure that images of Vrysinoch could be easily seen. The tapestry in the chamber of Prince Herod served only to torment the haunted man.

Herod stood and rubbed the weariness from his eyes. He slid his cold feet into a pair of animal skin slippers and stretched his back. His bedchamber was located right next to the royal reception hall that housed the throne. That was perhaps the worst part of his daily awakening, walking past the empty throne where his brother was supposed to sit and reign. The old king and queen from Herod's dreams were long since buried in the royal mausoleum, enjoying their eternal flight through the heavens on the wings of Vrysinoch.

Herod's brother, Prince Lucius Firesbane, ascended to the throne in his late twenties, ruling the kingdom through an age of unrivaled prosperity. Then, one spring, King Lucius set out to travel with one of the kingdom's many trade caravans, a wagon train of resources and finished goods leaving Talonrend and heading south to do business with the various villages along the Clawflow River. Lucius always believed that a great king must walk among his subjects. The trading caravans were the best way to mingle with the common folk.

That caravan was over a year ago. His trips usually lasted a few months or a season at the most. No word ever came back about the King's whereabouts; no traveler from the south ever said a word about the king passing through. It is as if the king of Talonrend disappeared.

Herod stopped a moment before opening the iron-banded door of his bedchamber. His tabard hung on peg next to the door and a pair of swords dangled in their sheaths underneath the cloth. An array of training weapons, some dulled and some with edges fine enough to shave with, leaned in a wooden rack next to the door. Herod glanced at the two swords hanging on the peg as he pulled the tabard over his head. A fine layer of dust coated the leather belt and the two sheaths. The weapons, a matched pair of enchanted swords crafted by Talonrend's most respected smith, had not moved in years. The training weapons were covered in pits and dents from countless hours of martial practice but the enchanted swords, Maelstrom and Regret by name, had never been drawn. Herod mulled over the idea of strapping the swords onto his waist and setting out to find his lost brother himself. The prince shook his head. The idea was fleeting and fled his mind as soon as he opened the door and walked into the throne room.

"Good morning, sir. Sleep well?" The king's steward was always awake before anyone in the castle and eternally in a good mood. Something about the way in which the young servant conducted himself, being perfectly dressed and composed day after day, bothered Herod. The steward was too clean, too well dressed, and too handsome. It was disconcerting for Herod to see the man every day when he woke up. The prince had always been cautious though, seeing a treasonous spy from another kingdom behind every smiling face.

"Yes, of course. I slept just as well last night as the night before. It's getting to be damned cold in that room though. Tell someone to bring up the winter sheets from storage." Prince Herod tried to wave the eager steward away as he took a seat at the long table beneath his brother's empty throne.

"Yes, I fear that the nights are becoming a bit chilly," the steward replied, standing uncomfortably close to the prince. "Perhaps, if my king would prefer to have a woman warm his bed, or even a wife to give the kingdom an heir—" Herod slammed his fist into the large wooden table and made bowls and platters of food shake from the force.

"This is the last time I am going to tell you this!" Herod screamed, far beyond his breaking point with the annoying steward. "I am not going to marry or produce any sort of legitimate or illegitimate heir to my brother's throne! It is impossible! I am NOT the king!" He accentuated the word 'not' with a slam of his fist, this time into the chest of the unsuspecting steward. "Lucius still reigns in Talonrend. I merely serve as his regent until his return. No progeny of mine will ever rule from that throne."

The kingdom was in disarray without Lucius to lead them. Everyone assumed that he was dead or never planning on returning. The people looked to Herod to lead them. Every time anyone in the castle referred to him as their king or bowed before him, Herod heard the soft words of Vrysinoch echoing through his head—*you will never be king*. With every decree and edict that Prince Herod signed in his brother's name, the winged god reminded him of his fate. *You will never sit upon your brother's throne.* The words tormented him and relentlessly coursed through his brain.

Herod grabbed a small chunk of bread and shoved the rest of his food away. He rose from the table, motioning for the castle's guard commander to join him. Darius, clad in his usual coat of mail with a great helm by his side, stood at once and walked next to the troubled prince. "Did you have another dream from Vrysinoch, my liege?" He asked, falling into step with Herod.

"The same as always, Darius. It never changes." The two of them walked out of the castle and onto the immense wooden drawbridge. Herod stopped next to one of the many banners that bordered the castle walls and leaned against the parapet, gazing out into the morning.

"If my god does not wish for me to rule this kingdom, why is it that my brother has not returned from his journey? Where is Lucius? Why has there been no word of his trip from anyone?" Herod began to tear little bits of bread from his chunk and toss them into the moat below. Feeding the ducks that lived in the moat was always comforting to Herod. Even when he was a little boy, Herod would save some portion of his meal and take it out to the ducks. Something about the way they ate the scraps that he dropped into the moat was serene and calming. The ducks had no idea that Herod was tormented. They didn't understand the dilemma that the kingdom was forced to endure. They simply ate little scraps of food and kept on swimming.

"I have no answer for you, Herod. I have never heard the voice of Vrysinoch. I go to the temple al-

19

most every day and pray that Vrysinoch guides my path, but I fear that the words of the priests are as close to god as I can get. Most men in the realm would give their arm to hear the voice of Vrysinoch." The captain of the guard set his helmet down atop the parapet where the morning sun made the polished metal shine. Darius rubbed his fingers on the hilt of his short sword and wondered why Vrysinoch had never spoken to him. The sword, his symbol of office, had a hilt carved into the image of a bird's claw. The sharp talons ended in a small emerald that was the symbol of the kingdom's religion.

"Look out at the city, Darius. All the houses, all the people going about their lives, look at them." Herod spread his arm out wide and soaked in the sight of his brother's kingdom. Castle Talon had been built on the closest thing to a hill in a hundred miles. Its foundation stood only twenty or thirty feet above the rest of the kingdom, but it was enough elevation to give a fantastic view of the city. The most prominent structure, the Tower of Wings, which served as the public temple to Vrysinoch at the heart of the city, was always magnificent in the bright morning sun.

Rising a hundred feet above the ground, the beautiful work of art was a pillar of sculptures more than it was a temple. Priests had constructed the building out of black stone taken from the caves under Castle Talon. Somehow, the cold black stone reflected the bright light of the sun with a searing intensity while at the same time offering a sort of translucent quality to the tower. Anyone looking at the tower would feel blinded by the light reflected from the walls but, at the same moment, they could see all the way through the walls to the other side. Not even the priests could explain the phenomenon without calling it a miracle.

The tower was intricately carved, every single inch of the exterior walls being crafted into wings. The wings wrapped around the whole building, interlocking with one another, to form a perfectly cylindrical tower. The top of the structure resembled the hilt of the guard captain's sword, a talon clutching an emerald.

The most interesting part of the city, at least in Herod's mind, was the wall. It was formally named the Wall of Lucius but the common folk all referred to the massive defensive structure as Terror's Lament. The wall, designed and built at the hand of Lucius, was an amazing work of military genius. It rose sixty feet above the city, a monstrous behemoth of smooth stone. Terror's Lament was so much more than just a tall barrier to guard the city. It was actually constructed of three walls, the outermost and innermost being a full sixty feet in height. The wall in the center was only forty feet high, and, instead of having a flat walkway on the top for archers and other soldiers to be stationed, it tapered into a rounded edge no wider than a few inches.

Any invader would first be tasked with scaling the smooth outer wall, climbing the full sixty feet with either a ladder or ropes. The ascent would be made under the direct fire of archers from the walls and ballistae from the towers that marked the corners of the square city. The inside face of the outermost wall was covered in barbed spikes, set at an angle to catch anyone attempting to jump or rappel down to the ground. The shorter and rounded middle wall had much the same defenses as the exterior wall. It was smooth on the side facing away from the city but held an array of upward reaching spikes on the interior face.

The interior wall, the thickest of the three, was hollow. It contained hundreds of archer slots, ballistae dotting the top of its parapet, and two thick chains attached to either side of each section. The chains were stretched taut from the top of each tower, two on each exterior face of the four sides of the square wall. At the end of each chain dangled a solid iron ball, covered in tiny dimples. The chains could be released from the ball end, causing the heavy metal to sweep like a pendulum down the face of the wall, clearing all invaders attempting to climb into the city. Although those defense mechanisms had never been used, many of the guards had taken bets on how far an unfortunate soldier would be thrown by the massive iron balls as they swung.

Further adding to the city's seemingly impregnable defenses, a maze of sorts was constructed for all of the traffic moving through the wall's gates. Only two gates existed that would take anyone beyond the walls altogether, but several other gates were present between the layers. None of them ever lined up evenly with another gate at a different layer and all were spaced far enough apart to prevent a battering ram from being able to turn and maneuver. The reason for the intricate defenses wasn't because of any sort of impending doom or overt threat to the city, but was merely a result of King Lucius' desire to protect his people at all costs. The resources and labor were available, so the king had the walls constructed.

Lucius always wanted to be remembered by the name King Lucius the Builder, but of late he was only referred to as King Lucius the Missing.

Prince Herod let his gaze fall, settling back on the ducks swimming around the moat. "What are we going to do, Darius? I fear that if I proclaim my brother to be lost and take his throne, Vrysinoch will strike me down before I make it up the steps to the royal seat. That is my dilemma."

The wizened guard captain had been pondering that circumstance for weeks now, ever since Herod confided in him. "I do not know, sir. I would not want to be the one to make your decision. We can probably delay any sort of action until a second year has passed without sign of your brother. I do not know how long the peasants will be satisfied, having a regent ruling over them and collecting their taxes." Darius started to inch his sword out of its scabbard, a nervous tick that betrayed the fear behind his calm eyes.

"It isn't the peasants that I am worried about. How long will it be before word of a leaderless city reaches the ears of those who would do us harm? It isn't another kingdom I fear, Darius. We are on the frontier! There isn't another city large enough to have an army within two hundred miles. But that is exactly what I fear." The prince clenched his fist, crumbling the remaining piece of bread to crumbs in his hand.

"What do you mean, sir? We don't have much contact with the other castles of the realm and I know of none that wish us ill will," the dutiful captain replied.

"The monsters, they are who I fear, the creatures that live in the wilderness." The prince let the ball of bread crumbs fall into the water below and pointed at Kanebullar Mountain, far on the horizon. "There. That is where evil lurks. We are the only castle that the villains of the wilds have ever seen. We are their only enemy, the only beacon that holds the darkness at bay. When my ancestors left the Green City, they followed a prophet for years until they found this spot. People flocked to their cause, blindly pursuing the dreams of a religious zealot. That is why I fear the monsters of the wilds so much. If they come against us in force and breach our walls, no rescue will ever come." He let his hand fall back to his side, brushing the remaining crumbs off of his tabard.

"Let us pray that Vrysinoch will never let an enemy breach our walls. The only creatures of the night who would dare to risk Terror's Lament are the goblins, too stupid to know any better. In the twenty years since the wall's construction, the goblins are the only enemies who have tried to attack our city." Darius put a hand on his prince's shoulder, hoping to comfort him and bring him some sort of peace, however fleeting it may be.

"Yes, I know. Those walls should stand for hundreds of years. No land army could ever climb our walls or knock them down..." Herod envisioned the death that would accompany such an attack and shuddered. "What would happen if the goblins, in league with some necromancer or powerful wizard, were able to summon and control a dragon? Will our walls save us from that? A million goblins? That is an army we could destroy against our gates. A thousand goblins with a single dragon? That is an army that would surely consume our city in a matter of moments." Herod turned to walk back inside the castle, his voice shaking with worry.

"Then perhaps it is time to test the words of Vrysinoch. Sit on the throne and take your brother's place. Claim your birthright. The coronation of a new king in Talonrend would show the wilds that we are not leaderless. They will fear the might with which you rule your lands," Darius told him plainly.

"Crossbows," Herod called back to the drawbridge where Darius stood. "Start training your troops to use longer-ranged crossbows. We need something that can kill a dragon." Herod walked into the castle and let the heavy doors of the keep close behind him.

"I know we need something to stop a dragon, but a crossbow won't do it, my liege," Darius mumbled to the morning air. "I will go to the artificers and the craftsmen and see if they have any better ideas than crossbows." The guard captain made his way down the drawbridge and into the city with his eyes cautiously darting up toward the sky to look for signs of fire.

Still mindlessly playing with the hilt of his jewel encrusted sword, Darius crossed onto the cobblestone street and into the city, heading in the direction of the artificer's guild house. The streets were busy with people going about their everyday business. Merchants of all sorts called out prices for their wares and women stood in the windows of brothels, blatantly showing theirs. Everything was in order.

Lately, tensions were high in the city. The public was starting to grow concerned with the absence of their king and many people blamed Darius. The trade caravan that King Lucius had departed with was escorted by a heavily armed contingent of Darius' soldiers. Many of the common folk suspected that Darius had ordered the assassination of the king on the road in some sort of planned coup. Luckily for Darius, no one in any position of real power believed the rumors.

Darius decided that the time had come for him to step up the search effort for the king's missing caravan. He took a detour on his way to the artificer's guild, stopping by one of the seedier taverns on the city's south side. The bar, aptly named "Terror's Legs" for its position against the great stone wall, was always full of patrons willing to trade some information for a few coins. Even early in the morning on a bright sunny day, the stench of alcohol and vomit assaulted the dignified captain's nostrils as he opened the rickety door to the tavern.

"What are you doing back in here, Darius? I thought I told you to never come back in my tavern again!" Nancy, the old and hobbled barkeep, hated Darius. The guard captain wasn't fond of her either. The last time that Darius had ventured into Terror's Legs, a fight had broken out. Darius didn't often drink, but when he did, he usually got into a brawl or duel with someone. Darius did not take insults to his honor or dignity lightly. Most negative things spoken his way were met with a gauntlet tossed in the offender's face.

"Oh, come now Nancy, you can't still be upset! It was just a little fight, nothing out of the ordinary. This is a bar, after all." The guard captain took a seat at the wooden counter and looked around the room for someone who might give him information. Not too many of the patrons left in the tavern were conscious enough to be of any use.

"Just a little fight?" the haggard wench yelled back at him, "you killed two of my customers! Stabbed them in the alley! If you weren't in charge of the jail, I would have you arrested!" The woman did have a point, Darius silently agreed.

"To be fair," he responded calmly, "they were the ones who said that I couldn't even swing a sword after drinking three pitchers of your spiced ale." He grinned at Nancy, leaning over the bar and motioning for her to do the same so he could whisper to her. "I'm looking for someone. A warrior," Darius whispered to her.

"We get a lot of men in here who claim to be warriors. You're gonna' have to be more specific than that if you want to find anyone useful." Nancy was holding her hand out on the bar as she leaned in close to talk to the captain.

"Maybe this will jog your memory," Darius said as he dropped a coin into her hand. "I need someone to find a king. Someone I can trust. Know anyone?"

Nancy pulled back and bit the coin to make sure it was real before putting it into a pocket on her apron. She put a finger to the edge of her mouth and pondered the question. After a few moments of mindlessly cleaning the bar with a dirty towel, Nancy returned to the captain. "See that man in the back of the bar?" she whispered, motioning with a nod to one of the passed out patrons in the corner. Darius smiled and got up from his stool and talk to the man.

A forceful hand on his arm stopped him before he left his seat. "No, not him," Nancy scolded. "He isn't the warrior you are looking for. He can connect you though. I get it; you don't want to send another search party after the king publicly. The peasants would be in uproar if they thought the government was desperate. Talk to that man in the back. He knows everyone with the skills you are looking for. I think he used to be a pit fighter or something. He can arrange the meeting." Darius dropped another coin onto the bar and rose from his seat, smiling as he made his way to the blacked-out man.

It took a few shakes before the slumped patron managed to open his eyes and look at Darius. "Hey, what do you want?" he groaned. The weary man shielded his eyes from the sun that came in through the open window set into the door.

Darius sat down with a thud in the stool opposite the drunken man and let the armor plates of his gear clang against the wood. The captain drew forth his sword from its scabbard, making the motion slowly, and forced the metal of the weapon to ring as it was drawn. He placed the sword on the gouged wooden table with the point aimed directly for the drunken man's chest. "I am Darius. This sword marks my station within Castle Talon. Do you know of me?" The captain didn't know where to begin soliciting information.

"Hey, am I being arrested?" The man began to rise from his seat, the alcohol in his blood obviously impairing his efforts. A quick shove of Darius' sword had the man sitting down again in a hurry.

"I am captain of the royal guard. No, you are not being arrested, sir. I am here to speak to you about some information." Darius took a small silver coin out from the pouch on his waist and laid it down on the table, tantalizing the drunken man.

Without taking his eyes off the coin, the drunken man seemed to sober up a little and brushed some of the sweat from his brow. "What sort of information are you coming here to find, oh gracious guard captain?" the man slurred. His head swaying back and forth as he spoke.

"I need to find a fighter," Darius said, keeping his voice low and a hand on the hilt of his drawn weapon.

"Should o' been here last night!" the drunk replied, laughing and nearly throwing up on himself as his chortle quickly turned into a cough.

"Not a brawler, not that sort of fighter. I need a champion, someone who can fight out in the wilds. Someone who can fight alone. I was told that you were the one to see. Now, can you help me or am I wasting my time?" Darius pulled his sword back and slid it into its sheath, taking comfort in the familiarity of the cold metal against his hip. He never liked to have his weapon drawn.

"I know of a man," the drunkard responded and reached for the coin. His grimy fingers got halfway across the table before Darius snatched the money up.

"This man," the captain said, skeptical, "are you sure he is a true champion? I need someone resourceful, someone cunning and lithe, but with the strength and prowess of a veteran pit fighter." He let the coin drop back to the table and roll to the drunk.

The stinking man snatched it up in an instant and clutched it tight to his face as he spoke. "Yes, of course. You need a crusader, a real paladin. I know of one, trained by the Tower of Wings, a perfect fighter. He just isn't one for... well, talking. Most people don't get along with him. I can arrange a meeting with you. Just tell me the time and place." The drunken man grinned and stared at his coin with sheer delight.

"I am going to believe you. Against my better judgment, I will trust this man. Tell him to be at the drawbridge to Castle Talon tomorrow at sunrise. Make sure he comes prepared with full arms and armor. He will be tested." Much to the delight of the drunken man, Darius dropped a second coin onto the table and left the tavern without another word.

Darius spent the rest of the day fruitlessly trying to figure out a way to defend the city against a possible aerial assault involving a dragon. The artificer's guild turned him away as soon the captain told them that it was a dragon he feared. In all of the histories of the various kingdoms around the world, a dragon had only ever been seen once. It ravaged the Green City, the home of Talonrend's ancestors, but that was thousands of years ago. Darius accepted the fact that no one in the city would help him build defenses against a dragon and went to tell his prince of the meeting scheduled for the next morning.

"My liege," Darius knocked on the door to Prince Herod's bedchamber. "I might have found someone to go and fetch our beloved king," he said as the door opened. Herod was visibly intrigued by the idea.

"Who is it?" he asked excitedly. "Have you hired another band of mercenaries to go and find Lucius and bring him back to his throne?"

"Not exactly," Darius said as he stepped into the prince's room. "I have a man coming here tomorrow at dawn to prove his worth. He has the reputation of a champion, a true fighter. Self-reliant, resourceful, cunning, strong—he should be what we are looking for to go and fetch your brother."

"What is his name? Is he one of the pit fighters?"

"His name is... well, actually... I never got his name. I haven't met him yet either," Darius confessed. "I am told that he is a paladin, trained by the clergy in the tower. I was also told that he isn't too good with socializing and doesn't get along well with others." That brought a frown to the prince's sullen face.

"You haven't even met this man? You hired some ruffian off the street to go and find the ruler of our kingdom?" Herod was visibly upset and paced the room nervously.

"I haven't hired him yet!" Darius explained, trying to calm the prince. "I want to test him before I pay him. He will be at the drawbridge at dawn. If he is the right person for the job, we will take him to the cave to be blessed." The guard captain left the room with a flourish of his cloak, angered by the prince's lack of trust in his decision.

Thankfully, the acclaimed champion arrived at dawn the next morning. Darius stood right outside the castle doors and watched the man's approach from the end of the drawbridge. The brawny stranger cut an impressive image. He was tall, not freakishly tall, but a full head taller than the guard captain with shoulders as wide as the length of Darius' sword. His head was shaved bald but he sported a long black beard, braided at his chin and hanging down well past his waist. He wore a thick leather belt attached to loose, flowing pants that indicated function over fashion. The belt connected to a harness on his chest that supported the man's minimal armor. Instead of a breastplate or other traditional protection, the man strode toward the drawbridge wearing two leather straps crisscrossing his chest and a sleeve of chainmail covering his left arm and ending in a thick steel gauntlet. A set of large throwing axes hung loosely from the man's side. His right arm, back, and his chest were entirely unprotected.

The hilt of a hand-and-a-half sword could be seen sticking up above the man's muscled shoulders and neck. He walked with the steady pace of a seasoned veteran, slowly making his approach while never taking his eyes off of Darius. "I hope you have come prepared!" the guard captain called out across the bridge before ducking back into the castle.

A bowstring thrummed from the parapet above the castle doors. The warrior's head jerked up with the sound as an arrow flew from the ledge and headed right for the hulking man. He crouched, just slightly, waiting until the last moment to spring out of the way and clear of the shot. The arrow bit deep into the wood of the bridge and vibrated where it was lodged. Stepping up his pace, the warrior saw a second archer drawing back his bowstring but he was easily able to dodge the poorly aimed projectile.

Grimacing, the warrior lowered his head and charged for the castle doors. Two more arrows plunked into the wood behind him but he made it to the entrance unharmed. The heavy doors of Castle Talon swung open easily behind the weight of the man's armored shoulder as he barged through. Much to his surprise, there wasn't an army waiting for him to battle on the other side of the door.

The ferocious warrior straightened and extended to his full height. He strode into the throne room, ready for single combat against his solitary opponent. Prince Herod stood in front of the empty throne, clad in full plate emblazoned with runes and symbols of Vrysinoch. In one hand the Prince held a falchion, the bottom half of the blade cruelly serrated. His other hand held a small dagger with a large crossbar designed for defensive parrying. The prince lifted his falchion up to his great helm, bowed, and began to charge.

The warrior in the doorway growled and set his feet in a defensive posture while he brought one of the throwing axes up from his side. The first whirling axe cleared the charging prince's head, sailing far too high and landing at the foot of the throne. A second axe went soaring in at the prince, its path perfectly in line with the royal seal of Vrysinoch on the front of Herod's breastplate.

Attempting to use the parrying dagger to knock the axe away, Herod dropped his hand and swung, solidly connecting with the deadly projectile. The axe's course diverted, causing it to ricochet harmlessly off of Herod's thick armor. With speed surprising for someone so heavily armored, Herod closed the gap between the two fighters before a third axe could even be readied.

The stranger, attempting to take advantage of the heavily armored prince, turned and pivoted at the last second, flattening his back against the stone of the castle's wall. Herod read the man's foot movements and anticipated the move flawlessly. The prince spread his arms out wide and hit the man squarely in the jaw with the hilt of the falchion as he passed by. Having less mobility, it took Herod a second to fully turn around and look for his prey.

A plated gauntlet connected with the back of Herod's helm in a resounding crash of metal against metal. The ornate great helm, now dented, flew from the prince's head and skittered to a stop against the wooden door. Grunting, Herod swung both of his weapons in wide from the sides and right for the gut of his attacker.

The nimble fighter was able to quickly bring his armored left arm into the path of the falchion and turn the blade away before it could bite into his flesh. His longer arms and larger physique allowed the man to grab the armored wrist of the prince and stop the dagger a full foot short of its mark. Wasting no time, the warrior reared back and delivered a devastating headbutt to the prince's unarmored face that sent him flying against the doors.

Blood oozed from the prince's ruined nose in thick spurts. He tossed the dagger down to the ground and charged in with both hands on the hilt of his falchion. Herod led with a stab that was easily sidestepped by the more agile fighter. Thinking to slice the larger man in half, Herod pulled his hands in and moved the blade in a vicious loop toward his dodging opponent. Metal rang out against metal as the blade of the falchion connected with the armored left arm of the fighter. The well protected arm rolled with the blow and deflected it rather than trying to absorb the hit.

Before Herod could pull his weapon back to strike again, a plated fist crunched into his breastplate, startling him and knocking him back. The man struck out again, kicking Herod's leg and forcing him to shift his weight to his back foot. The next blow came in the form of an armored punch to the wrist of Herod's primary sword hand and sent the falchion flying to the ground. The man dropped low and rushed the prince. He lowered his head at the last moment which allowed the hilt of the sword still strapped to his back to land solidly on the prince's exposed neck.

Herod doubled over in pain. With his back against the castle doors, he had nowhere to run. Fighting out of desperation, Herod attempted to grapple the larger man and wrestle him to the floor. In the blink of an eye, the prince was sprawled out on his back. Herod's face was smeared with blood and the hulking stranger stood over him and laughed.

"Congratulations," came the voice of Darius as he walked out from his hiding spot behind the throne. "Herod, my liege, I do believe that we have found ourselves a champion." The guard captain helped his prince up off his back and returned his weapons to him. Looking at the unknown warrior, he smiled and said, "Well met, good sir. You fought wonderfully, besting your own prince in single combat without even drawing your sword. Might we have the honor of learning your name, brave stranger?"

"Gideon," the stranger said with a gravelly voice.

Herod patted Gideon on the shoulder. "You fought well," he said as he inspected the dent on the back of his great helm.

"Why have you brought me here?" Gideon asked. His voice sounded like the low rumble of a landslide.

"I was told that you are a paladin, trained by the tower in the holy art of war. Is that accurate? I saw no use of holy magic in your duel with the prince." Darius was skeptical of Gideon's training. He had never seen someone so easily best a seasoned warrior without drawing a blade.

"I was trained by the tower, that is correct," was the only response the man offered.

"And what are you now, besides just strong and large?" Herod asked, nursing his bruised neck.

"I left the tower after my training," Gideon explained. "They train men to fight side by side, tower shields and maces forming an impenetrable wall. As far as I am concerned, in order for a warrior to excel to the heights of fighting perfection, he must learn to do combat alone."

"Yes, our legions are trained to fight as a cohesive unit," Darius said, considering the lone nature of the warrior before him. "If you were selected for training at the tower, that must mean Vrysinoch speaks to you. Can you still manipulate the holy powers of Vrysinoch?"

"The winged one speaks to me still, although it seems to be more at his pleasure than mine. When I was training with the other paladins, I could command the holy energies at my will, bending them to strike my foes at any moment. Now, it is only in times of great need that Vrysinoch chooses to aid my cause. I do not consider myself a paladin." Darius moved around the man and inspected his muscled frame for the distinctive tattoo of the paladins.

Just above Gideon's right shoulder blade, partially obscured by the hilt of his sword, was a small mark: a talon clutching an emerald. "Your mark has not faded. Vrysinoch still names you among his

41

elite. You are a paladin, by all accounts. You are just..." Darius paused, searching for the right word. "Unique," he continued, "the most unique paladin I have ever met."

"We need you to go out into the wilderness, alone, and find my brother, the king." Herod liked this warrior, especially because a man with few friends ran little risk of telling the wrong person about his mission.

"So, the rumors are true then," Gideon said, looking past the prince and his guard to the empty throne at the center of the room.

"Yes, well," Darius said, "we aren't exactly sure where the king is. We have no reason to believe that he is dead, but if you find that to be the case, bring back proof."

"You will be paid on your return," Herod was quick to put in, "double if you bring the king back to his castle. We don't want to financially encourage you to kill my dear brother..."

"I will need equipment, provisions, gear for a long journey," Gideon remarked, looking to Darius to arrange supplies for his trip.

"Along those lines, we would like you to come to the royal temple, the cavern underneath Castle Talon. We are hoping that the high priest in the temple will facilitate your blessing." Darius turned around and led the trio to a door at the back of the throne room that led to the caverns.

"Who knows," Gideon mumbled, "maybe Vrysinoch would enjoy seeing me again." The group made their way down the steep tunnels underneath the castle in silence.

After the long trek, the three arrived at the edge of the room that housed the statue of Vrysinoch. The interlocking wings that created the entranceway into the temple were too low for Gideon to stride through and forced him to duck to enter the cave. The priest was there, standing beneath the statue, waiting for the group.

"We have come to seek the blessing of Vrysinoch," Herod said, making his way to stand next to a bowl at the foot of the winged god.

"Yes, yes," the old and withered priest said, "I knew you would come to me today." When the high priest spoke, the emerald light in the room seemed to shift and dance with every word, settling down as soon as the man stopped talking.

"This one, however," the priest continued, "is already blessed by the winged god. I'm afraid that I am unable to help. No blessing of mine could improve the powers already bestowed upon this man by Vrysinoch himself." That news was shocking to everyone, including Gideon. The three surprised men stood dumbfounded in front of the priest.

"You are the highest priest in the kingdom, the chosen of our lord. Certainly there is something that you can do?" Darius was at a loss for words. He looked from the priest and back to Gideon for some sort of answer.

"Well, there might be something that I can do," the priest said in a mystic tone. "I might be able to convince Vrysinoch to bestow his blessing upon your weapons instead. The usual weapon enchantments that the tower gives to the paladins are for their shields. This one carries no such shield." The old priest pointed a crooked finger up toward the hilt of the hand-and-a-half sword strapped to the warriors muscled back. "Yes," he continued, "if you would just place your sword inside the bowl at the foot of the statue, we can try."

Gideon took a step away from the priest. "I do not think that would be wise," he said with a grating tone.

"And why is that?" Darius inquired with sudden curiosity.

"My sword is already enchanted," the warrior said, "and quite powerfully so." Gideon took another step back from the priest with his hands up in a defensive posture.

"Do you doubt the powers of Vrysinoch, warrior?" the priest asked. His voice dripped with accusation. "That sword looks sturdy enough to bear multiple enchantments, even one as strong as the blessing of a god."

Gideon took another step back and bumped his head into the stone wings of the statue that formed the entry into the cavern. "You don't understand," he said, glaring at the priest. "My sword is honor-bound to my hands. I cannot draw it here." Darius' eyes jumped to the weapon with a hint of recognition.

"What does that mean?" Herod asked the guard captain. The prince's hands moved nervously to the hilts of his own weapons.

"An honor-bound weapon," Darius explained in frightful tones, "is magically entwined with the soul of its owner. It is a powerful enchantment, the properties of which are still largely a mystery. The priests of the tower seldom imbue a weapon with so strong an enchantment. While the power given to an honor-bound warrior and his weapon is certainly significant, so is the cost." Herod leaned closer to the captain, hanging on every word.

"The cost is immense," Gideon interrupted, finishing the explanation. "Every time I draw the weapon from its sheath, it drains part of my soul, feasting upon my life energy. True, it makes the weapon incredibly powerful, but if I do not allow the sword to take the life of another after I have drawn it, I cannot let it leave my hand. In essence, from the moment I draw my sword, it begins to kill me. Unless it kills someone else quickly, I will be consumed by it. My life force is strong enough to resist the sword for an hour, maybe two, but then I will die. The only way to return the sword to its sheath is to sate its hunger for souls."

There was a long pause in the cavern. Gideon stared at the statue of Vrysinoch and everyone else stared at him. "Best not to take it out, then…" Herod said quietly to break the silence.

"If you don't kill, you will die," the priest said, "every single time you bring it forth. Vrysinoch protect you, my son." The wrinkled hands of the priest ushered the group out of the temple, obviously eager to be far away from the sword.

"Does your sword have a name, Gideon?" Darius asked when they reached the drawbridge once more.

Walking out of the castle, his sword on his back and axes by his side, Gideon glanced over his shoulder and nodded.

Three

GRAVLOX AWOKE THE next morning long before the sun's rays began to warm the mountain. Vorst was waiting for him by the time he collected his gear and opened the door to his cave. "Hi Grav!" she said, bright and chipper. For a moment, Gravlox considered the fact that she might be so willing to follow him into the wild for the sake of murdering him for her own advancement, but the thought was fleeting and melted away as soon as Vorst smiled.

"I decided to leave the other poison ingredients here, in my cave, just in case," Gravlox said as he shut the wooden door behind him.

"Probably a good idea." Vorst nodded her head in agreement as she inspected the heavy pack that

Gravlox wore on his back. "What all did you bring? How long do you think this journey is going to take?" The burlap sack on the hunched goblin's shoulders was bulging.

"Food, mostly," Gravlox responded, hefting the sack in an attempt to impress Vorst with how easily he could lift it.

"Are you really not bringing any weapons?" Vorst asked.

Gravlox stammered, not knowing what to say. "I actually don't own any," was all he could think to say. While fights and killings were commonplace anywhere in the mountain, Gravlox always felt safe in his mine and had never given the need for a weapon serious consideration.

Vorst set her small travelling pack down on the ground and produced two squat short swords, complete with scabbards and belts. She tossed one of the weapons to Gravlox who embarrassingly fumbled it to the ground.

"Here, let me do it," Vorst said, kneeling down and buckling the sword around the waist of her travelling companion. After the awkward moment passed, Vorst patted Gravlox on the shoulder and smiled. The female goblin turned, starting toward the exit of the mountain complex.

Gravlox, being a mining foreman, lived near to where he worked in the heart of the mountain. "Come on," Vorst said, waving to him, "the exit is over this way." Vorst bounded down the dark tunnels, full of excitement and the lust for adventure.

When they reached an area bathed in sunlight from the outside world, Gravlox stopped.

"You have been outside before?" he asked, trying unsuccessfully to hide his surprise. Miners had no need of visiting the outside world and goblins in general rarely left the mountain.

"Of course, silly. Who do you think goes and gathers up all the supplies for the store? I do!" Gravlox stood in a shadow, not wanting to exit the mountain, unsure of his every step.

"Come on," Vorst continued, turning back and grabbing Gravlox by the hand, leading him to the end of the tunnel and the outside world. "You miner goblins never leave the darkness? Doesn't it get boring, being cooped up all the time in the dark?"

Gravlox shook his head. He was at a loss for words, a sensation that he was quickly becoming used to around Vorst.

The bright sunlight at the end of the tunnel stung the miner's eyes, causing him to lift his hand and squint painfully ahead. Gravlox hesitated in the cavern, fearing that the sunlight might burn his skin and reduce him to a pile of ash. "Hurry up, Grav!" Vorst called to him, dancing in the warm sunlight.

Gravlox took a tentative step into the open air, gazing upon the farming terraces that lined the southern side of Kanebullar Mountain. Everywhere he looked, Gravlox saw goblins going about their work in the harsh sunlight, farming the land, tending to livestock, or simply resting. He moved another step out of the tunnel, letting the sun wash over his pale skin and heat his body.

Within a moment, Gravlox was running and skipping, trying to keep up with Vorst as she bounded down the terraces. Farming goblins yelled and cursed at the pair, who trampled more than a few crops as they continued their gallivanting. Nearly halfway down the sculpted mountain face, Vorst stopped, panting heavily. She sat down hard upon a rock, throwing her hands in the air, and let out a contented sigh.

Gravlox was right behind her, collapsing to the ground in his jubilant exhaustion. Both of the goblins were sweating and breathing heavily, staring up into the sky. A long moment passed before either of them spoke.

"How do you like being outside?" Vorst asked, her voice sounding small and far away, as if she was lost in some sort of ethereal daydream.

"Wonderful. The outside is just wonderful," Gravlox replied. "I can't believe that I have never left the tunnels before..." He let his voice trail off, closing his eyes and thoroughly enjoying the warmth and beauty of the outside world. "Everything is just so warm," Gravlox said, barely audible.

"And dry. I can't stand being stuck in the wet caves and tunnels of the mountain. Everything out here is just so fresh and beautiful and dry. I love it here." Vorst was lying down next to Gravlox on the grassy terrace, her head casually brushing up against the edge of the foreman's shoulder.

"Look, up in the sky, there!" Vorst pointed at a small black object fluttering through the milky white clouds.

Following her hand, Gravlox peered into the sky. "What is it?" he asked, a hint of fear in his voice. "Should we get back into the mountain and warn the others?"

Vorst laughed aloud, rolling in the grass. "No, silly," she said between her laughter, "that's an eagle." As if on cue, the great bird of prey loosed a piercing shriek, breaking the sky and shattering the serenity of the moment. The eagle caused many of the goblins to look up into the sky, wondering what they had just heard. Eagles were not uncommon around the mountain, but the way that the bird overhead had cawed, it set everyone's nerves on edge. The eagle sounded like it had screamed, as if out of pain or hatred. There was anger behind the piercing screech of the great winged beast and all the goblins standing in the terraces could feel it.

"Let's get moving along," Vorst said, cautiously standing and keeping her eyes peeled on the sky. "That was peculiar." The two goblins rose up from the grassy terrace and continued down the mountain face, eventually arriving at the edge of the heavily wooded plain that surrounded their home.

"So," Gravlox said, stopping before entering the tree line, "where should we start to look for necrotic dust? Where can we find a necromancer?" He tried to hide his nervousness, but failed miserably.

"I know a place where ghost flowers grow," Vorst replied, skipping past the first few trees and into the forest. "There is a graveyard not too far from here. I think it is only a few days walk from the mountain, near one of the human villages along the riverbank." She drew her sword and used it to point the way.

"Lead on, Vorst!" Gravlox said with a smile, bounding after her once more. He spent the entire day trying to keep up with his spry companion. Vorst led him through the forest in the direction of the riverbank, always a few steps ahead of him.

Gravlox tried to stop many times, usually to investigate some plant or animal he had never seen before. Vorst was eager though, relentlessly leading him farther away from the safety of the mountain.

"Shhh," Vorst whispered when she finally came to a stop, motioning for Gravlox to be quiet. The two goblins crept up to an open glen, a grassy area void of the tall trees that made up the rest of the forest. "Look there, Grav, look at those stumps." Vorst was crouched behind a small bush, pointing to four tree stumps in the clearing.

"What about them?" Gravlox asked, not realizing the significance of the stumps. He peered around the bush, trying to get a better look into the glen.

"They were cut down," Vorst explained, making a motion with her hand to resemble a forester with an axe. "Humans do that. They cut the trees down for timber, just like we do."

Gravlox shrank down behind the bush, trying to remain as stealthy as possible. "What do we do? Are there humans nearby? I can't smell them." The frightened goblin drew his short sword, not even sure how to hold it properly. Vorst put a hand on Gravlox's shoulder, keeping him back while she stood up and looked around the edge of the bushes into the clearing.

"No one is here," she said, standing up fully and bounding into the glen with her normal excitement. Gravlox stood up slowly, still tightly clutching the hilt of his weapon. The glen was large, with a small stream running between the tree stumps and back into the woods. "Let's camp here tonight," Vorst said.

"Alright," Gravlox replied, grateful for a break. He sat down on one of the stumps, rubbing his weary feet with one hand while still grasping his sword with the other.

"Grav, check out these tracks. Some animals have been through here, probably to drink from the stream. We should follow their tracks and see if we can find them." Vorst bent low over the tracks, following the large prints closely.

"What are the tracks from?" Gravlox asked, "Humans?" He walked over to the tracks slowly, unsure of himself.

"Those aren't human feet," Vorst said skeptically, pointing to the impressions in the mud. "Humans usually wear cloth on their feet, from what I've heard. These prints look like two big and pointy toes." The two goblins stared at the tracks, having no idea that they were made by a rather large elk.

"Alright, let's go find this animal." Gravlox stood up straight, looking down the path of the tracks, trying to impress Vorst with his bravery. They started to follow the tracks, attempting to remain silent and undetected by the animal they were stalking. It didn't take long before they came upon a cave, its smell indicating that more than one animal lived inside.

"That is where we should camp," Gravlox said, desiring the familiarity of the cave to the open air of the forest.

Out from behind the cave emerged the elk, towering over the goblins, its antlers each the size of a goblin and half. Gravlox shrieked in fear, turning to run from the menacing creature.

Vorst, much calmer in the presence of danger, rolled to her side, coming to a crouch behind a small boulder and taking her short bow from her back. The elk, disturbed and threatened by the terrified shouts of Gravlox, lowered its head and began pawing at the ground with its hoofs.

"Gravlox!" Vorst called out, trying to get the poor goblin's attention. "Run, but not too far from here. Lead the beast in a circle!" A smile broke out on the younger goblin's face as Gravlox took off, the elk pursuing. Steadying her hands, Vorst nocked an arrow. Her breathing slowed to a deep, calm serenity. She pulled the bowstring back, just slightly, testing the tension, feeling the supple wood in her hand. Vorst's body moved with the path of the elk, tracking her shot perfectly.

In a split second, Vorst exploded into action, closing her eyes and loosing three shots into the elk over the course of a single exhale. The massive beast hit the ground hard, sliding from its own momentum, and coming to rest just inches behind Gravlox. Opening her eyes, Vorst returned her bow to her shoulder and stood from her crouched position, calmly striding over to the fallen animal. It took a few moments for Gravlox to even realize that the elk had fallen. He turned around, shock and awe plastered plainly on his face at the sight of Vorst removing her arrows from the body of the slain creature.

"What the... How did you..." Gravlox threw his hands in the air, letting his sword fall to the ground. "Where did you learn to do that?" he muttered under his breath as he approached the dead elk. Vorst stood, her three arrows dripping blood onto the soft ground.

"Don't worry about it, Gravlox, I've got your back. Nice work." She cleaned the arrow heads off on the hide of the animal and replaced them in her quiver.

"How do you know how to shoot like that?" Gravlox was truly stunned. The impressive archer standing before him shrugged like it was nothing, pulling a small knife from her pack and starting to cut into the flesh of the elk.

"You pick up certain skills when you spend a lot of time outside the mountain," she said nonchalantly. Vorst continued to cut the elk, removing the hide in large chunks. Gravlox sat down on the grass beside her, watching her work, admiring her familiarity with the carcass. "Here, try this," she said, holding out a piece of the elk's meat in her bloody hands.

Gravlox took the chunk of meat and brought it to his mouth, biting in. Blood dribbled down his chin as he ate the morsel, savoring the flavor. "If you like that, you should try it cooked. It tastes even better when you roast it over a fire," Vorst explained, wrapping a massive section of meat in the cut pieces of elk hide. She continued to dress the animal, removing the antlers and as much meat as she could carry.

After an hour or so with the dead elk, the two goblins made their way back to the grassy clearing and began to prepare a fire. The sun was low in the sky and the sounds of roasting elk meat filled the air by the time they finished setting their campsite. Vorst had cleaned the hides, setting them down on the grass to use as cushioned mats. Gravlox, not knowing the meaning of night and day as it related to the sun, became frightened with the onset of darkness.

Even though he could see perfectly fine in almost any environment, and the darkness actually aided his vision, he fidgeted nervously with the hilt of his blade. "I've never actually met a human, Vorst. I don't know anything about them. Well, to be honest, I don't know anything about anything out here. I have lived my entire life in the mines beneath the mountain. Do humans hunt at night?"

Vorst laughed aloud, shaking her head and sending hot droplets of grease all over their campsite. "No, silly. Humans are weak. Their bodies tire after even the most meaningless activity. Whenever it gets dark, humans lie down and sleep, like an animal." She demonstrated a human sleeping by lying down and crossing her arms over her bare chest.

"Why do they do that? Couldn't someone just walk up to them and kill them while they sleep?" Gravlox didn't understand the need for sleep, never having felt the need himself.

"They just do it," Vorst explained. "And humans do other strange things, too," she continued, sitting up on the hide.

"They sound primitive," Gravlox mused, wondering how the humans could get anything done. In

Kanebullar Mountain, the fluctuating temperatures caused by the sun's rise and fall dictated separations between days.

"You haven't seen a human yet," Vorst said. "They aren't as primitive as you might think."

Gravlox and Vorst waited in the glen for some time, lying down or sitting on the hides, eating roasted elk meat and drinking from the stream. As goblins, they did not need to sleep as humans did, but they still had to rest for a few hours in order for their bodies to recover.

"We should follow the stream," Vorst said a long while later, heading in that direction. "If we walk alongside the stream, we should be able to follow it to the river. From there, I think we can find the graveyard with the ghost flowers. I haven't been there in a long time, but I should remember where it is." Gravlox simply nodded his head, the knuckles of his hand turning white as he clutched the hilt of his sword. He hoped that he would never have to meet a human. He tried in vain to telepathically beg Lady Scrapple to keep him safe from the humans, a goblin prayer of sorts.

It was around midday by the time that the goblin pair arrived at a small ridge with a clear view to the graveyard. "What exactly are we doing here?" Gravlox asked, his eyes darting about the area, searching for humans. The village that buried their dead in the graveyard was just on the other side of the Clawflow. Gravlox and Vorst could see people walking about the streets of the small village, keeping to themselves and never bothering to look across the river at the distant spies.

"Ghost flowers are the closest thing I know to necrotic dust," Vorst explained, pointing at the graves. "I was thinking that if we start pulling up the ghost flowers, maybe some necromancer will come to try and stop us." The way she laid out the plan so casually terrified Gravlox.

"So, you want to anger a necromancer into coming to us? That seems…" Gravlox paused, trying to think of a way to politely explain his apprehension. "Dangerous. Yes, that plan feels very risky. What happens if the necromancer shows up? Do we just ask him for some dust?" Gravlox was shaking his head, wanting more than anything to just return to his mountain lair.

"Look, ghost flowers aren't used for much. The only things that goblins ever need them for is dark magic. I imagine that human necromancers must harvest the flowers regularly for their spells," Vorst said nonchalantly, as though she were just explaining an everyday activity. "As for when one would arrive to check on the flowers, I figured you would just be the hero and kill him," she continued, patting the hilt of Gravlox's sword.

The scared goblin swallowed hard, trying to be brave. "Sounds like a good plan to me," he muttered.

"Where are these ghost flowers, anyway? All I see are normal flowers," Gravlox wondered, inspecting the graves as best he could from the ridge.

"They only appear at night!" Vorst hit him lightly on the shoulder, "don't you know anything?" The female goblin stood, peering across the river to the human settlement. "I wonder what that town is called. Humans always give interesting names to their little villages."

"What should we do while we wait for night?" Gravlox asked tentatively, fearing the answer.

Vorst looked at their surroundings, pondering the question. She walked around the small clearing behind the ridge, out of view of the river and graveyard, and picked up two fairly long sticks. "Here," she said, tossing one to Gravlox, "spar with me. I want to see if you are any good or not." Before she even finished her sentence, Vorst charged, catching the terrified foreman off guard.

Gravlox had just enough time to shrug his heavy pack off of his shoulders and roll out of the way of Vorst's first swing. He could feel the wind from the stick rushing over his head and his eyes grew wide. He knew that the blow would have hurt and maybe even have knocked him out. Gravlox saw only the sky from his back and kicked out wildly, knocking Vorst back and keeping her momentarily at bay.

Using the temporary pause to remove her bow and pack, Vorst began to jump on her feet, loosening her limbs for combat. Thinking to turn the surprise to his favor, Gravlox leapt forward, his arms spread wide, the stick in his right hand. Already light on her feet, Vorst dodged the lunge with ease, striking out at the back of the soaring goblin as he missed his mark. Gravlox hit the ground on his chest, groaning loudly and sending up a cloud of dust.

Vorst took a few steps back, letting Gravlox get to his feet. She charged in again, swinging the stick for Gravlox's head, allowing him to easily duck out of the way.

With a yell that surprised both of them, Gravlox swung his own weapon, a large sweeping motion he hoped would take the younger goblin's legs out from under her. Vorst, instead of jumping over the strike, rolled over the stick as it passed underneath her. She attempted to continue the roll and come up on the side of Gravlox, ready to strike at his exposed flank, but the sharp crack of a stick on her back changed her mind.

Gravlox scored a hit, bringing his branch in close when he saw the roll and hitting Vorst on the back. "Sorry," he breathed, not wanting to hurt his friend.

Vorst, more surprised than hurt by the hit, scrambled away and rose to her feet a few paces from Gravlox. She pulled her arm back and launched the stick at Gravlox, sending it whirling end over end. Much to her delight, Gravlox slapped the missile out of the air and then rushed in, leading with a stab that pushed Vorst back to the outside edge of the clearing.

A quick series of stabs followed the initial thrust, slowly putting Vorst's back to a tree. Gravlox stabbed in low, thinking he had won the duel. With a smile on her face, Vorst stepped down hard on the branch, snapping it in half against the ground. At the same time, she reached her hands up behind her head and grabbed the lowest branches of the tree. Using her upper body, Vorst was able to quickly flip upwards, her foot catching Gravlox in the chin and sending him sprawling to the ground.

Vorst, completely inverted, used her curled legs to fly out from the tree, landing on Gravlox with a cruel headbutt. He dropped his stick, the wind knocked out of his small lungs. Seizing the opportunity, Vorst grabbed the tip of the branch she had broken off of Gravlox's makeshift sword and pressed it tightly to his neck.

"You're dead," she said with a grin before tossing the stick away and standing. "That wasn't too bad though, for your first time."

Gravlox, nursing a bruise that was quickly turning black on his chest, stood up and stretched. "At least I managed to get a hit," he said playfully. "I'm hungry. Can we eat more of that meat?" He moved over to Vorst's pack, opening it and taking out a large chunk of elk. He tossed half of it to Vorst and sat down to consume his portion, blood running freely down his chin.

The two goblins ate in silence and waited for night to fall. Vorst scavenged around for wood appropriate for her to fletch arrows and set to work. Gravlox, wanting to feel useful, attempted to fletch arrows himself, but ended up ruining every piece of wood he touched.

Nightfall found the two goblins sitting on the ridge, a dozen fresh arrows in Vorst's quiver, a frightful expression on Gravlox's face. As the sun disappeared behind the horizon, small red flowers growing on the graves began to glow a soft blue.

Wisps of ethereal smoke drifted up from a patch of the flowers, slowly drifting into the night sky.

The blue glow began to grow, consuming the red flowers, shifting in the moonlight and making the shadows of the gravestones dance. "Just wait," Vorst said, mesmerized by the lights. The glowing images surrounding the red flowers expanded, slithering into the air, vines of soft light spreading out to surround the tombstones. Little blue flowers of light began to bloom on the tops of the tombstones, each one opening with a gentle sucking sound, as though the flowers were absorbing the very energy of the air.

"The flowers are beautiful," Gravlox murmured. He was truly awestruck. "We can't go and smash those," he continued, his voice small. "They are too beautiful. Why don't those grow in the caves of Kanebullar Mountain?" The light was dancing off of the two goblins in eerie, shifting patterns.

Footsteps crunched through the underbrush on the other side of the graveyard. Vorst grabbed the back of Gravlox's neck and pulled him back behind the ridge, tucking into a roll to avoid being seen. "Someone is here," is all she said, reaching for her short bow.

"Where?" Gravlox asked, not having heard the footsteps. He looked around frantically, drawing his sword from its sheath at his side. The two goblins crawled on their bellies back up to the top of the ridge, trying to get a better look at their visitor.

"It could be the necromancer we need to find." Vorst sounded excited. Gravlox wished with all of his heart that she was wrong.

Out from the woods on the other side of the graveyard stepped a human wearing a dark robe. The figure moved silently, swiftly approaching the graves. The robe's hood was pulled down low over the human's face, completely masking the person's identity.

Vorst slowly took an arrow out of her quiver and set it against her bowstring. The feathers tied to the shaft brushed her cheek as Vorst pulled on the bowstring, slowly adding tension, never taking her eyes from the cloaked figure.

The human approached one of the graves and produced a small metal lantern from somewhere deep inside the robe. Vorst held her bow steady, the arrow nocked and aimed for the hooded person. The human opened a small door on the front of the lantern, spoke a line of words completely foreign to the goblins, and motioned with a hand for the flowers to enter the lantern. They obeyed. Ghost flowers from the tombstone began to drift slowly into the lantern, tendrils of blue light playfully encircling the human.

Vorst exhaled, her breath hot and heavy. The small goblin closed her eyes as she pulled the bowstring back further, drawing the arrowhead against the wood of the bow's handle. The hooded figure bent slightly, beckoning to the flowers, welcoming them into the lantern where their soft light was extinguished.

The thrum of Vorst's bowstring broke the halcyon serenity of the night air. The arrow flew, passing through the ghastly tendrils of a ghost flower and causing the wisps to scatter into the wind. The robed figure jerked forward and dropped the lantern onto the grass, leaning heavily on the top of the tomb stone. Vorst nocked another arrow, pulling the bowstring back to loose again.

"Wait," Gravlox whispered, "you wounded it already. Shouldn't we just capture the thing?" He put a hand on Vorst's arm, lowering her bow. The female goblin opened her eyes and saw Gravlox staring at her, begging for her to spare the life of the human she had just shot.

"Let's go," she said, slinging the bow over her shoulder and jumping down the ridge to the graveyard. Gravlox followed quickly behind, his sword in hand. The goblin pair descended upon the wounded human quickly, knocking the person to the ground. Gravlox swung his sword, connecting the heavy hilt of the weapon with the soft back of the human's head. The hooded figure slumped to the ground, twitching a few times before lying still.

"Did you kill it?" Vorst asked, hardly believing what she had just seen from the timid foreman. Gravlox simply shook his head and began to lift the human off the ground. The two of them carried the unconscious figure back over the ridge and into the grassy clearing. Vorst worked quickly to remove her arrow and patch the wound, tossing the bloody arrowhead into her pack to reuse later.

Blood stained the human's black robe, but the wound was not deep enough to be fatal.

Four

GIDEON STRODE TO the gates beneath Terror's Lament with his sword strapped to his back. His travelling gear was light, nothing more than some simple traps and snares and his gleaming armor. The four throwing axes on Gideon's hip clanged together with his stride like the high-pitched ring of funeral bells.

Not many enemies were known to Talonrend, so the guardhouses along the walls were never heavily manned. The people trusted their thick walls more than the reach of any guardsman's pike or sword.

Without much to go on, Gideon couldn't be positive which direction to take outside the city gates. The king's caravan had originally set out to the south, to visit the smaller villages on the edges of the Clawflow. Having long ago lost his horse in an arena bet, Gideon was forced to travel on foot, something he hated doing. He had no friends to ask along on the journey, so Gideon simply set out to the south, leaving the city of Talonrend behind him.

The landscape was pleasant although ultimately boring. For miles around the high walls of the city, nothing was visible except for grassy plains in all directions. Kanebullar Mountain stood high on the horizon, surrounded by a thick forest of hills and trees. Mountains stood far to the north, but only after journeying through the plains for days could anyone even make out enough of their shape to know they existed. Most of the plains around the city of Talonrend had been plowed and built into farms to sustain the population, but some areas of the countryside were too stony and lacked the proper topsoil for agriculture.

Gideon stuck to the barren section of the plains, preferring to walk atop the stony cave ceilings that ran under the entire kingdom than to trudge along the road. Travelers and farmers always wanted to speak to people like Gideon, seeing his sword and asking if he was coming from the arena. The gladiator pits were immensely popular in Talonrend. Every stocky farm boy and drunken blacksmith in the entire kingdom eventually made their way to the great pit in the center of the city. In order to save the kingdom's population, some king or other a long time ago set forth an edict that outlawed fighting to the death against other men. The ban on mortal matches was lifted on a fighter after he survived a full year in the arena against non-human opponents. Too many farm boys and blacksmiths never returned to their villages and the country side had suffered.

Gideon had made his life in the pits before being trained as a paladin at the tower. When he was young, he worked in a smith's shop. He was never allowed to work on any of the projects, but the master smith paid him to carry the materials around the shop. Gideon spent his days hauling carts of raw ore, moving rods of metal around the shop, and bringing heavy hammers to and from the smiths at their anvils.

When he turned sixteen, Gideon signed up for his first fight in the pits. A fighting agent had approached him at the smith's shop after noticing the bulging muscles in the young man's back and arms. He recruited Gideon without even testing him, bringing him into the arena with a broadsword to fight against wolves and bulls and other beasts of the wild. Gideon didn't know it at the time, but the arena agent had paid the owner of the blacksmith shop handsomely to take the boy in and get him ready for combat.

In his first year in the pit, Gideon astounded the crowd. He slew handfuls of wolves with his sword, knocking them out of the air with great sweeps of his weapon and keeping them at bay with his reach. His final trial before entering into mortal combat with other men had been harrowing to say the least. Gideon stood in the center of the arena with the sand beneath his boots and his broadsword in hand. The arena agent had arranged everything, spending an amazing amount of money to coordinate the fight.

The crowd went into a frenzy when the iron gate at the end of the arena lowered. In his usual stoic style, Gideon watched the monster emerge without so much as a flinch. A hundred paces away, standing over nine feet tall, strode a minotaur. The beast was covered in thick, matted hair, with gnarled horns twisting and curving their way to the sky. He wore two heavy chains on his shoulders that crossed over his chest. The minotaur's heavy hooves thundered on the dry floor of the arena and left clouds of dust in its wake.

Gideon's immense opponent was wielding two weapons, both with wicked edges that gleamed in the sun. His right hand grasped a long metal bar, the top of which was edged with five razor blades, each the length of a sword, running vertically parallel to the shaft of the pole. The staff itself was nearly as tall as Gideon, but the minotaur swung it effortlessly, as if it were made of air. In the four meaty fingers of his left hand, the beast held a magnificent scimitar, its hilt encrusted with jewels.

The brawny blacksmith's assistant was armed with a two-handed broadsword and a sleeve of plate armor covering the left side of his body that ended in a heavy gauntlet. The crowd roared to life at the sight of the two opponents facing each other in the sand. Gideon stood at the center of it all, determined to make a name for himself in the pits and earn his glory. He didn't fight for the fame of a gladiator's life and he certainly wasn't trying to impress anyone in particular. He fought simply for himself - he wanted to be the best at everything he did.

With a strange calmness, Gideon stood in the center of the sand that day and waited for the minotaur to come to him. The broadsword was heavy and its wrapped leather handle fit nicely into the palm of his hand. The minotaur snorted, his breath fogging the air before his immense snout. The crowd held its breath for what felt like an eternity as the two opponents stood motionless, scrutinizing each other from a distance.

Finally breaking the tension, the minotaur began to move forward with the five-bladed pole cocked behind his head. Just twenty or thirty paces from the solitary man, the minotaur let loose. The crowd hushed, expecting the warrior to be impaled on the spot. Gideon judged the shot as it left the meaty hand, his eyes never leaving the wicked staff as it sailed over his head and missed the mark by inches. Sand splashed in a great wave as the unorthodox javelin bit into the ground and buried itself far behind Gideon. The minotaur tightened his strong grip on his sword and continued forward. Something about the small size of the jeweled scimitar made it look almost comical in the hands of such a hulking beast.

Gideon, not wanting to underestimate his opponent, rolled out of range of the first swing, ducking and dodging, keeping his own weapon low to prevent the massive hooves from caving in his chest. He knew that it would only take one solid hit from the minotaur to lay him out. After a full minute of avoiding the minotaur's heavy swings, Gideon realized that he could not tire the beast. A minotaur's endurance would last for days, especially when driven by the adrenaline of single combat.

The warrior strode along his path out of Talon-rend, not even realizing that his feet were mimicking his own movements of his fight in the pit with the minotaur. He turned and rolled along the rocky ground, dodging the scimitar, ducking under strikes, reliving the entire combat from memory.

Gideon tried to think of a plan while he dodged, tried to come up with some sort of offense that would get him inside the swinging scimitar before his own endurance gave out and he collapsed to the sand. He had never fought a minotaur, never even seen a minotaur before, but he knew enough just from the corded muscles of the beast's body that he would not survive a direct test of strength.

A swing came in for Gideon's head, the tip of the curved blade entering his vision from the left. The warrior feigned a dodge, moving his feet to jump back and to his right and outside the weapon's deadly reach. At the last moment, Gideon pivoted into the swing, bringing his own weapon up to block the attack, hoping to surprise the minotaur. The beast slashed across its body, wielding the scimitar in its left hand, and was able to quickly follow the parry with a brutal punch to Gideon's chest.

The warrior staggered backward and tried to catch his breath after the mighty blow. The roar of the crowd around him was deafening. Relentless, the creature pressed his advantage, swinging wildly at the retreating man. Gideon dodged most of the attacks, parried the few that came in too close, and continued to move away from his snarling foe.

Finally, Gideon saw an opportunity. He had retreated far enough to catch a glimpse of the heavy metal javelin protruding from the sand to his right. His first thought was to retrieve it and use the length of the weapon to keep the monster back. No, he thought, the minotaur's reach with the small sword would still best the length of the heavy pole.

The minotaur pressed him again, unleashing a chain of fast attacks that Gideon was forced to parry. The man planted his feet, determined to not let the shaft of the javelin out of his sight. His broadsword came up in a flash, barely catching the scimitar's point on the hilt. Using the exact same maneuver that had scored a hit on himself, Gideon pressed the weapons together and punched out with his left hand, catching the beast in its hairy chest. If the minotaur noticed the blow, he didn't show it.

Hoping to impose a test of brawn, the minotaur leaned in and pressed with all of his might against the smaller warrior, forcing the blade of the scimitar closer and closer to the man's neck. At the last moment, Gideon turned his shoulder hard, dropping the blade of his own sword into the sand and letting the overbalanced minotaur crush through the block. Had Gideon not ducked into the attack, he would have been eviscerated where he stood.

The smaller man had slipped under the large minotaur's arms and managed to get the blade of his sword on the creature's shoulder, slashing a long gash from the top of his arm to the chain at the center of his muscled chest. The infuriated minotaur spun quickly and blasted Gideon's jaw with his hand and narrowly missed with the scimitar that followed, a strike that surely would have decapitated the man. Gideon had timed it all perfectly. Collecting his wits and rubbing his jaw, the warrior managed to escape to the buried javelin as the monster howled in pain, much to the delight of the crowd. Blood oozed from the wound and dripped into the sand.

Gideon dropped his sword at the base of the javelin and used both of his strong arms to tear the weapon free. The arena floor let go of its prize in a whirl of sand that temporarily blinded the minotaur. Not wasting the opportunity, Gideon charged in with the weapon, swinging wildly with the butt of the heavy pole at his hip. The long and slender blades cut a deep wound into the side of the minotaur, causing more blood to spill forth. The beast howled again but did not fall.

Surprisingly, the minotaur reached down and tore the strange spear from Gideon's grip, dropping his own scimitar in the process. Scrambling, Gideon launched himself to the ground and grasped after the hilt of his broadsword. His hand found it, but not in time. The heavy pole smashed down on the back of Gideon's legs, rending his flesh. The clever beast then revealed the true function of the weapon, rotating it in his fierce grip and using the five blades to shave the skin from the back of Gideon's legs.

The pain was dizzying, but Gideon fought on. He knew that he didn't have much time left; the next blow from the pole would likely shred his skull to bloody ribbons. The minotaur lifted the weapon high to the roar of the frenzied crowd, seeking to make the final strike more dramatic.

Gideon took the chance to roll, sending waves of pain from his legs all the way to his eyes. His vision began to fade. Dark spots formed wherever he looked but he had his broadsword grasped firmly in hand. The beast bent over to strike, putting all of his bulk into the attack. The young blacksmith's assistant set the broadsword's hilt against his side in the sand and used the leverage to lift the sharp blade at the last second. The massive minotaur wasn't quick enough to shift his feet and avoid the blade.

The screams of the beast could be heard for miles. It wrenched away, covering the downed Gideon in blood, and howled into the sky. The two handed sword had impaled the mighty creature. Half of the blade protruding from the beast's back, half from the front. Gideon slowly climbed to his knees, his torn legs barely supporting his weight.

Suddenly, a mighty fist crashed into his neck, sending him sprawling back to the sand. The minotaur was laughing with the sword still plunged deep into his bloody chest. Gideon grabbed the ground with his hands and used the strength of his upper body to roll forward into a crouch. Standing upright just a few paces away was the laughing minotaur. It reached down, one hand grabbing the hilt of the sword and the other grasping the blade close to his body. Gideon scrambled on his hands and knees, trying to get away but never taking his eyes from the gruesome sight.

The crowd went quiet, expecting to see the bloody giant rip the sword from his own chest and fight on. Instead, the minotaur used his brute strength to break the forged blade in half. He tossed the bloody hilt to the crowd and began to shake, arching his back and convulsing. The second half of the blade dropped to the sand with a spurt of thick blood.

Gideon managed to get to his feet as he watched the astounding spectacle. With the minotaur's own scimitar in hand, he slowly began to circle the beast. The crowd went wild at the sight of both combatants leaking blood all over the sand, the minotaur unaware of the warrior standing behind him. Gideon raised the scimitar up, thinking to cut the gruesome head from the hairy shoulders of the minotaur, but the beast sensed him at the last moment and turned. The monster couldn't get the javelin in line to spike Gideon but was able to dodge the killing blow, losing only a horn in the process.

Gideon was quick to retrieve the twisted, severed horn from the sand and used it in his left hand as a dagger. The minotaur took the offensive again, attempting to charge Gideon and open his gut with the end of the pole. Blood loss from the sword wound in the minotaur's chest slowed him and caused him to stagger as the thick, dark blood began to fall from the beast's mouth. Mustering his last reserves of energy, Gideon struck out with one quick, low feint with the scimitar to force the beast to lower the pole. A flick of his wrist brought the sharp horn up under the minotaur's chin. A singular, powerful flex of Gideon's arm had the end of the horn protruding from the top of the creature's skull and the minotaur fell to the sand, lifelessly twitching as the crowd screamed for more.

In dramatic fashion, Gideon dropped the jeweled scimitar down on the top of the minotaur's lifeless chest and collapsed to the sand next to the slain beast, exhausted and nearly dead.

It took the warrior three weeks under the care of the Vrysinoch priests at the tower before he was able to stand unassisted. It was at the tower that Gideon was recruited to fight for the city as a paladin. He spent ten years living there, training with the other paladins and becoming a true warrior. Holy paladins of Vrysinoch are trained to use large shields and maces and to fight side by side, using each other for support on the battlefield.

After his decade of rigorous training, Gideon took his weapons and left the tower, never entering it again. Typically, a paladin who has graduated from the tower either receives a commission in the royal army as an officer or is chosen to be one of the king's guards. Not wanting to dedicate his life to the service of one man or even one city, Gideon abandoned his life as a paladin.

He took his tower shield and his enchanted mace to the blacksmith where he used to work and sought to have something better crafted. Not being able to pay for his gear, Gideon returned to his old job hauling ore and materials. It took him almost two years to pay for the re-forging of his holy weapons. The shield and mace, along with a decent portion of Gideon's blood, were melted down into a single sword entwined with the warrior's powerful soul.

A screech brought Gideon back to the road in front of him, shattering his peaceful memories. His eyes immediately shot skyward, searching for the bird that had screamed. An eagle, the divine beast of Vrysinoch, was a fortuitous portent for the wandering warrior. Gideon listened, hearing the powerful call of the eagle echoing off of the high city walls behind him. The screech was full of violence and strength, mimicking the blood in Gideon's own veins. His pace quickened to a light jog, adrenaline coursing through the great warrior's body.

"Vrysinoch!" Gideon called to the sky, yelling at a black spot on the horizon he assumed to be the distant eagle. "Grant me your blessing!" he shouted, breaking out in a run. The axes on his side thudded against his powerful thighs with each hulking stride and his sword bounced up and down in the leather scabbard on his back.

Gideon did not know why he had begun running. Something about the way the eagle had cawed ignited a holy passion in the paladin. The divine symbol etched into his back from his training at the tower began to glow and radiate with heat. The warrior kept his pace, jogging for a few miles before finally coming to a rest outside a small hamlet on the edge of the Clawflow. He made his camp outside the town, not wanting to spend money on a room at an inn or tavern. He waited until the dawn before beginning his search for information concerning the lost king.

The villages along the Clawflow River all belonged to Talonrend and swore allegiance to Castle Talon, but few citizens from the small towns frequented their capitol city. The river ran from north to south, beginning somewhere in the snowy mountains to the north of Talonrend and continuing through the land for hundreds of miles before splitting into many tributaries. The Clawflow not only served as the lifeblood of the villages, but also created a natural barrier to the wilds. All of the human settlements were located on the western bank of the river; no villagers wanted to brave the untamed wilderness of the great forest in the east. Always dominating the horizon, the massive form of Kanebullar Mountain could be seen from almost anywhere, towering above the shadowy forest.

There was another kingdom far to the south of Talonrend and beyond the reaches of the Clawflow.

Reikall was only a few days' ride on horseback to the south of the river but the two kingdoms had almost no communication or trade between them. Gideon had a sneaking suspicion that his southerly neighbors were somehow behind the disappearance of King Lucius.

Every five years, dignitaries from Reikall made the trip to Castle Talon to partake in diplomatic discussions. Well, that was the agreement at least. It had been over twenty years since anyone from Reikall had been seen. Geographically, the two cities were not far from each other, but in the minds of the citizens of Talonrend, Reikall was all but forgotten. The two kingdoms had no trade between them and had never been at war. It was whispered, of course, that King Lucius would send the worst criminals of the realm to exile in Reikall, a statement that the rumormongers could never prove true or false.

Like everyone else, Gideon had only heard rumors of the kingdom of Reikall, but even so, a nagging feeling tugged at his gut and caused him to turn his gaze upon the southern horizon.

Gideon welcomed the journey with a sigh of contentment.

Five

DARIUS WATCHED AN interrogation through the heavy iron bars of the cell. The guard captain held a small silk cloth over his mouth, a futile effort to keep the pervading stench at bay. Under Terror's Lament, buried hundreds of feet below the massive stone walls and tucked away in a cavern that few knew existed, was the dungeon. The man being interrogated was nearly dead, having offered up no pertinent information. Darius was still no closer to finding King Lucius.

"Death is such a flirt," King Lucius' steward mused, grabbing a small piece of iron with a heavily gloved hand. "You never know just how much one man can take before death comes for him. Sometimes it feels like I've been doing this for hours, sometimes they die with the first tiny cut. Interrogation is such an imperfect science, wouldn't you say?"

The tortured man tied to the bloody table in front of the steward didn't respond. He merely whimpered, barely even attempting to struggle. The king's royal steward, Jan by name, although most everyone used his title when addressing him, also served as the dungeon's primary interrogator. The steward lifted the heavy piece of iron out of the fire and pressed it gently to the bound man's eyelid, laughing quietly as the skin began to crackle and pop.

"One more time, good sir," the steward taunted, lifting the iron from the smoldering face, "where is the king? Everyone knows that you went with him in the caravan, your own family will attest to that." The man's face contorted in horror at the mention of his family.

"Tell me where the king has run off to, and I will end this. One stab of my dagger, deep into your heart, and this all ends. Your daughter won't have to answer any questions, your wife won't have to answer any questions..." Jan was twirling his dagger around in his hand, staring at the ceiling as though he were discussing the weather with an old friend over a casual game of chess. The steward lifted the small strap of hemp from the man's mouth, prompting him to speak.

"I... I already told..." the words came out in between violent sobs that sent blood splattering to the table.

"Yes, yes, the king left the caravan before you arrived at the southern village of Cobblestreet," Jan interrupted. Darius shook his head at the bars, looking away, knowing what was coming next. "It seems that everyone who has wandered back into Talonrend from that caravan has the same sad tale to tell. The only problem is, I don't believe it. I say you killed our dear Lucius. You and your merchant band united and slew the king and his guards and now all spin the same pathetic web of lies." The steward reached under the table to a thick wooden crank and began turning it, lifting the table up to a vertical position. "Your lies will not save you. Not here."

With a flick of his practiced wrist, Jan replaced the rope in the merchant's mouth, looping the ends of the hemp around a hook on the back of the table and completely immobilizing the man. The look of sheer terror on the man's burnt face was enough to make Darius leave the room. This was the third interrogation he had seen in as many hours, having lost the contents of his stomach only minutes into the first.

With the table in position perpendicular to the floor, Jan picked up a heavy axe from the floor, its edge heavily stained with old blood. He held the axe up against the man's pale neck, gently rubbing it back and forth, bringing a thin red line of fresh blood to the blade. The tortured man closed what was left of his eyelids, waiting for the end. Jan started to laugh. His victims never understood. "You only get to die quickly if you give me what I want!" he bellowed, cackling away with evil, sadistic joy.

One perfectly placed blow severed both of the man's ankles, dropping his bloody feet to the floor. Jan's leather boot kicked the feet away, burying them in a pile of filth and other rotting parts. "Now, just to let you know what is happening, although I don't suspect that you have much time left in the first place," Jan picked up a large bucket from a table behind him and placed it under the man's bleeding stumps as he spoke. The steward had to use both hands to lift a heavy bag from the table, pouring its white contents into the bucket, filling it to the top with fine salt. The bloody stumps writhed in pain just an inch above the grains.

"Now, this bucket here is full of salt," Jan explained, wiping the blood and grime from his hands onto a towel. "Right now, that isn't much of a problem for you. I tied the ropes too tightly for you to fall into it." King Lucius' steward bent down and took a pinch of salt from the bucket and sprinkled it into the savage burn on the man's face. "I assure you, you do *not* want to end up in that bucket." The man howled through clenched teeth, fighting against his restraints at the new wave of pain.

Jan walked to the corner of the room to a set of a dozen ropes attached to pulleys in the stone ceiling. After sorting through them for a moment, he grasped one of the ropes and smiled at the man on the table. "Better flex," he said in a melodic voice, yanking down firmly on the rope. In the blink of an eye, the hook at the back of the table released, causing the man to violently jerk downward, no longer supported by the ropes but still unable to escape the table with his arms tied out wide.

Jan hurried out of the small chamber, locking the door behind him. "I'll send the wolves in tomorrow to clean up your mess," he called back over his shoulder as he continued down the hallway past the other cells.

"Do you always have to be so dramatic at the end?" Darius asked, falling into step beside the king's steward. The captain kept his silk cloth over his mouth until the pair exited the dungeon entirely.

"I like the drama of a good interrogation," the man replied, his voice dripping with malice. "Besides, that's what the king pays me to do, to interrogate people and then make them disappear."

"Yes," the captain said solemnly, disgusted by the horror of it all, "judging by the smell in that room, you don't bury the bodies. Ever." Darius was glad to step into the sunlight of the warm afternoon and breathe the fresh air. "We still don't know much about the king. All of the merchants that have wandered back to Talonrend just say that the king left the caravan with some of his guards at some little village along the Clawflow."

Jan stopped at the exit to the tunnel, leaning against the smooth stone of Terror's Lament as he thought. "They said that the king left somewhere around Cobblestreet. That pathetic village is quite a long ways from Castle Talon, one of the southernmost settlements along the river. What could he be looking for? Where is the rest of the caravan?"

Darius fiddled with the hilt of his sword, pondering the situation. After a moment, he simply threw his hands up in the air, defeated. "None of this makes sense," he said, exasperated. "Why have some of the merchants left the caravan, but others have not returned? I truly believe that those men I saw you torture hid nothing. They honestly have no more answers than we do..." Darius' voice trailed off as he shook his head.

"Thank you, good captain of the guard. I take pride in my work. No one hides their secrets from me. No one." Jan took off the heavy leather apron he was wearing and hung it on a wooden peg just inside the iron door to the dungeon. It took him a few moments to produce the proper key from a deep pocket on his royal finery and lock the door. The two men took a few steps away from the wall before turning. Jan spoke a simple arcane command word and the door vanished into the wall so thoroughly that it was as if the portal never existed.

"I will never understand how you do that, Jan." For what seemed like the thousandth time that day, Darius shook his head in disbelief. Jan simply nodded to the captain, folding his hands behind his back and assuming his regal posture before departing for the castle. The guard captain continued out from the wall in the direction of the artificer's guild, hoping to find some answers through less violent means.

The artificer's guild hall was an interesting structure. When Talonrend was first settled hundreds of years ago by the refugees from the Green City, the building was a small palace. The residence had two turrets flanking the ornate wooden door with leering stone gargoyles keeping watch from above. The guild hall ran east to west within the city, each end marked by a formidable round tower molded to the shape of an eagle's grasping talons. No one has ever been quite sure how the artificer's guild came to possess the palace, but it had been their home since before the birth of King Lucius' parents.

Darius approached the guild hall quickly; he never enjoyed his meetings with the arrogant artificers and he wanted the whole affair to be concluded quickly. As was normal with every visit to the strange guild hall, the door opened before Darius was in range to knock.

"Hello again, good captain Darius," the porter said in a mellow voice, beckoning to Darius with one hand as he held the door ajar. "So good it is to see you today. Shall I inform my master of your arrival?"

"Yes, yes, of course," Darius muttered as he strode into the ornately decorated foyer. In the blink of an eye, the master of the artificer's guild stood in the foyer as well, right in front of the startled captain, a tiny wisp of smoke dancing to the ceiling.

"Please," Darius said with a start, "Lady Keturah, your sudden arrivals only serve to frighten me. Perhaps you could..." Darius tried to clear his head and recover from the frightening appearance of the guild master he so despised dealing with. "Knock...

or something… before you just show up like that…"
Truly at a loss for words, Darius simply took a step
back from the imposing woman and produced a
small leather sack full of coins from his belt.

"What exactly would you like me to knock upon, guard captain Darius?" Keturah's voice had a
melodic quality to it that sounded almost incorporeal, like a beautiful ghost was whispering her words
just after she spoke them. "Your head, perhaps?"
Keturah lifted a slender, gloved hand into the air,
making a knocking motion a foot from Darius' forehead. The guard captain felt the magical hand tapping on his head as surely as he felt the wooden
floor beneath his boots.

With a flick of his wrist, Darius tossed the sack
of coins to the intoxicatingly beautiful woman. Keturah was dressed in a flowing silk dress the deep
color of blood with a black corset laced up her chest.
Her long, curly red tresses matched the color of her
raiment perfectly, almost blending into the soft fabric itself. Keturah's hair bounced playfully as she
reached up and caught the flying coins, allowing
Darius to catch a few glimpses of the woman's striking green eyes. She was unerringly attractive, her
pale, lithe arms ending in black leather gloves covered in runes.

Keturah snatched the money out of the air and looked at it intensely, weighing the contents in her mind. She smiled, sending a wave a relief through the nervous captain. With a snap of her fingers, the gold vanished. "So, you are serious this time. You brought enough gold to convince me that either you have actually spotted a dragon or this meeting is about something else altogether." Darius lost himself in the thin, ghostly echo of Keturah's words, barely understanding them as the woman spoke.

"I need you to find the king," Darius stammered, never taking his eyes from the lovely mouth of the guild master.

"An interesting proposition. Just where do you think our precious Lucius has run off to?" The woman smiled as she spoke, her thin red lips nearly hypnotizing the enamored captain. "Surely you do not expect to find him here, yes?" Darius didn't miss the subtle glance of Keturah's eyes to an ornate door on the side of the room. Still, the man's increased heart rate betrayed him, turning his face red. "Follow me," Keturah whispered, echoed by her high-pitched ethereal counterpart. She reached out, taking the rough hand of the guard captain in her delicate, gloved grasp.

Keturah led Darius deeper into the guild hall, heading East, through corridors lined with statues and portraits of famous, and sometimes infamous, artificers. Darius was barely able to take the sights in, having never been beyond the foyer of the grand building. Keturah moved quickly, guiding him by the hand through the various twist and turns of the mansion. Finally, they arrived in front of a solid stone wall, the base of the eastern round tower.

With a gentle shove, Keturah pushed the man away from the stone and squared her shoulders to it. "Get behind me," she said, using a tone that brokered no alternative. Darius nervously toyed with the hilt of his short sword, honestly wondering if he was about to die. The woman, and the guild she represented, terrified him. Darius had never been blessed with any powers beyond the martial, divine or arcane. Magic and magic wielders, especially beautiful ones, held a distinct advantage over the anxious man.

Keturah spoke her name to the wall forcefully, projecting her voice much louder than Darius thought possible given her slender frame. Something about her astral echo changed when she spoke to the stones. The ghastly quality hidden underneath the woman's melodious voice grew in volume and speed, pronouncing Keturah's name even before her natural voice did.

The stones of the tower's base shifted ever so slightly, quivering with energy, before erupting into flame. The gout of liquid inferno washed over Keturah, blinding Darius momentarily as he ducked down behind her. Lines of fire continued down the hallway behind the pair, congealing onto the floor in a pool of sublimated flame.

Darius could feel the intense blast of heat licking at the edges of his body. He quickly retracted his arms in to his chest, curling up as tightly as he could against the dizzying onslaught. Much to his disbelief, his skin was not burned. With Keturah in front of him, Darius was able to endure the fire without any serious injury.

As quickly as the geyser had erupted, the hallway calmed. Everything looked just as it had a moment before, without a burn or char to be seen anywhere. Keturah turned and lifted the man from his crouch, brushing his shoulders off and smilingly sweetly. "See, I told you to stay behind me." Her voice had returned to normal; well, as normal as her voice ever was. The woman was unscathed by the maelstrom of fire, looking perhaps even more radiant than before.

The two continued up a dark, unlit staircase winding tightly around itself as it ascended. Keturah took the pitch black steps two at a time, her footfalls placed perfectly on the stone. After several full rotations, they arrived at the top of the tower, its stone walls set with intricate stained glass. There was a bronze telescope on a tripod standing in the center of the room, facing east.

"Based on everything I have already seen in this place, I'm betting that telescope is no ordinary device." Darius took a hesitant step forward, approaching the telescope with a measure of reverence.

"That would be correct," Keturah said, moving swiftly to position herself behind the fine bronze instrument. "Now, where should we begin our search?" The graceful woman swiveled the telescope back and forth, aiming it at the stained glass windows, one after another. Darius then realized that she wasn't looking through the scenes painted on the glass, she was looking into them.

"We have learned that the king left the merchant caravan he was travelling with around the town of Cobblestreet. You might try starting there." Keturah turned the bronze telescope to a window depicting the small village of Cobblestreet and watched for a long moment. Darius watched the woman with anticipation, hoping she would be able to locate the missing king with ease.

"Well," she said, standing up and returning her gaze to the captain, "he is not in Cobblestreet. Most of the merchants are still there, camped outside of the village, milling about and doing nothing. The king's royal banners and his large tent are clearly visible, but peering inside the tent reveals nothing."

"What about my men stationed to guard the king? Is there any sign of the twenty armed soldiers that served as Lucius' escort?" The captain's mind raced with possibilities. He had learned of the king's departure from the caravan already and with the amount of money he had paid the guild master, Darius expected more information.

Keturah leaned over the telescope again, further examining the area surrounding the small riverfront village. "I see a few armed men, nothing the level of a royal escort though." The woman turned the telescope just slightly, aiming it at the very edges of the stained glass window. "There are tracks in the mud from horses, leaving out to the south of the encampment," she said, shaking her head. "I do not have the range to follow them. The windows are only so big."

"Continue to search. I want to know every single thing about the town. There must be other clues around the village." Darius was impatiently pacing the small tower room, his right hand fidgeting with the hilt of his sword.

Keturah continued to scan the telescope over the window, inspecting every street in the muddy village. Darius was quick to notice the sudden quickening in the woman's breathing as the telescope aimed at the far edge of the town, opposite the camp.

"What is it?" he asked in a frantic voice, "have you found something?" Darius moved behind the woman, hoping to look through the scope and see the king, alive and well.

Keturah shook her head, continuing to look through the instrument as she spoke. "This is certainly interesting. It appears as though the little town of Cobblestreet has some uninvited guests." She moved the scope even further to the edge of window, straining her vision to its magical limits.

"I can't quite make out what is happening, but on the other side of the river..." Keturah stopped her scan, rubbing her eyes before returning to the telescope. "Yes, there are two goblins camped out on the fringes of the town in a small clearing. Right next to the Cobblestreet graveyard, it seems this pair of armed goblins is spying on the city. Certainly is unusual behavior for such an unintelligent race."

Keturah stood up, letting Darius view the bizarre scene for himself.

The image was cut off at the edge, not showing the entire clearing, but Darius could easily see two small goblins sitting down on the grass. "Why would there only be two of the wretched vermin?" Darius muttered to himself, trying to look beyond the small clearing to see the rest of the area. Something at the edge of his vision caught the guard captain's attentive gaze.

"Did you see the boots at the very edge of the view?" he asked, looking back to Keturah. The expression on her confused face told Darius that she had not.

Keturah shoved the man aside, peering back into the stained glass. "Those aren't goblin boots. As far as I know, goblins don't even wear boots. Those feet belong to a humanoid, either a man or an elf, perhaps a cleric of some sort, judging by the hem of the robe. That is all I can see. The stained glass images don't extend far enough."

"What do we do?" Darius asked, fearing that a goblin raiding party was waiting just beyond their vision.

"We send a scout. That is what we do." Keturah's voice, amplified by the ethereal echo behind it, was commanding. "I trust that you have already sent an expedition to find the dear king? They must be warned."

"Yes," Darius agreed. "Our fastest scouts will be dispatched to warn the town."

"I have someone faster," Keturah said with a sly grin. She cupped her hands in front of her mouth, whispering arcane words of evocation into them. When she revealed her hands again, a large black scorpion sat upon her fingers, clicking its massive claws together. Keturah set the creature down upon the stone of the tower and breathed on its back, a thick cloud of billowing smoke escaping her mouth and enveloping the scorpion.

"Taurnil," Keturah whispered to the swirling wisps with her ghostly, disembodied voice. "Taurnil, arise, my champion, awaken from the abyss." Keturah and Darius both took a step back, giving the scorpion as much room as possible in the small chamber at the top of the guild hall's eastern tower.

The smoke swirled about the black scorpion faster and faster, the insect's body beginning to pop and crack with the magic of transformation. Obsidian flakes of the scorpion's exoskeleton fell to the floor and dissolved as a humanoid shape grew within the smoke. Taurnil stood five and half feet tall, his sinewy flesh pulled taut over thick lengths of corded muscle. His body was completely devoid of hair, his skin the color of pale ash mixed with acrid snow. The room smelled strongly of sulfur, the pungent odor stinging Darius' nostrils.

The demon, or whatever Taurnil truly was, grinned, showing his jagged teeth stained brown and red from years of eating flesh. The beast's face was flat, with a wide nose so stretched over the underlying bone that it appeared as two gaping holes in the center of its head. His eyes were dramatic enough to send Darius running from the room, had Keturah's command over the creature not been so apparent. The monstrous being craned its neck about the room, its eyes showing nothing but the deepest black. The room reflected blurry off of the crystalline eyes, giving a haunting, soulless aura to the foul humanoid.

Keturah moved to the creature's side, placing an arm gently on its boney shoulder in a loving manner. "Taurnil, my dearest champion, go now. Fly to the settlement of Cobblestreet, southeast of this place, along the Clawflow River. Go there, warn the king's soldiers of goblin activity in the region. Then go across the river, near the human graveyard, and kill every goblin you can find." Taurnil smiled devilishly at his last command.

"I do as you command." The creature's voice was more a hiss than recognizable speech. Taurnil bowed his head in obedience to his master. Keturah pushed up a small section of the stone, causing the wall to swing open and revealing a sizeable door in the tower between two of the stained glass windows. "I shall return once I have gorged upon the souls of goblins," the beast hissed, turning for the door.

Taurnil's back shifted and churned, the taut flesh splitting on either side of the demon's distinct vertebrae. Two massive wings unfolded themselves from beneath the flesh, hooked spikes of bone accenting the bottom of each leathery appendage. Taurnil spread the wings wide, filling the small chamber, flexing with raw power. The thin wings were translucent, bulging veins showing clearly throughout. The wings were torn in places, small holes letting the sunlight of the morning shine through them.

"A powerful and winged lich died near Talonrend once," Keturah explained, recognizing the shocked expression on Darius' face. "Of course, I couldn't just let the wings go to waste. Taurnil here was most appreciative." Turning back to her champion, Keturah bade him to leave with a calm wave of her gloved hand.

"I have seen too much for a man my age," Darius muttered to himself. Keturah simply laughed, watching her demonic companion fly out of the tower.

Six

"WHY HASN'T HE woken up yet, Vorst? I thought he would be awake by now..." Gravlox was nervous. Even though the man's chest still rose and fell with steady, rhythmic breathing, Gravlox feared for the man's life.

"It has been a full night. I figured that he would wake up with dawn, most humans do anyway." Vorst sounded inquisitive rather than nervous like her companion. "Go to the river and get some water. Maybe if we splash it on him, he will realize that I didn't kill him. Humans are so stupid."

A few moments later the man was coughing up a runny mixture of river water and blood, frightfully looking about the clearing at his captors. The man was almost six feet tall, greatly dwarfing the goblins that held him hostage. He continued to cough, struggling against the ropes that bound his body.

"Wha—? Goblins!" the man shouted when his eyes fell upon the image of Vorst holding her bow. It was clear from the sneer in the man's voice that his initial surprise was replaced with disgust.

"Yes, goblins," Vorst responded in a halting version of the human tongue. "Just goblins," she said calmly. Vorst lowered her bow slightly and sounded out the word 'necromancer' in the man's direction.

Gravlox nearly fell over dead from shock at hearing Vorst's beautiful voice speak the human language. His mind started to ask her how she came to speak their language, but his mouth would not move. Gravlox sat slack-jawed on the grass, dumbfounded.

"Necromancer?" the man questioned, rising up to a sitting position. If he felt any fear or apprehension toward his captors, he did a fine job of hiding it. "I can assure you," he continued, "I am no necromancer, nor do I have any desire to become such an abomination."

The calm manner with which he conversed with the goblins alerted Vorst to how powerful the man must be. She drew an arrow from her quiver and began to take aim at the man. Gravlox caught the man glancing toward the lantern sitting next to Vorst's pack. Not sure what powers it might possess, Gravlox drew his sword and walked to the magical lantern, ready to smash it if need be.

The man leaned forward in his bindings, staring hard at Vorst. "What are you?" she said, unsure as to just how dangerous her captive was. A smile broke out on the man's face as Vorst finished her question.

Kill him. Without a moment of hesitation, Vorst loosed her arrow, taking the man full in the chest and knocking him to the ground. He sputtered just once before his life ended. *Keep the lantern, toss the body into the river where the current is strong.* Vorst stood, placing her bow over her shoulder, and moved to grab the man by his ankles.

"Help me dump him, Gravlox," she said, dragging the man through the clearing toward the river.

"What is going on? Why did you kill him?" Gravlox remained frozen in place, standing above the lantern with his sword drawn.

"Lady Scrapple commanded it. I am not one to go against her orders." The tone of Vorst's voice indicated that she had disobeyed the Mistress of the Mountain sometime in the past and did not entertain the possibility of ever doing it again.

"She speaks to you? Lady Scrapple speaks to you?" Gravlox was amazed. He had never heard the voice of his mother.

"She does, on occasion. Only when I am in trouble, it seems." Vorst had the corpse almost to the river by the time Gravlox managed to pick up the man's arms and help.

"Why does she protect you?" Gravlox asked after they had tossed the body into the river.

"I assumed she spoke to all goblins," Vorst replied calmly, rubbing her hands against the grass to try to remove the stench of human. Gravlox knew she was lying, but decided it was better to let it go and ask his questions later. If Lady Scrapple talked to all goblins, why had she never spoken to him?

"We should get going," Vorst said as she gathered up their supplies. "I do not like this place. It reeks of humans. Grab the lantern, I know enough about ghost flowers to make a potent enough poison." Her command was final and sucked all the joyful life from her voice.

The two goblins didn't speak as they headed out of the clearing in the direction of Kanebullar Mountain.

They had been on the trail for about an hour before Gravlox finally found the courage to break the silence. "Vorst, you aren't acting like yourself.

What is going on?" He didn't know how to phrase the question properly. He really just wanted to know who his companion actually was and how she came to speak the human language.

Vorst sighed. "Grav, I think you need to ask that question to yourself. *You* are more than *you* let on." Vorst stopped on the trail, turning to face Gravlox and look him in the eye. "Lady Scrapple has me watching you."

"Why?" he pleaded more than asked. It was clear from his expression that Gravlox assumed he was about to die. "For plotting to kill a miner?" He put his hands in the air, ready to defend himself.

"No, silly Gravlox, of course not!" Vorst laughed, "You weren't made to be just a foreman, or even the leader of a mine. You were born with certain…. powers." She paused a moment before continuing. "Lady Scrapple made sure of it."

"What sort of powers?" Gravlox asked, looking at his hands, expecting them to suddenly feel stronger and bulge with muscle.

"Alright Gravlox, I don't know if you are ready for this or not, but I will try to show you." Vorst closed her eyes, silently conversing with Lady Scrapple and seeking her approval. She drew her short sword from its scabbard at her side, holding it firmly in her hand. "Close your eyes and imagine the ground right behind you. Picture yourself five feet from me, instead of just two."

Trusting fully in Vorst's judgment, Gravlox did just that. Vorst stabbed out hard with her sword, aiming for Gravlox's vulnerable neck. Faster than Vorst's mind and eyes could even register, Gravlox was standing further away, out of her sword's biting reach.

"Open your eyes, silly," Vorst said in her usual voice, full of life and melody. The gasp that escaped Gravlox's mouth sent birds fluttering from the trees.

Gravlox simply stood on the trail, a dumbfounded expression etched onto his hairless face. "How did you do that?" he finally stammered, barely audible. The frightened goblin touched his body, wondering if he was even real.

"*I* didn't do that, Grav, *you* did!" Vorst jumped about, excited that Gravlox was finally discovering his powers. "You were created by Lady Scrapple to be a shaman, Gravlox. You just never figured it out on your own. Some goblins need a little pushing."

Gravlox let the explanation sink in, wondering how he had lived his entire life without knowing he was a shaman. "What else can I do?" he asked, eager to learn of his abilities.

"I can't help you there. Goblin shaman aren't like human mages or wizards. Goblins don't spend years in a school learning all of their powers, they just kind of come to us when we are ready. You have to discover things for yourself." Vorst started to skip down the path back toward Kanebullar Mountain.

"How long have you known?" Gravlox asked, running to catch up to Vorst as his mind raced. "About me, that is," he clarified.

"Lady Scrapple told me a while ago," Vorst called back over her shoulder, vaulting a fallen log that blocked the path. The two goblins sped off through the forest, Gravlox trying hard to keep pace with his lithe companion, eventually arriving at the small creek where they had previously felled the elk.

Gravlox ran with his head down, breathing heavily and not even aware that Vorst had abruptly stopped at the edge of the small clearing. The two goblins rolled into the glen, fully entangled. Gravlox was too absorbed in his thoughts and emotions to have noticed the line of human crossbowmen kneeling on the other side of the grass.

Gravlox did, however, manage to hear the click they made as the bolts fired out from their bows, cutting a horizontal line of death through the afternoon air. Had it not been for his ungraceful tumble into the back of his friend, the two goblins would have surely been cut to ribbons by the volley. Fourteen crossbow bolts sailed above the goblin pair, thudding into the trees and other brush behind them.

The foreman froze, not sure what course of action he should take. Vorst didn't waste a single moment, leaping into action with her usual confidence. The crossbows, taking time to reload, had used up all of their effectiveness in the first volley. Vorst's short bow was much more mobile, ripping the life from three of the men before they even drew their swords.

"Get up!" Vorst called to Gravlox, still lying prone on the grass. The nearest two crossbowmen charged, their gleaming sword points leading the way. Vorst swung her bow, more of an attempt to distract the men than deal any damage. It worked, buying the goblin a split second to draw her own sword and toss her travelling pack to the ground. Gravlox was up by the time the soldiers closed the gap, squaring off against the two. Vorst barely rose to the height of the average man's waist, so she used her shortness to her advantage, ducking in under the sweeping strikes of the soldiers.

Both swords crossed above her head harmlessly as she scored a hit on the back of one knee, rolling out to the other side, near the reloading crossbowmen. Moving purely out of desperation, Gravlox parried the first strike high, knocking the blade away and stepping into the attack, bringing his body right up against the shining armor of the human soldier. The goblin foreman reached within himself, trying to find his inner wellspring of power, the conduit between the realm of magic and his pale fingertips.

Blood showered from the back of the soldier, pieces of his metal chain armor flying all over the grass and bits of gore splattering the man's comrades. Gravlox slowly withdrew his hand from the far side of the man's chest cavity. Blood dripped from his fingers to stain the green grass. A few of the crossbowmen paused, lowering their weapons as they watched the corpse of the man fall. A large hole gaped in the soldier's chest. Gravlox stood behind the torn remnants of the human, staring at the lines of blood on his own arm.

The man fighting against Vorst stopped, staring slack jawed at the scene, allowing her plenty of time to put her sword to deadly work.

Sensing a lull in the combat, the leader of the guard patrol stepped forward, calling for his soldiers to stay their weapons. The leader, designated by the bright white cape he wore, kept his hands in the air before him and made no moves to unsheathe his sword. "Taurnil!" he called out with a smile.

The heavy beating of wings heralded the demon's arrival. Taurnil landed softly on the grass in front of the humans, just an arm's length from the small goblins. The beast's skin was eerily similar in color and texture to that of the goblins, but that is where the similarities ended.

Taurnil opened his mouth, revealing a circular maw of jagged teeth, three elongated tongues dancing about happily. Gravlox could make out the terrified face of one of the crossbowmen through a ragged tear in the monster's huge wing. Bone claws at the bottom of each wing pulsated with energy, hungry for a kill. The ashen-skinned nightmare wore no armor, its long claws serving as its only conventional weapons.

Gravlox and Vorst stood close to each other, both expecting the other to act first. Vorst looked at her wooden bow longingly, the weapon lying just inches behind one of Taurnil's pale feet. Gravlox glanced down at his own weapon, the hilt of his sword clutched tightly in his shaking hand.

Taurnil stretched his muscled arms out wide and clicked his claws violently in the air. The demon rushed in, using one beat of his wings to lift him from the ground. Taurnil's scything talons creased the air, screaming in from the sides, wide enough to decapitate both goblins at once. Gravlox lifted his arm to block the coming death, not wanting to look the demon in the face.

Taurnil's mighty claw struck Gravlox's arm, hitting him with full force. The short goblin felt the pulse of energy within him, the magic racing to his limb, absorbing the entire attack without the claw even breaking his skin. Taurnil used his winged speed to continue over the goblins and landed down behind them.

Gravlox felt the well of magic within him begin to dwindle, having spent almost all of his remaining energy blocking the first attack. Taurnil reared his head back and spat, launching a spray of green bile toward the goblins. Thinking fast, Vorst pushed Gravlox to the side and rolled the opposite direction. The acid began to smolder and melt the ground where it landed.

The pale demon strode in, heading directly for Vorst, thinking his victory nigh with the two opponents split on the battlefield. Vorst lifted her sword in front of her and readied her defense. The great winged beast slashed out at the small goblin, his muscled arm sweeping in above the sword. Vorst jerked her defense skyward at the last moment, hoping to sever the claws from the demon, but only succeed in entangling her blade.

Taurnil was stronger than Vorst could have ever imagined, wrapping his sinewy fingers around the blade and disarming her with a flick of his powerful wrist. Vorst could only watch in horror as her weapon tumbled to the grass. Her peripheral vision picked up the action of Taurnil's wing, but it was too late. Vorst was disarmed, with no way to block and nowhere to dodge.

The barbed end of Taurnil's right wing came driving up, the demon having pulled his wings in suddenly and arching his back. The bone spear bit deeply into the soft flesh of Vorst's hip, rending it open and spilling forth her blood in a great rush of agony. Vorst howled in pain.

Gravlox was behind the beast, hoping to decapitate the demon while it struck. His short sword came down in a flurry, all of the goblin's strength behind the blow. Just inches from the taut and ashen neck, the left wing of the monster snapped in tight, the top of it coming into perfect line with the descending blade. Gravlox chopped down and cut a deep wound in the top of the leathery wing.

Taurnil pulled back, dislodging his barb from Vorst's side, and curling away. One flap of his wings sent him high into the air, relative to the short goblins, and placed him safely out of their reach. Blood flowed freely from the top of Taurnil's wing but it flowed faster from Vorst's hip.

Vorst tried to roll and retrieve her bow, hoping to shoot the flying demon from the air. She didn't get far, her leg failing beneath her the moment she put weight upon it.

Gravlox watched her crumble to the bloody grass, clutching her wound. The rage welled up inside him, a red wall of seething anger. Gravlox swung his sword about in the grip of his hand, letting his acrimony build. With a fierce, primal growl, Gravlox leveled his blade and charged, intent on skewering the beast where he hovered.

The goblin foreman leaped from the ground, his small but powerful miner's legs catapulting him into range. He stabbed out, a vicious thrust aimed right for the grey chest of his foe. Taurnil curled his wings in tightly about his body, rolling in the air to deflect the blow, gravity pulling him to the ground. Gravlox's sword struck true, slicing a clean path through both wings and pinning them to the beast's chest. Taurnil's roll rent the sword from the goblin's hand, the hilt of the weapon acting as the head of a nail, keeping the monster's arms pinned inside his wings.

Gravlox fell to his back on the bloodstained grass, coming up quickly in a roll. Taurnil began to retreat back to the line of crossbowmen. The line of soldiers had reloaded by then and leveled their bows at the two goblins. Gravlox, his adrenaline-fueled bloodlust all but dissipated, looked upon the line of soldiers and despaired. He could not stand against that volley.

The shaman fell to his knees beside his writhing companion, expecting the end to come swiftly. He bent low over Vorst, attempting to apologize for getting them both killed, but the beautiful goblin female was already gone, her mind having fled to the peaceful sanctuary of the unconscious.

Eight crossbows clicked. The soldiers fired a hail of deadly bolts into the air. Gravlox felt the last remnants of energy deep inside his body fading; the well of power was nearly dry. His hands clutched at the slick ground, the dirt and blood feeling sickeningly warm beneath his pale fingers. With a cry, Gravlox ripped two handfuls of dirt from the ground, throwing them into the path of the iron-tipped bolts as one last act of desperation. The ground beneath the small clumps of earth rolled and a roiling temblor rose up from the goblin's fingertips, racing toward the soldiers. The wall of vibrating grass and soil shot forth, sending a turbid column of dust into the air.

The growing tremor absorbed the bolts, soaking up their added energy. The captain, being the singular standing soldier of the group, was the only human fortunate enough to have the time to escape before the shockwave of earth hit the line. Soldiers flew from their crouched positions with wild abandon, the sheer energy of the wave blowing apart their weapons and bones like twigs in a tornado.

Taurnil and the lone surviving soldier ran for their lives. The wave of earth dissipated far from the fleeing pair, its magic spent. Gravlox collapsed to his back, truly exhausted, the power within him utterly depleted. In the same belabored heartbeat, two score of additional soldiers sprinted into the clearing, weapons at the ready.

They were goblin soldiers though, coming to aid the fallen pair. Their leader, a heroic goblin warchief by the name of Yael, rushed to Vorst, quickly tending to her grievous wound. The goblin soldiers secured the area, making sure that Taurnil and the human had fled and no other men were nearby.

It took nearly two hours to return Vorst to consciousness. Her hip was patched with rugged strips of leather, an herbal poultice filling in the wound and aiding the healing process. Gravlox merely sat next to the wounded goblin, watching the other goblins work to save her life, not speaking a word. Finally, Yael approached the shaken foreman. "Lady Scrapple sent me here with a warband of drones to help you," he explained. When she saw the vision of Vorst killing the man by the river, she knew there would be a fight. Yael sat on the ground next to Gravlox.

"Why does Lady Scrapple only speak to her? Why is it that I have never heard her voice?" Gravlox was staring in the direction of Kanebullar Mountain, his mind reeling with a thousand questions.

Yael let out a long sigh. "Lady Scrapple cannot feel you. You are not connected to her by the magical bonds that unite all of the goblins. The drones, these soldiers I brought with me, they are merely manifestations of Lady Scrapple's will. They do not think, they do not make decisions, they are simply tools, like the crude weapons they wield." Gravlox spent a long moment digesting the profound words.

"What have I done to so offend the Mistress of the Mountain? I never wanted to be cast out from her favor..." Gravlox let his head fall, staring into the dried blood beneath him, sorrow stamped clearly on his face.

Yael shook his head. "You were not cast out by our mother, never that," he reached a hand out to

Gravlox's shoulder, trying to comfort the troubled goblin. "The well of magic that resides inside you is limitless. It is too powerful for even Lady Scrapple to hope to comprehend. Her psionic magic has no hold over you. You, foreman Gravlox, are the first goblin that is truly free. No part of your will is bound to that of our common creator." Yael stood, returning to help the injured Vorst as her mind returned to her corporeal body.

Gravlox gazed into his hands, clenching his fists and trying to call upon the energy within him. The shamanistic power was unresponsive. "Your friend here is a high ranking associate of the Ministry of Assassination," Yael said as he checked the bandage on Vorst's side. "She was assigned to keep tabs on you, reporting your life to Lady Scrapple, and to kill you if the need arose. Clearly, that need has not yet arisen." Yael was gathering his warband together, calling the mindless soldiers to his side.

"What am I to do?" Gravlox asked, still looking at his hands more than anything.

"Lady Scrapple wishes you to head south. A very tentative alliance has been formed between the goblins and a powerful, ancient necromancer. Go to Reikall, that is where you will find him. I cannot guarantee your safety though, for the robed man you captured and killed earlier was the necro-

mancer's son, sent to be a spy among the humans."
Yael drew his sword as he spoke, tossing it to the
ground at Gravlox's feet. "You may need a new
weapon when you get to Reikall. Try to salvage
what alliance you can with the necromancer. We
need him. Lady Scrapple needs him. All goblins
need him. For whatever reason, our mother determined that Vorst's life was worth more than the life
of the necromancer's son and possibly the alliance."

Gravlox could hardly believe the words he was
hearing. Yael started to march his warband out of
the small clearing, leaving the looted remnants of
the human squad scattered about the grass and up-
turned dirt. "I will use these drones to keep the humans busy. This necromancer with which Lady
Scrapple has entangled us captured the human's
leader, their beloved King Lucius. We cannot be
sure what will become of him, especially now, but
war is brewing between our races."

Vorst was sitting up by then, looking at Gravlox, trying to gauge his reaction. "We are the children of fire, the heroes born of the sacred mountain," she said, her voice small and riddled with
pain. "Will you rise to the challenge, Grav? Will you
travel through the immense forest to the far away
kingdom of Reikall with me?"

"Limitless," Gravlox muttered, nodding his head.

Seven

IN A DARK cave a hundred feet below the elaborate guild house, Keturah waited impatiently. Her delicate foot tapped, the sole of her slipper rapidly clicking against the wet stone of the chamber. The cave was completely lightless, a black dome devoid of torches at the very depths of the extensive cave system beneath all of Talonrend.

Keturah's footfalls echoed off the walls of the empty cavern, a hollow sound accompanied by the slow dripping of water somewhere in the distance. The woman paced back and forth, her gloved hands running through her long hair. A delicate lace band was wrapped tightly about her head, fully covering the woman's lovely green eyes. The thin white fabric, commonly referred to as moonlace, illuminated the sight of the wearer so long as the darkness itself was not magically imbued.

The tall guild master used her magically enhanced vision to look about the cavern, trying to discern the slightest ripple in the air that would indicate the arrival of her overdue guest. At the back of the chamber, the stagnant air finally began to shimmer and swirl. Keturah walked quickly to the spot, enacting a minor enchantment to protect herself from the heat of the teleportation.

The air began to split as if invisible hands were pulling it apart like a thick curtain. A tiny scarlet bead of magical energy appeared on the floor and slowly rose toward the ceiling. The orb passed through the air with a crackle, surrounding Keturah with magical heat.

As the portal opened, it offered a stunning view of the other side. The portal connected to the top of a high castle tower, far to the south. The panoramic view of the wasteland beneath the stone tower was breathtaking. Plumes of acrid smoke danced with the charred rain of brimstone and hellfire that covered the kingdom of Reikall. Burnt frames of farmhouses and stables dotted the countryside like lonely tombstones standing guard in an empty cemetery. The smoke billowing up from great fissures in the ground was laced with toxic poison, suffocating what little flora remained in the dead kingdom.

A man walked into view of the portal, dressed in simple clothing with a heavy cloth bandana covering his mouth. With a smile, Keturah reached her hand through the red portal, welcoming the tingling sensation of spatial dislocation that shocked her body. The man on top of the tower touched her own, using it to balance himself as he took a small step that moved him over a hundred miles in a heartbeat. The portal stayed open, continuing to swirl and shimmer in the dark air of the cavern, displaying a constant background of fiery carnage.

"Well met, fair sister Keturah," the man said with a grin.

"You're late, brother," was all that Keturah said in response. Her scowl showed clearly how little she tolerated tardiness.

"How fares our intrigue with the crown?" the man asked, trying his best to ignore Keturah's frown.

"Darius is a persistent bastard," Keturah sneered with a shake of her head. "I had to show him our goblin associates outside of Cobblestreet. He only sent one man to find the king, some long forgotten paladin. I have Taurnil out as well, a more capable hero by far."

"You showed him the goblins, the ones who killed my son? I will flay the skin from their bones myself if I ever see those two." He spat as he spoke, wondering how a pair of goblins could have killed his own child; even a fledgling magician should have been able to deal with a pair of goblin scouts. "No matter, I have other sons. Any child of mine who cannot defend himself against two goblins is not worthy to inherit the kingdom I am building. How much did you tell Darius? I always believed our plan to rely on the element of surprise, a unified strike to quickly overwhelm the city."

Keturah wondered in the back of her mind just how much the ties of family meant to her brother. "I haven't spoken to the goblins in some time, but I believe they will understand this latest development. The plan has changed slightly, not in concept but perhaps in timing. If I can instill enough fear in Herod, he will issue a call to arms and send forth the army. With the Vrysinoch Guard deployed to the field against our goblin allies, your own army will meet little resistance inside the city. Darius' tenacity might work in our favor, dear brother."

"I have never liked that little whelp. He goes on and on about honor and valor, things that have no place in the proper scheme of leadership. The king should be the most powerful man in the realm, not just the one lucky enough to have been born a prince."

"Or the most powerful woman, brother," Keturah laughed. "Do not forget our agreement. Reikall is yours, as it already is. Talonrend will bend its weary knees to me. I wish to rule over a kingdom of living subjects, not a scarred land of mindless undead." Keturah let her gaze fall again on the ruin of Reikall visible through the rippling portal. Something about all that fire and sulfur *was* appealing, she thought, picturing Talonrend suffering from equal destruction.

As if reading her thoughts, the tyrant of Reikall smiled. "Yes, the intoxicating aroma of death appeals to everyone, whether they admit it or not. So, if we can get the goblins to assemble an army in the field, we are certain that Darius will send the Vrysinoch Guard to meet it? I like the sound of that plan. You always find ways to please me, sister."

"Yes, well, the only problem remains with Herod. No matter how much Darius begs the king to dispatch the army, Herod will likely wait, evacuating the villages along the Clawflow to the safety of his high walls. The prince will not assume the throne until he sees his brother's bloody corpse. According to the priests, only the rightful king can dispatch the holy army of Vrysinoch. Our prince is so weak that he would never go against the priests lest he lose favor with the city. We can prevent Herod from evacuating the villages by downplaying the goblin presence. With any luck, we can force Herod to move the army out of the city when our own machinations have come to fruition."

"Yes, Herod is a tricky one. He will not produce an heir of his own and he will not sit on that damned seat himself. I have been trying for months to get him or anyone to claim himself as king. Without a king, the army will never leave the city. If he recalls the villagers and does not meet the goblin army head on, our plan may fail. Now that Darius has seen our little friends, he will surely begin to ready the city's own defenses. I do not want to waste a hundred thousand of my soldiers just to get ten of them over the walls." The man's tone was stern, leaving no room for debate on the topic.

"I understand, brother," Keturah said, her eyes still scanning the destruction of Reikall. "We will not move until every piece is precisely in place. Taurnil should have no trouble dispatching the two goblin scouts, which will ease the fears of the villagers. Once they are pacified, I will have the goblin army move from their mountain lair and march north, assembling quickly in the field, a force that will demand the entire attention of Talonrend. With the villagers so vulnerable, Herod will have no choice but to move the Vrysinoch Guard out of the city, whether he has the approval of the priests or not."

"It would certainly be easier if Herod would just accept that fact that he is the king. If that were the case, the priests would demand that he send the army to war, not prevent it." He let out a long sigh, frustrated that the tenacious guard captain was impeding his plan. I trust that you have already instructed Taurnil to kill the paladin that is at this moment heading for my borders?"

"Why certainly, brother," Keturah responded, the ghostly echo behind her voice filling the dark chamber with confident laughter. "That poor paladin is likely lying dead in the field at this very moment."

"Good," the man said with a nod, "I don't want anyone wandering into my kingdom uninvited."

Keturah noticed a fresh spray of blood on her brother's shirt and harrumphed. "You've been recruiting more troops, I take it?" she said, pointing out the small splatter. "You warlocks use such barbaric methods of coercion."

The man smiled, inspecting the blood stain. "How many times have I told you, Keturah? I am no simple warlock. A warlock is but an average wizard who prefers a darker taint on his magic. A powerful necromancer such as myself creates the very essence of undeath. I have an entire kingdom of perfectly obedient undead thralls at my command!" He lifted his hands above his head, sending a narrow bolt of dark grey fire leaping from one open palm to the other. The small ball of energy congealed in his left hand, slowly taking the shape of an eyeless creature about the size of a dog with long, black claws like a jungle cat and festering wounds covering its hide.

Yawning, the beast took life, moving its sightless head about the air, its jagged teeth dripping with black saliva. In one fluid motion, the necromancer broke the beast in half, releasing a wave of magical energy much larger than the one that had created it. With a snap of his finger, Keturah's brother absorbed the energy into his hands, leaving no evidence that the small creature ever existed.

"Power begets power," he said with a grin.

Keturah could only watch then as he stepped back through the portal and left. The cave darkened as the portal closed, leaving her standing in the dark. "Goodbye, Jan," she said as she began the spell that would return her to her chambers in the guild hall above.

LATER THAT DAY, just after nightfall, Darius sat behind his large desk in the center of the barracks that housed the Talonrend city guards. His familiar sword sat on the desk next to a stack of leather bound books, one of which was opened to a list of names. Candles and torches hung on wall sconces around the stone room but Darius was alone.

"I cannot bother the prince with this goblin nonsense until I am sure it is more than just a simple pair of creatures sent to scout," he mused aloud. He had been sitting behind the desk since dawn, looking through ledgers that were filled with the names and ranks of each soldier serving in the guard. Another book, much smaller than the one open before him, held the identities of all the guards that had attended the king on his journey.

"There is too much coincidence here..." he pushed through more pages, running his fingers over the names. "Why would two lone goblins appear outside the city where the king disappeared?" Darius mindlessly flipped his feather pen into the air, trying to play it all out in his head.

A cricket began to chirp somewhere in the room, breaking the man's concentration. "Someone has to be cooperating with either the goblins or whatever kidnapped the king! Goblins do not target royalty and they certainly do not hold hostages for ransom!" he yelled, more to hear himself say it than for any real gain. Darius had been thinking that very thought since the moment Keturah had shown the goblins to him.

It can't be the goblins, they are too dim-witted to formulate complex plans with other races, Darius thought, tossing his weighted pen from one hand to the other as he stared into the flames of the candle on his desk.

The guard captain scanned through the names on the page for what felt like the hundredth time that hour. "Someone has to be on the inside, some-one! Kings do not simply vanish and goblins do not simply appear *when* kings vanish." Darius knew every name on the list of guards personally. He had recruited each and every soldier himself. As far as he knew, they were men loyal to the throne to their last breath.

"Maybe it was just a simple coincidence..." Da-rius said, closing the book with a thud. "Maybe these two goblins got lost or separated from their tribe and wandered near the village." Darius knew in the back of his mind that a mere coincidence was not the case. He regretted not taking more action when the king had first gone missing.

The guard captain had sent a search party out, of course, but no word has been heard from them either. *I should have sent runners to every single village, sent a dozen search parties in every direction. This all could have been avoided.*

He spun his sword around idly on his desk as he thought. *Where would the king have gone? Why would he leave his caravan?* Not paying much attention to his actions, the tip of Darius' short sword bumped into his inkwell, knocking it to the floor where it shattered.

"Ugh..." Darius mumbled as he bent over to collect the broken glass. It wasn't the first time he had knocked over an inkwell.

His hands full of inky, black glass, it took the man a moment to notice that the stones of the floor were stained with some other than his mess. Blood was dripping onto the hard rock just a few feet from where the inkwell had shattered.

"What on earth..." his voice trailed off as his gaze locked on the growing pool of crimson blood. Slowly, his eyes followed the dripping up to the high stone ceiling of the barracks. "Lieutenant!" he barked, hoping that someone would hear him and come to his aid. "Guards!" he shouted, unable to take his eyes from the black pool of shadows on the ceiling. "Anyone!" came the final ring of his panicked voice.

Darius crouched on the floor by his desk, his hands covered in ink and broken glass, and knew that he was about to die. The tight collection of shadows on the ceiling was darker than it should have been, darker than the darkest night Darius had ever seen. His jaw tightened. His stomach tensed.

Slowly, the shadows began to move. Darius stood and reached for his sword, bits of glass biting into his hand as they were crushed against the hilt. He lifted the weapon in front of his chest and set his feet solidly underneath him. Fear rattled his mind and confused his senses.

Two ragged wings stretched forth from the abyssal darkness. Blood dripped from vicious wounds the beast had recently received. Its powerful claws dug into the stone, holding his body firm as it turned its head to glare at the man.

"Taurnil," Darius said, defiantly. He locked stares with the awful creature. His own blood began to run down his arm from the shards of glass tearing open his flesh.

"Darius," the monster hissed back at him. Taurnil's mouth was full of jagged teeth and his three long tongues licked the air with anticipation.

"This is where it ends," Darius said with a slight moment of resolve. "At least now I know what happened to my king. I welcome this reaping, that I may join Lucius in Vrysinoch's paradise." His eyes never left Taurnil's black orbs as the winged demon let go of the ceiling and charged.

The ragged wings beat the air with ferocity, blowing loose sheaves of paper from the desk onto the floor. Darius tried to mount a valiant last defense, but he was quickly overwhelmed. The strong beast held every advantage and Darius' feeble sword was easily slapped from his grip. Black ink splattered the demon's face, only adding to the terror the pale monster evoked.

Three tongues latched onto the captain's forehead and face, oozing vile poison into the man's body. Darius struggled under the powerful grip of the monster, trying to get enough room to stab. His struggle was brief. The poison coursed through his veins, turning his innards to nothing more than smoldering ash. Darius' body shuddered twice and then went limp in Taurnil's arms.

One scything sweep of his massive claw severed the captain's head from his shoulders. The bloody captain hit the stone floor in two pieces with a wet thud, like a thick leather boot being pulled out of mud.

Taurnil took a step back before letting the rest of the body slide from his powerful arms. The beast smiled. He walked to the head, staring at it for a long while before bending down and lifting the bloody lump from the stone. "So this is what an honorable man looks like," Taurnil hissed, inspecting the disembodied head.

He kicked Darius' sword across the room where it clanged against the wall. "I fight without your useless steel, without your cowardly armor, and yet I have never fallen to a human in single combat." Taurnil turned the head over in his hands, inspecting every inch of it. "Perhaps it is not tools your species lacks, but courage."

Taurnil remembered the two goblins that had bested him at Cobblestreet. "That goblin loved its companion and would have gladly sacrificed itself for another," he said to the head, looking again into Darius' dead eyes. With a smirk, Taurnil nudged the bloody corpse with his naked foot.

"No," he hissed through a smile of jagged teeth, "I have never been weak enough to feel such primal emotion. That is not what makes someone strong. True power can only come from the abyss, and I am its chosen avatar, the singular paragon of might in this world and all others." Taurnil lifted off from the stone floor and exited the barracks through a broken window set high in the stone.

The beast met its master in the dark of night behind the artificer's guild hall. Casually, Taurnil tossed the head to the ground at Keturah's feet like he was throwing a coin to a beggar. "Behold your captain," he hissed.

"Rally around his feet," she responded with a chuckle, "or perhaps just his head."

Eight

*Y*OU WILL NEVER be king. You will never sit
upon your brother's throne. Your fate is not in
this kingdom. Your destiny has been written
elsewhere. You will never be king.

Herod awoke in the middle of the night with
cold sweat covering his brow. Vrysinoch would not
let him find rest. The castle was quiet. Shadows
danced along the walls from the few torches that
still burned low. The prince stood and pulled his
robe tight about his chest to ward off the cold night
air.

He pulled a torch from the wall and started to
leave the bedchamber before turning for his sword
belt. Herod often went for walks about the castle at
night but the hairs standing on the back of his neck

told him to go armed. His sweaty hands rubbed the remaining sleep from his eyes and he strapped his sword to his left hip, a matching dagger to his right.

The prince of Talonrend did not know exactly where he was going, but he left his room nonetheless, locking the heavy wooden door behind him. He walked down the short hallway that connected his personal quarters to the throne room and stood in front of the empty chair that had consumed his life.

In the dim, scattered torchlight of the airy castle, the throne's green cushions danced with life. It was an immense chair, carved from the very stone of the castle and much wider than any of the kings who had ever sat upon it. The back displayed a pattern of wings, an interlocking design resembling the tower in the city's center.

"Why do you torment me, Vrysinoch?" Herod asked the empty throne. The prince's fingers slowly traced the great talon that protruded from the arm of the chair, its claws clutching an old white skull. "The priests in the tower tell me that you are a good god, providing for all of my needs, protecting me when I am weak." The emerald placed in the skull's eye socket was cold to the touch.

"Why can I not find peace and rest? Why do you torment me?" Herod drew his sword and pointed it right at the center of the throne. His glare and threatening posture challenged Vrysinoch. "If you weren't made from the very stone of the floor I would throw you in the moat myself." Herod spun his sword around in his hand and slid it back into the scabbard at his hip. The sound of the metal ringing against his leather sheath echoed in the empty chamber.

Herod turned from the throne swiftly, his robe fanning out behind him. He stormed to the door with a great scowl stamped on his royal face. The prince had never left the castle in the dead of night before, at least not without a formal guard and good reason. The heavy wood and iron doors were locked. Herod took a step back, thinking to simply return to his room or perhaps walk about the parapet, but a thought struck him and he turned back to the door.

Reaching inside a deep pocket on his robe he produced the key to his personal chamber. Without thinking about it, he pushed the key into the iron lock on the door and turned it. A subtle clicking sound accompanied the opening of the door. He felt the cool breeze of the night air brush against his cheek and heard footsteps coming from the drawbridge. Herod drew both of his weapons and pushed the door open quietly, standing in the entryway with visible defiance.

A huddled figure hurriedly moved to the castle. Whoever it was, they hadn't noticed Herod, likely absorbed in their own thoughts. The prince stepped quickly to the side and closed the heavy door behind him, waiting in the shadows of the parapet for the person to approach.

Herod exhaled a long breath, steadying his nerves and calming the rise and fall of his chest. The prince was a seasoned warrior, a veteran of many hunting skirmishes with beasts in the wild. He waited, watching every step of his foe before springing into action. Like a cat leaping upon an unsuspecting field mouse, Herod launched his body into action. The muscular prince quickly overpowered his prey, knocking the man to the ground.

Sentries on the parapet above heard the commotion and began shouting. Herod wrestled the smaller man to his back in moment, the point of his dagger coming to rest right beneath the fool's chin. The prince's sword hovered just over the man's scalp, both weapons poised for an easy kill.

"Jan…" came the exasperated and surprised voice of the prince as he untangled himself from the king's steward. "What in Vrysinoch's name are you doing out here?"

The terrified man picked himself up, dusting his robes off and collecting his thoughts. "My apologies, my liege. I did not mean to frighten you," he said as Herod replaced the weapons in their sheaths.

"And why are you outside at this hour? Why are you awake?" Herod scrutinized the man's appearance trying in vain to find anything out of place.

"Well, sir, I may live in the castle but I do not spend every single moment of my time in it. I was out in the city on personal business." Jan began to walk into the castle, leaving Herod standing in front of the doors with a confused expression on his face.

"I could have killed you," the prince called to the steward.

"Yes, my prince, I am well aware," Jan smiled, showing no signs of fatigue for the late hour. "I am glad you chose not to."

Herod nodded and took a few steps away from the castle doors to stand on the wooden drawbridge. The man stood there, leaning on one of the draw-bridge's heavy chains, and stared into the calm water of the moat below. None of the ducks that often floated atop the water could be seen.

Something in the back of Herod's mind told him to be worried. He fumbled through the pocket of his robe and pulled out the metal key to his bed-chamber.

"The key to my personal quarters is the same key that opened the front door to the castle..." Herod turned on his heels and moved swiftly to the castle doors, testing the key again. Sure enough, the key turned easily in the lock and the door opened on its heavy hinges.

"I knew I should have never trusted that one..." Herod returned the key to his pocket and took a step back, looking up to the sentries on the parapet above.

"Where can I find a locksmith?" he called to them, barely making out their faces in the dancing torchlight.

"There is an armorsmith that makes doors and chests just right down the road, not far at all, the building with the red roof," the drowsy sentry pointed toward a huge structure that towered over the other buildings in the area.

"Yes, I know the place well," the prince shouted back to the sentry. "Master Brenning, the head smith of that forge, crafted my armor for me. I did not know he made locks." Herod began walking toward the smith's shop, his hand subconsciously fondling the top of the metal key inside his pocket. "If Jan comes back out of the castle before dawn, shoot him down and then come get me." Herod's expression was as solid as a statue. The two sentries on the parapet did not question his order. "I want to know every time that man leaves the castle and when he returns. Someone find Darius for me, go wake him and send him to Master Brenning, I need to speak with him at once." Herod walked from the castle with a quick burst of energy filling his step, his robes fanning out behind him.

Master Brenning's forge, Dragon's Breath Armory, was a colossal business. The burly armorsmith employed a score or more of the city's best weapon and armor crafters. Herod arrived at the door to the business and found it unlocked. Two of the four stone chimneys were billowing thick black smoke into the night air.

The ring of metal against metal and a stinging burst of heat greeted the prince as he entered the busy forge. Even in the dead of night, a few smiths stood at their anvils and forges practicing their art. The fires at each of the stations bathed the room in a soft orange light, shadows growing and dying on every wall as the artisans moved.

None of the smiths took notice of Herod's entry and the prince moved quickly to the staircase at the back of the room. Master Brenning worked on the top floor of Dragon's Breath Armory by himself. Herod passed by the second floor, a space that served as a storage area for raw materials, and arrived in front of a heavy steel door that barred entry into the highest level. The prince knocked on the door sharply and waited a few moments before a small hatch on the metal surface opened.

Master Brenning's bearded face filled the tiny portal like a grizzly bear peering into a pot of honey. With a gruff nod the master smith opened the entire door and stood aside as Herod walked into his chambers. The room was sweltering from the heat of the active forges below but no fire burned within the room save one lonely candle held in the smith's right hand. Master Brenning hadn't bothered to put the candle on a tray; rather, he held it and let the hot wax drip onto his bare hand. If it bothered him in the least, he didn't show it.

"Your captain of guards allows you to wander the streets of Talonrend without armor or escort?" The gruff man was covered in a thick mane of curly black hair that barely revealed his mouth when he spoke.

"Master Brenning," Herod said, clapping the strong smith on the shoulder. "Long ago you taught me that not every protection is visible in the form of a steel breastplate or an armed man at my side." The two men sat down at a small wooden table next to the smith's tiny cot against the far wall of the room.

Remnants of the smith's uneaten dinner were still strewn about the surface.

Master Brenning used the lit nub of a candle to light a candelabra on his table before extinguishing the nub in the palm of his hand with a grunt. "Something must be troubling you greatly. Princes do not simply knock on my door in the middle of the night. What's on your mind, Herod?" Master Brenning spoke in a monotone base that sounded vaguely of a wagon wheel rolling over a bed of crushed rocks.

Herod placed the key from his pocket on the table between them and slid it over to the smith. "I need to know who made this key." Master Brenning didn't even bother to pick the thing up before asserting that it was not his work.

"I haven't made keys since I was an apprentice, before you were born, I would bet." Brenning's eyes never left the prince. "What does this key unlock?"

"It is the key to my personal chambers," Herod replied, taking the key back and holding it in front of the candle flames. "It also unlocks the main castle doors, as I learned tonight."

The smith's eyes closed for a moment as he digested the words. "Where is your escort? As the last living heir to the throne, you should be guarded at all times."

Herod's fist slammed into the tabletop. "Lucius will return! He is not dead!" the prince shouted in a brief outburst of rage. "I am not the king… I will never be king…" The prince hung his head, his thoughts fixated on his brother.

"It is the castle steward that holds a copy of this key, is it not?" Master Brenning acted as though the prince's outburst was nothing more than a passing gust of wind.

"King Lucius' steward, not mine. Darius, the guard captain, serves as my personal assistant, not that I have ever found much need for him in that capacity. What business does that conniving little man have in keeping a key to my personal chambers?" Herod tried to recall in his mind if he had ever noticed anything amiss in his chamber.

"You cannot trust that coward. I would suggest that you have your man Darius arrest him at once. It was a clever disguise, changing your lock instead of carrying two keys." Master Brenning took a tankard of warm ale from the table and finished it in one long draught.

"I know, I rarely leave the castle when the door is locked, I have no idea how long he has had access to my room."

"So," the bearded smith said as he wiped the foaming ale from his mouth, "I assume that you came to me for a new lock on your door. I would suggest perhaps a new piece of armor as well. You have enemies here, Herod." The burly man looked around the room nervously. "Especially since the disappearance of your brother. The whole city is on edge, most of them wondering when you will become their king."

Herod sneered, anticipating the voice of Vrysinoch in his head. He knew every word that the winged god would say to him. "I cannot become king. Not until I see my brother's corpse will I even consider it." The prince shook his head. "You make the armor for the tower's paladins, what are the priests saying about our situation? Have you heard any rumors there?"

Master Brenning laughed, a great booming sound that shook the small table. "The priests are always talking, Herod. You should know better than anyone about that. The priests and clerics in the tower don't respect you at all. The people may love you and love for you to be their king, but the holy men would never allow it."

"You tell me nothing that I do not already know." Herod stood, wanting to leave the hot room. "Can you make me a new lock by tomorrow? You said something about new armor as well. If it fits under my tabard, I'll take it." Master Brenning nodded with excitement.

"Hey, rumor at the forge is that you sent one of my assistants to go fetch your brother!" Brenning was up and about, rummaging through his cupboards for more ale, no doubt.

Herod stopped and scratched his head, not sure at first what the old smith was even talking about. "Gideon?" he asked, remembering the warrior's name.

"The very same!" Master Brenning found what he was looking for, a large silver horn filled with frothy dark beer. He took a healthy swig before continuing. "He was one of my best. He helped me build things that most smiths can only dream about. That one is strong, he will find your king if there is anything left of him to be found."

Herod watched in amazement as Master Brenning finished his ale and moved to put on his heavy leather apron, wasting no time getting to work. The prince left the hairy man's chamber and continued out of the building. He was just past the front door when he realized that Darius had not found him yet.

The prince made his way quickly to the barracks where Darius worked. One of the sentries from atop the castle parapet was standing in front of the large wooden door that blocked the entrance to the barracks.

"Prince Herod," the man called out, tipping his helmet as he spoke. "We have not located the guard captain yet. He was not in the barracks and there are no signs of a struggle within. It seems he is simply out and about this night."

Herod shook his head. "Alright," he said, saluting the soldier. "Notify me the moment he appears. I must speak with him."

The guard nodded. "I sent two soldiers out into the town to look for him but it is unlikely that they will find him tonight. He will show up in the morning and I will send him to you personally, sir."

The prince liked this soldier. For some reason, Herod felt like the man could be trusted. That feeling of trust was quickly soured by the growing knot of fear in Herod's stomach. It was unlike Darius to vanish without having told anyone where he could be found or when he would return.

Nine

GRAVLOX AND VORST left Yael and his band of goblins with fresh supplies, heading south toward Reikall. Despite the goblin's best efforts, Vorst still needed time to let her body recover from the battle with Taurnil. The two adventurers made slow progress through the thick forest that bordered the river. Gravlox, intently focused on helping the wounded female clutching to his side for support, failed to notice the paladin and his dark companion shadowing the goblin's every move.

The beating of leathery wings often heralded Taurnil's arrival. No rush of air accompanied the thin red portal that rippled through the light of dawn next to Gideon. The alert paladin was on his feet in a moment, a throwing axe instantly in his strong hand. He took several steps away from the portal and pulled his arm back to throw. A scantily clad female leg slipped through the portal, slowly testing the ground, before two gloved hands appeared and widened the shimmering red crease of magic.

Gideon's arm lowered just slightly as the full form of Keturah stepped through the magical portal. The soft glow of dawn played with her red hair, causing it to shimmer, a color somewhere between the deep hues of golden wheat and the slick crimson shine of fresh blood.

Seeing the axe poised to fly at her head, Keturah quickly held up a hand. "Wait!" she called to the warrior, closing the portal behind her with a flick of her delicate wrist. "I am a friend." Keturah tried to assume the friendliest pose she could, a stance that the seasoned paladin interpreted as ill-intentioned seduction.

Gideon grinned, knowing that his target was too close to dodge and completely devoid of armor in her sheer red dress. The axe spun from his hand with expert precision. Keturah's eyes went wide with surprise. In a flurry of red she spun as the axe neared her face, catching the wooden handle as it passed her vision.

The beautiful woman plucked the flying axe out of the air and completed her spin, using her own momentum to toss the axe back at Gideon's feet. "Is that how you greet all women?" The spin maneuver had kicked some dust up onto the bottom of her elegant dress, something the woman quickly fixed. "It is no wonder that most of you brutish warrior types don't breed. Or does the tower require that all paladins be celibate?" Keturah smirked and stood straight, watching the confused expression on Gideon's face.

The warrior's muscled arm reached to the hilt of his sword, the familiar leather and steel giving him comfort. "Darius, the captain of the guard sent me!" the woman shouted, tired of defending herself and not wanting the man to waste any energy.

Gideon's hand stayed on the hilt of his sword and his gaze bore into the woman relentlessly. "Gideon, I'm not here to hurt you!" Keturah said, holding her arms out wide for the man's inspection.

The paladin took his hand from the weapon on his back and picked his throwing axe up from the ground. "Who are you and why have you come to me?" Gideon resolved not to charge the woman where she stood, partly because she knew his name and partly because she should not have been able to avoid his axe. It was a perfect throw and the ease with which she had denied it frightened the paladin greatly.

"My name is Keturah," the mysterious woman replied. She placed a delicate hand into a seamless pocket on her flowing gown. "Darius wants me to help you find the king. Although I cannot personally join you on your quest, I have someone who might help." She withdrew her hand from the pocket and revealed a jet black scorpion that skittered around her glove.

Placing the creature on the ground, Keturah whispered to it, summoning Taurnil. The demon was somewhat dwarfed by the hulking paladin, standing between the two humans and flexing its healed wings.

For the first time in his life, Gideon thought he was about to die. The sinewy creature before him assaulted every divine sensibility the paladin had. He could smell the stink of the abyss washing the area in a foul haze.

"Begone, demon," Gideon growled under his breath, feeling the holy energy of Vrysinoch filling his body. The symbol on his back flared to life in the presence of such a foul creature.

"Do not worry, paladin," Keturah said sharply. "Taurnil lives in the abyss, yes, but he is not a denizen of that place. I created him, I control him."

Taurnil turned his head just slightly to look over his shoulder at the woman, his three tongues moving eerily around his pale lips. "We have reason to believe that the goblins are behind the disappearance of the king," she continued, moving to the beast's side and placing a hand on his shoulder. "Two of them were spotted on the other side of the river and have escaped."

"So I heard," was Gideon's gruff response. "I spent the entire day yesterday talking to the village, gathering information. I also heard a rumor that your pet couldn't even handle two puny goblins, even with support from the militia." Gideon spat on the ground at Taurnil's feet, an open challenge. The beast spread his wings wide and hissed in return. Green acid flew from the creature's tongues and landed on the ground with a sizzle.

"These goblins aren't like anything we have ever encountered," Keturah answered. "One of them is a powerful shaman. Do not underestimate those two. They are heading south along the Clawflow, presumably toward Reikall. Follow them. Taurnil can scout from the air. Find out what you can, bring the king back if he still lives." Keturah didn't wait for a response before snapping her fingers and vanishing.

Taurnil and Gideon stood in the drowsy light of morning and stared at each other. The intensity of the paladin's eyes evaporated in the inky blackness of the pale demon's lightless orbs. Gideon looked away.

"The moment I sense your treachery, demon, I will not hesitate to cut you down." Gideon began walking toward the riverbank, heading south.

"I could kill you with a thought," Taurnil hissed back through his jagged maw. It was a lie, but one that Gideon had no way of knowing. Taurnil, a creature created from pure magical essence, could not use much magic himself. He had command over shadows and could manipulate light, but his arcane abilities were very limited beyond the realms of optical illusion.

"We will shadow these goblins, all the way to Reikall if we must. I will pursue from the eastern bank of the river, to protect the villages we pass." Gideon pointed toward the forest with his armored hand. "You will fly above the forest and track them. We meet up every night at dusk and every morning at dawn. You have the advantage of mobility, so I expect you to come and find me."

Taurnil was already a few feet above Gideon's head when the paladin finished speaking. He lowered his head and took off for the distant shore, wanting more than anything to find vengeance on the other side of the river.

Gideon shook his head, glad to be rid of the demonic beast for a while. His muscled body was warm in the morning sun and the gleaming steel covering his left arm reflected the summer brightly. Patches of brilliant white light danced about the man's leather boots as he walked.

The riverbank still wet with morning dew, the tall grasses rising up beyond the tall man's belted waist. Gideon crouched down low, trying to make out any signs of the goblin pair on the other side. No movement on the other riverbank betrayed the presence of enemies. Still holding his crouch, Gideon moved further south through the tall grasses, his body getting soaked by dew with every step. A large shadow darted among the tree tops on the other side, something Gideon could only hope was Taurnil.

Having no clear sign to follow other than the airborne demon, Gideon subtly made his way back from the edge of the Clawflow and took off in a jog, trying to match Taurnil's pace from a distance.

The small goblins were easy for Taurnil to spot. The demon was perched quietly in the upper boughs of a tree, waiting for the pair to move by underneath them. Green turned to brown and then to black on the leaves beneath the sinewy beast's ashen skin. The very presence of such evil tainted the living plants around him.

Gravlox came into view beneath the tree first, leading Vorst behind him. They were moving slowly, their pace diminished by the jagged gash on Vorst's hip. Taurnil looked down to the barb on the end of his leathery wing and smiled, remembering the hit that nearly impaled the goblin. The three humanoids were barely more than two miles south of Cobblestreet but it was clear that Vorst needed to rest her aching side.

Gravlox gingerly set the female goblin down against the base of the tree and took his travelling pack off. He produced some sort of food from the pack and fed it to his injured companion one piece at a time. Vorst's eyes slowly rolled back in her head as she ate and Taurnil quickly straightened his back and turned to put a thick branch between her vision and his skin. Taurnil was quick and Vorst was slightly delirious—she didn't notice the beast in the tree above her.

The goblin foreman sat down on the grass beside the female, letting go a long sigh. Vorst leaned her head to rest it on Gravlox's shoulder, a gesture that clearly unsettled the recipient. Gravlox put a tentative arm around Vorst's back and pulled her in close, trying his best to comfort the wounded goblin. Taurnil cocked his head to the side, having no way of comprehending the scene unfolding beneath him.

Keturah often placed her arms on the demon's back and shoulders much the way the two goblins did, but Taurnil did not know why. He always understood the gesture to be one of ownership and control, nothing more. Taurnil's mind raced, thinking back to the times when Keturah had touched him, wondering if there was any ulterior motive behind the woman's actions. The beast did not feel the pangs of physical attraction and was immune to all of the softer emotions that accompanied such feelings.

Inquisitively, Taurnil continued to stare down at the goblins from his high perch. The two goblins were speaking to each other in soft tones, a language that reminded Taurnil of the high-pitched wails of tormented souls in the abyss. The wounded goblin moved herself closer to her companion, nestling her head next to his. Even the emotionless beast in the tree could tell that Gravlox felt unnerved and cautious. Taurnil, sensing the trepidation underneath Gravlox's shaking hands, readied his wings for flight. He expected some sort of trick or other form of treachery aimed at himself or the male goblin.

Everything felt like an elaborate trap, one that Taurnil had no way of anticipating.

The demon did not like feeling powerless.

Much to the surprise of both Taurnil and Gravlox, the wounded female goblin reached an arm up behind her companion's bald head and their lips met. The kiss lingered for what felt like an eternity to all three of them. Taurnil fully expected a dagger to flash up and rip the life from the male goblin. Why else would the wounded one have gotten so close to him if not to kill him? "Goblin, you are more a fool than I had thought, letting your guard down," Taurnil whispered past his jagged teeth. The three tongues within his maw writhed, playing out the beast's frustrated confusion.

Gravlox's hand grasped the rugged bark of the tree, supporting Vorst as their limbs became entangled. Something around the two goblins was different. The air became charged as though lightning had just struck the ground. The leaves on the ground swirled through the air, ever so slightly, dancing softly on the warm earth. Taurnil could feel the magic seeping from the goblin's hand and climbing up the tree. Leaves began to grow anew beneath the demon's feet.

It took a conscious effort for Taurnil not to lose his connection to the foul magic of the abyss, so strong was the energy washing over him through the tree branches. The emotion accompanying the pure magic was completely foreign to Taurnil, an exotic rush of heat that caused his wings to flex and his arms to tighten. He tried to conjure a wave of ethereal darkness around his feet, hoping to stem the flow of energy into his body, but no magic would obey his call. The abyss felt so far away, like a distant memory of a dream.

Miraculously, the seeping wound on Vorst's hip closed and the flesh knitted itself back together. Taurnil could only watch in bewilderment as the leaves around the pair swirled faster and faster. The beast closed his black eyes and tried to conjure forth a vivid image of his home in the maelstrom darkness of the abyss. Fleeting images of blackened evil approached the edges of his mind but Taurnil could not hold them.

Suddenly, as quickly as the warm energy had assaulted the demon, it retreated. Wave after wave of magic left the beast and coursed back through the bark and into Gravlox's hand. The goblins pulled away from each other and Vorst stood. The female goblin offered a hand to her mate and pulled him from the ground. The two of them continued to speak but Taurnil did not understand. Within a moment, Vorst had darted out of view with Gravlox fast on her heels.

Taurnil looked up at the sky, the strong summer sun stinging his soulless eyes. Acid pumped from his tongues and filled his mouth with bile, a familiar and comforting taste. Taurnil spat the glob of poison out, dissolving the nearest tree branch to toxic ash. He smiled, truly enjoying the decay that radiated from his corrupted body. The abyss called to Taurnil, filling his physical form and wrapping his mind in a cold embrace. His wings shot out, shredding the dying leaves and cutting through the branches as he thrashed. With the goblins out of sight, the abyss was alive inside him again.

Taurnil dropped to the ground with a thud, sending a cloud of dark grey ash into the air. "Yes," he bellowed, feeling the magical connection solidifying in the area of his being where a soul should have been. "These two are strong," he cackled, "but whatever magic connects them can be severed by the black claws of the abyss."

The monster clicked his sharp claws together and flexed. A wide smile covered his face as he leapt into the air and took flight.

Ten

GRAVLOX BREATHED HEAVILY, his chest rising and falling with the crunch of leaves and twigs under his naked feet. Vorst was always a few steps ahead of him, running with boundless energy. The two goblins had been moving at a frantic pace for the entire day, slowing only once to cross a small stream. Somehow the healing magic that Gravlox had called forth during their kiss had energized Vorst and brought a new lust for life into her step. Gravlox *thought* it was the result of magic, at least.

It wasn't until around midnight that their bodies started to tire and Vorst had to stop. Gravlox arrived at the creek where Vorst had stopped, a tributary of the mighty Clawflow, just a few steps behind her. Vorst was already floating on her back in the calm stream, casually splashing around with her delicate arms. Her travelling pack was resting on the mossy shore, along with the short leather pants that the female goblin always wore.

Gravlox quickly came to a halt and removed his own animal hide vest and studded skirt, tossing them to ground before jumping into the stream. The water was cool against his pale skin, making what little hair he had stand on end. Vorst swam over to him, splashing water on his face and jumping about. The stream wasn't deep, but there was plenty of water for Vorst to latch onto Gravlox's shoulders and dunk his head beneath the surface.

The taller goblin planted his strong feet on the slick pebbles of the streambed and pushed upwards, grabbing onto Vorst's legs and sending her vaulting skyward. The two goblins landed with a splash but came up quickly, locked in a kiss. A warm moment passed before Vorst pulled away.

"Um, Grav?" she said in a small voice, her eyes intently probing the surface of the water.

"Yeah, Vorst?" Gravlox was staring at her beautiful head, bald and gleaming with water. He loved when she whispered to him. Her voice sounded like the gentle hum of the stream around them, high-pitched and airy, full of life.

"When we get back to Kanebullar Mountain…" Vorst's voice trailed off but she lifted her head from the water and looked into Gravlox's eyes. "Will you live with me? We can find a new cave, a bigger one, and live together?" The smaller goblin was embarrassed as soon as she said it and pulled Gravlox in tight to avoid looking at him when he responded.

"I would love to do that, Vorst." He kissed her on the top of her head, pulling her in as tightly as possible. "Maybe we could even be married…" Gravlox could feel Vorst nodding slowly into his chest. Both of them smiled.

Marriage was a concept stolen from the human kingdoms and adapted to a goblin society that naturally devalued the family unit due to the inability for goblin pairs to reproduce. Rather than wearing wedding bands like the human corpses that goblins often looted after a raid, Lady Scrapple's progeny practiced a much more permanent symbol of union. Two goblins, after falling in love with one another, were expected to proclaim that love by cutting the pinky finger of their spouse's left hand off. The removal of the finger could never be undone or easily hidden. Everyone knew that a nine-fingered goblin was married. The pain associated with the ritual only served to solidify the bonds of love, a willing sacrifice between two goblins.

After an attack on a human settlement or caravan, goblins would loot the bodies of the fallen soldiers, taking every scrap of metal they could, wedding bands included. The ease with which a human could hide his marriage from the world or have the evidence of such a bond stolen after death is what led goblins to design their own physical manifestation of marriage.

Vorst subconsciously rubbed the pinky of her left hand, running her fingertips over the knobby joint that signified her availability. "I would like that, Grav," she said, giving him another kiss.

The two goblins spent another moment together in the stream before climbing to the grass and collecting their belongings. Having no need for sleep, they simply slowed their pace to a casual walk in order for their bodies to recover, following the small stream to the south. The darkness of night was thick about the pair, muffling their footfalls and making the world disappear. They walked in silence, hand in hand, and listened to the calm sounds of the stream and forest.

After nightfall Gravlox spotted a small cave opening farther down the path that piqued his curiosity. His natural night-vision was enhanced by years of working in the dark mines of Kanebullar Mountain and allowed him a good view of the cave.

The opening was a slight hole in the ground, partially covered by fallen branches and leaves. Putting a hand on Vorst's shoulder, Gravlox balanced himself and peered over the edge of the formation to get a better look.

"Looks like a cave vent, some sort of air passage to a larger chamber down below," Gravlox said, pushing the debris from the area. "Sometimes we drill chimneys like this in the ceilings of caverns so that air can move from chamber to chamber as the miners work," Gravlox explained.

"Is this a natural opening or something man-made?" Vorst got down on her belly, peering into the opening.

"It's hard to tell," Gravlox replied. He moved slowly about the hole on his hands and knees, using his weight to test the ground's stability. "Some animal probably lives down there and uses the opening to come out and hunt. Come on, Vorst, we should get going."

Gravlox reached a hand down and lifted Vorst from the ground. The female goblin jumped up and landed with a subtle thud that shifted the rocks beneath her feet. Gravlox took one step and, all of a sudden, the earth beneath their feet gave way. The small opening in the ground was instantly larger than both the small goblins combined, swallowing them in the blink of an eye.

Thinking quickly, Gravlox was able to wrap an arm around Vorst and the two slid down the falling cascade of stone together. The goblins were enveloped by the hail of small rocks and dirt and fell into a sloped chamber a dozen feet below the mossy surface of the forest floor. The slanted floor of the cavern was angled steeply, carrying the two goblins even further underground.

Gravlox was able to latch a hand around the base of a root protruding from the smooth stone but it gave way almost as quickly as he had touched it. A crumbling chunk of stony dirt hit Vorst in the shoulder, knocking her away from Gravlox. The goblins reached out to one another but there was nothing they could do. The slanted stone of the cavern acted as a natural slide, rushing the pair underground with mounting speed.

Despite the dirt in his eyes, Gravlox could make out the end of the slide in the dark cavern. The stone narrowed considerably, but with a natural partition separating him from Vorst. A similar taper existed a few feet below the falling form of Vorst. "Gravlox!" the terrified goblin called out through the sea of falling rock and dirt.

"Vorst! Take my hand!" Gravlox reached out and tried to find his falling companion but the stone partition between the two goblins was quickly approaching. He knew if he let his wrist hit the solid barrier, it would surely shatter. Gravlox closed his eyes and hoped for the best, crossing his arms over his chest as his feet went through the narrow gap in the cavern.

His head banged painfully off the stone ceiling and he shot through a nearly vertical tunnel. Stones pelted his head and chest but the sloped rock beneath him disappeared. Gravlox knew he was in free-fall.

Somewhere far beneath him, the shaman could hear the sounds of water flowing. His body slammed into a wall of solid limestone, scrambling his senses and boggling his mind. The world around the goblin spun in a dizzying haze of dark splotches that obscured his vision. Gravlox knew he was still falling but couldn't tell which direction. He was almost thankful when his bruised body finally came to a halt, face down in a very shallow pool of water.

Groggily, Gravlox managed to roll himself over. He wasn't sure if it was blood or cave water, but he coughed a stream of warm liquid out of his mouth and rubbed his eyes. A wave of sharp pain shot through his back as the battered goblin managed to bring himself to a sitting position. The cavern was huge, a large underground dome covered in slick moss and pale mushrooms.

He could see the opening in the ceiling above him, a small hole in the stone about thirty feet above his head. The sloped cavern he had first landed in was out of view, just a small pocket in the stone above the larger chamber. Following the route he had taken with his eyes, Gravlox traced out the likely path that Vorst had travelled. He knew that his beloved companion was in a different chamber but she could not have landed too far from him.

"There must be a tunnel that connects us," Gravlox mumbled as he got to his wobbly feet. The foreman drew his sword from the sheath at his hip, inspecting the weapon to ensure that it hadn't gotten damaged during his plummet. Luckily, it was intact and made a wonderful cane to support his bruised legs. Gravlox hobbled to the side of the chamber where he had fallen and tapped on the rock, hoping to hear a similar tapping from the other side to signify Vorst's presence.

Goblins, living in the dark chambers beneath Kanebullar Mountain, often communicated by tapping on the stone walls that separated the various passages from one another. Deep in the mines, goblins had developed a sophisticated language of tapping and scraping that the rest of the goblin society was quick to adapt.

Are you alright? Gravlox tapped on the wall. *Can you breathe? Are you alive?* No tapping came back from the other side. *Vorst, are you alive?* Gravlox tapped faster on the wall, panic gripping him fully. He endured another excruciating moment of silence. Using the hilt of his sword, Gravlox tapped even harder on the wall, throwing what remained of his strength into every blow. *Vorst!* His sword hilt cried out on the stone. *Where are you? Are you alive?* A tear streaked down his dirty face and fell to the floor.

Gravlox, came the slow reply from the wall. The taps were faint, almost impossible to hear above the sound of the underground stream in the chamber. *I am alive.* Gravlox was so overcome with joy that he simply collapsed to the floor and cried. *Are you badly hurt?* Vorst asked, her taps coming with more strength than before.

No, Gravlox replied with his sword hilt. *Are you?* He feared what the response might be.

Nothing that won't heal, came her characteristic response. Gravlox could see her smiling on the other side of the stone, grinning from ear to ear at his worry. *Is there a stream on your side?* Gravlox searched the cavern, hoping that the stream went under the rocks and into Vorst's cavern.

Yes, he tapped out excitedly, scrambling for the edge of the water. He dunked his head in, trying to see where the water went. It was nearly impossible to tell with certainty, but Gravlox felt the water rushing as though it was moving under the stone wall and into another chamber. The opening was narrow, less than a foot in diameter, but it gave him hope. *I am going to try to swim to you,* Gravlox tapped out as he removed his pack.

He attached his sword belt to the rest of his travelling gear and then fixed a long length of rope to his ankle, the other end tightly tied to his equipment. *Be careful,* Vorst tapped on the other side of the stone, *I can hear something. I think there are footsteps coming from another cavern. They sound close, getting louder.* Gravlox didn't waste a moment.

The goblin dove down on his belly in the shallow stream, pushing himself along the cavern floor as flat as he could. Thankfully, the stream deepened where it met the stone wall and he was able to slide a hand under the ledge and pull himself down. His eyes grew wide with panic when he realized how far he would have to crawl before the stone above his head gave way to air. Gravlox rotated in the water, placing his hands above his head and clawing his way through the submerged passage.

He was wedged into the stone tightly, his face smashed against the rock above him, his back being cut by the rock beneath him. Without being able to turn his head, the goblin had no idea how far the tunnel would take him. *Hurry,* came the tapping, barely understandable to the underwater goblin. The warm water coursed past his body, moving much faster than Gravlox.

Panic gave way to sheer terror in a matter of moments. Gravlox's small lungs burned. It took every fiber of his will to keep from screaming in the narrow tunnel and filling his body with cave water. Frantically, Gravlox clawed and scraped at the stone, pulling himself along, inch by painful inch. *Hurry,* Vorst repeated. *Hurry, something is coming.*

Gravlox grit his teeth and tried to pull himself further along the tunnel but his hips were stuck. *Gravlox... Hurry.*

Eleven

"STILL NO REPORT from Darius, sir." The soldier was impeccably dressed, his fine mail armor betraying his inexperience. Herod preferred a warrior with a few dents in his shield. There was a long pause before anyone in the throne room spoke again.

"Alright. Thank you for the update." Herod stood before the throne on the raised dais, his body clad in heavy steel plates. Herod's twin longswords, Maelstrom and Regret, dangled on his hips, their sharp points hovering right above the stone. No one had seen the prince's famed weapons in years. Their very presence indicated the gravity of the situation. "What is your name, soldier?" Herod's deep voice boomed through the stone hall, echoing with a new-found air of command.

"Apollonius, my liege," replied the well kempt man, offering a rigid bow. "I live to serve the throne."

Herod smiled. His right hand moved to his left hip, slowly drawing Maelstrom from its golden sheath. "You serve the throne..." Herod muttered. The room full of soldiers stood on edge, silently awaiting the prince's action.

Prince Herod lifted the blood-red blade before him, holding it up for everyone in the room to see. With a simple thought, the sword burst into flame in his hands. The fire was not real, in the physical sense, but ethereal. Black, translucent flames licked up the red steel and sent a thick plume of ash swirling toward the ceiling.

Maelstrom swung down with the prince's arm, cutting a line of incorporeal fire through the air, and connected with the seat of the throne with a re-sounding thunder. The stone of the royal seat was torn asunder. A thin line of molten rock seeped from the edges of the laceration as the throne crumbled to ruins on the dais. A chorus of hushed gasps met the prince's rigid gaze as he turned back to the assembly before him.

"You say you serve the throne." Herod looked as many men in the eyes as he could, striking fear into their very souls. "I ask you now to serve your city. Talonrend needs you, not the throne. This is the hour of her greatest weakness." A priest standing off to the side of the assembly opened his mouth to speak but an upraised hand from the prince stopped him cold.

"All of you assembled in this hall, you are the city guard. I ask you now to protect your city, as you have sworn to do. Darius, your leader and my friend, has been killed. Treachery held the blade that took his life. I do not know who commands such treachery, but we will discover them, and we will kill them. Trust no one but myself, Master Brenning, and each other. Anyone approaching the castle without my consent is to be considered hostile."

Master Brenning stood near the priest to the prince's right. He was wearing the traditional armor and tabard of the royal guard, signifying him as Darius' replacement. The proud smith stood slightly taller at the mention of his name.

"You soldiers are no longer the city guard of Talonrend. I commission you now as Templars of Peace, ordered to protect the city at all costs. All those who do not wish to be a part of this order may throw down your arms and leave the castle unharmed. You will not be exiled from the city, but you may no longer serve in its guard. All those who wish to serve as guardians of the people," Herod lifted Maelstrom high above his head, ordering the weapon to extinguish its fire so that the sunlight streaming in from the windows glinted on its dark crimson edge, "kneel!"

Every man in the large audience hall kneeled at once, without hesitation. Every man except for one. The priest of Vrysinoch stood steadfast next to Master Brenning's kneeling form, locking eyes with the prince.

"Only a king has the power to commission such an order," the old priest spat. He turned to face the crowd of kneeling templars but none of the armed men even glanced at him.

"Our rightful king is missing, likely dead. Our guard captain is missing, likely dead as well." Herod pointed his red sword at the withered priest menacingly. "Who are you to say that a prince cannot protect his castle and his city?"

"I am a holy priest of Vrysinoch!" the man cried out. "You cannot take such actions without the approval of Vrysinoch! The tower does not approve! You are not our king!" The wrinkled old man stretched his hand out in the direction of the prince, pointing a crooked finger, a sneer plastered to his ugly face.

"I have been tormented by Vrysinoch for far too long," Herod said with solemnity as he lowered Maelstrom back to his side. "It is time for your god to truly protect you, priest." The words of damnation rolled off of Herod's tongue and left a sweet taste in his mouth. The prince slashed Maelstrom through the air in the direction of the priest who instinctively raised his hands to defend himself. Thirty feet of open air separated the two men but Maelstrom understood the prince's intent.

Ethereal tendrils of acrid black smoke shot forward from the tip of the sword, circling about each other wildly as they sped toward the priest. The black smoke materialized into six clutching hands that latched onto the priest from all directions. Herod held the sword steady, leveled at the old man's splotched forehead.

Master Brenning, the man who had made the sword, knew what was about to happen. He closed his eyes tightly and kneeled lower to the stone, making his body as small as possible. One sharp tug of Herod's wrist pulled the sword back across his body and stretched the ghastly tendrils taut. When the sword reached the end of its arc, the black hands receded to their origin, taking six bloody chunks of the priest with them and depositing the remains of the shattered priest at Herod's feet. Blood splattered Master Brenning's armor as the priest exploded in a rain of gore. The man never had the chance to scream.

"Vrysinoch is no longer your guardian," Herod called to the kneeling soldiers. "The paladins who serve the tower have not shown themselves. With the command of my brother, I doubt they will leave their tower, even when it comes to open warfare in the streets of Talonrend. You must protect each other now." A wave of his hand commanded the templars to rise and they obeyed in unison. "Apollonius!" Herod called to the soldier standing in the front row.

"Yes, sir!" the loyal man barked back.

"Go to the tower. Tell those cowards what has happened here." The eager soldier nodded. "If the priests refuse to summon the Vrysinoch Guard, kill them until one of the priests agrees." Apollonius nodded again, more solemnly. "The army is to be gathered at once, inside the walls. Every paladin, healer, warrior, and pit fighter is henceforth called to serve." Herod scanned the room and searched the men's faces for any signs of doubt. "Failure to heed that call is treason."

Satisfied that none of the murmurs were of dissent, Herod continued his rousing speech. "Send runners to each of the villages. The militia is also called to serve. Every city along the Clawflow is required to send thirty able-bodied men, with arms and armor if possible. Organize the militia outside the walls in camps." Herod turned to Master Brenning and offered the man a stiff salute. "See to it that the militia is properly equipped and well fed. I feel a war on the horizon."

The burly smith returned the salute with a grim smile.

Some minutes later, after much cheering and applauding from the gathered templars, Herod left the audience chamber and returned to his personal chambers. Master Brenning hurried along behind the inspired prince. The two men stopped in front of the brand new steel door that barred the way to Herod's personal chambers.

The heavy door was inscribed with enchanted runes, every line weaving a strong magic that protected the room beyond from unwanted visitors. Two similar doors had also been installed on the front of the castle and the drawbridge was being modified by Master Brenning's chief smiths.

Herod waved his hand in front of the steel and the runes glowed to life, unlocking with a series of metallic clicks. "Master Brenning," the prince said with a smile before stepping into his chambers, "you are a genius. This door will only admit myself, no one else?"

The hairy man nodded with excitement, strands of his thick beard flying about his face. "Your command will allow visitors to enter, but only those you name specifically. Your new armor also awaits you in your chamber," Master Brenning chimed in. "And it is always good to see my favorite swords being put to use. Maelstrom and Regret have hidden in their sheaths for far too long."

"I wish that you still made weapons of their caliber, Master Brenning." Herod thumbed the hilts of his magnificent swords with nothing but true appreciation showing on his face.

"Those two swords are my masterwork, Herod. After I crafted those weapons, I turned my focus to armor. I have only made one weapon since, but it wasn't a longsword."

Prince Herod took a hesitant step into his room, but turned back to face the smith. "Your last weapon was not a hand-and-a-half sword, honor-bound to a disgruntled paladin, was it?"

Master Brenning's deep laugh resonated through the stone halls. "Indeed, my prince." The smith's eyes took on a glossy sheen and he looked through Herod rather than at him. "Nevidal, the sword is called. It simply means 'wonder', in the old language. Maelstrom and Regret may be the strongest paired weapons in the entire realm, but Nevidal is stronger still. Gideon could slay an entire army with that sword…"

Herod waited a moment before speaking, allowing the smith his moment of reverie. "Assuming that Gideon's own soul would not be destroyed in the process?" he asked.

"Yes," Master Brenning muttered, "there is that one small matter. Hopefully Gideon can learn to control the weapon before that happens. A blade like that is not something to be trifled with. In the hands of anyone else, it would reap nothing but disaster. The Blood Foundry can be a tricky forge, especially when it comes to weapons."

"Your sacred forge has never ceased to amaze me, Master Brenning. Your capabilities as a smith are only outshined by your undying loyalty." Prince Herod gave the man a rigid salute, showing him nothing but respect and friendship.

Master Brenning returned the gesture and spun on his heel to leave. As the new captain of the guard, Brenning had plenty of work to do around the castle. His smiths were almost finished installing new doors at the end of the drawbridge, enchanted plates of steel designed to keep out all forms of magical intrusion.

Brenning stood in front of the massive metal doors, staring at the parapet above. Two of his smiths were standing on the top of the stone wall, fitting an iron mount onto one of the crenellations so that a heavy ballista could be stationed there. With his mind's eye, Brenning imagined the new fortifications and defenses of Castle Talon. Ballistae lined the parapet, manned by seasoned soldiers of unflinching loyalty. The moat would be filled with large iron spikes rising up out of the water. Master Brenning imagined small catapults stationed near the castle's round towers, filled with loose sacks of caltrops that could be easily set on fire and launched onto the ground before the moat, slowing the assault of any army.

The smith's vision turned to the city itself. "All of these buildings will need to be removed," he whispered, not wanting anyone to hear. The row of houses and buildings closest to the castle were too close, Brenning thought. He could not see well past that first row and into the city proper. "Herod will not like that idea," he muttered, shaking his head. "But we need to have sight. A clear view of the enemy is the first step toward defeating the enemy, whoever that may turn out to be..."

"Sir!" a soldier behind Master Brenning called to him, interrupting the daydream. Brenning turned to see the man, a newly commissioned templar, standing on the top of the parapet with a crossbow in hand. The templar pointed and Brenning turned, drawing a short sword from his side in the process. The burly man was not a soldier by profession, but neither was he a novice to melee combat.

A man approached the drawbridge wearing a plain brown shirt with matching leather breeches, his head hung low in thought. "Fire at his feet and reload quickly," Master Brenning called to the templar. The man walking toward the castle was easily recognized by the smith as Jan. Apparently, the steward had not gotten wind of his exile from the castle. A heavy, steel tipped bolt thudded into the banded wood of the drawbridge, causing Jan to jerk back reflexively.

"Halt!" the templar called out from above. The clicking sound as the crossbow reloaded quickly followed the soldier's voice.

"What are you doing here, Jan?" Master Brenning took a step in front of the door, squaring off against the steward across the drawbridge.

"What in Vrysinoch's name is going on here?" Jan's eyes darted around the castle, examining the new fortifications and finally finding the stone cold stare of the burly smith. "I am the king's steward! Am I no longer permitted entry into the castle?" His tone was incredulous and spiteful.

"By order of the Sovereign Prince Herod, ruler of Talonrend and commander of both the Vrysinoch Guard and the Templars of Peace, you are hereby exiled from Castle Talon and from Talonrend herself, on pain of death. You are under arrest and will be escorted outside of the city." Jan's jaw dropped and his legs began to noticeably tremble.

Have they found me out? Did Keturah turn on me? Tentatively, he took a step back. Master Brenning matched his movement and took a confident step forward onto the drawbridge, openly challenging the smaller man.

Brenning motioned with his hand and the templar fired a second bolt. Jan saw the deadly missile speeding toward his chest and reached a hand out to block it. Dark magic swirled about his wrist and formed into a solid buckler of necrotic energy that easily shattered the bolt and then dissipated. Jan turned and began to run.

"It seems you've been hiding a great many secrets, traitor!" Master Brenning yelled, taking off in pursuit of Jan. The smith's powerful legs closed the gap quickly but all it took for Jan to escape was a few lines of arcane summoning. A bright orange portal ripped through the air, crackling and popping with energy. Without a moment of hesitation, Jan leapt through the portal and began to close it behind him.

Reaching out through the portal and trying to grasp Jan's arm to pull him back, Brenning was sucked through the closing gateway with a pop. A strange tingling energy rippled through the smith's muscular back and vibrated his beard hairs. The sensation of falling gripped his chest and caused him to grit his teeth, expecting the worst. Master Brenning landed on cold stone with a heavy thud and felt the wind rush out of his lungs. He was dazed but not severely injured.

Brenning got slowly to his knees, clutching his sword close to his chest and looked around in the darkness. At first, Master Brenning thought he must have missed the portal and landed on the other side of the stone walkway leading to the drawbridge. The inky blackness of the world around him assured him that he was no longer in Talonrend.

"Jan!" he called to the darkness, anger filling his gravelly voice. Master Brenning stood and swung his sword about in a wide arc. It clanged loudly against a stone to his right. The smith reached a muscled hand to the stone and felt the edges, the turn of a wall. Putting his back to the wet, mossy stone, Master Brenning waved his sword about in frustration. "Jan!" he shouted again, hearing his own voice echo around him.

A tiny ball of brilliant white light appeared somewhere in the distance, too small for Master Brenning to identify. Slowly, the glowing orb grew in size, illuminating the room. Brenning lowered his sword and shielded his eyes from the intense light as he scanned the prison. The area was circular, made of large stone blocks covered in a thick carpet of verdant moss. Everything was damp and glistened in the bright light with little drops of water. What Brenning had thought was the edge of a stone wall was actually the opening to a small passage. Water trickled over the stone lazily to slicken the moss at his feet. Three small metal bars were set into the stone at narrow intervals, effectively blocking the opening to anything as large as a human.

The stone walls of the circular chamber extended well over triple the smith's height but did not meet a ceiling there. The top of the chamber was high overhead, another twenty or thirty feet above the top of the cylindrical prison. Master Brenning could barely make out the dark outlines of roots poking through the stone ceiling. A brown drop of insipid water fell through the humid air to the mossy carpet below.

Jan stepped forward from the ball of brilliant light, placing a gigantic shadow over the trapped smith. The former steward hovered above his captive on a black disc of swirling energy. Jan's laughter filled the room.

"Master Brenning, so nice to see you again," he cackled, sending little bolts of black magic dancing from his fingertips and sinking into the stone. "Welcome to my kingdom!"

Brenning spat on the stone and averted his eyes. Defeated, the humbled smith sank to the mossy stone and rested his back against the wall.

Jan knew that he would never bring the smith to despair. He might kill the proud man, but he would never be able to break his spirit. Annoyed at the thought, Jan dispelled the magical light with a wave of his hand. "Enjoy your stay in the sewers of Reikall," he calmly said before disappearing through another portal of conjured magic.

Master Brenning closed his eyes and let his anger subside. There was nothing he could do to escape his stone prison. With a grunt of exasperation, Brenning pressed his ear to the wall to listen for anything that might give him hope.

Twelve

A SMALL GOBLIN hand grabbed the top of his bald head. He could feel it distinctly, but at the same time the touch felt like it was miles away. The pale fingers reached around his head and clenched down firmly on his scraped neck, closing with surprising strength. The hand began to pull, raking his battered body against the sharp stones, but the strong goblin hand would not relent. Slowly, his body began to move forward. Walls of solid rock closed in on his hips with every inch, adding a deep crimson to the rushing water.

Suddenly, the water disappeared. Gravlox felt only the cavern floor beneath his back as he gasped for air. Covered in cuts and bruises, the small goblin was thankful to be alive. Vorst pulled the rope behind her companion and retrieved his pack from the water.

They heard the footsteps resounding against the walls. The chamber was small, much smaller than the one Gravlox had come from, and it reeked of death. The echoing footfalls were coming from nearby but the sound was steady, neither approaching nor retreating.

We need to look, Gravlox tapped on the stone. The two goblins crawled on their hands and knees to an opening in the wall. Hesitantly, Gravlox placed a hand on Vorst's back as she peered around the corner. Almost instantly, the female goblin jerked her head back and rolled into the chamber.

Hundreds. Her fingers drilled the code into Gravlox's forearm in a silent panic. *Humans. They are marching. The tunnel extends far to the North, back toward their city.* Both goblins dared another look around the corner of the stone. Hundreds of human forms shambled through the rock tunnel. Some of them hit their heads on the ceiling above or scraped into the sides of the tunnel but none of them slowed or stopped.

Mindless, Gravlox signaled. *I don't think they will attack.* The two goblins straightened in the passageway and drew their weapons. Acting on instinct, Gravlox stabbed out with his short sword and impaled a thin human female. The tip of his weapon protruded garishly from the front of her chest but no blood spilled forth. The walking corpse turned and swung her arms out to claw at him but an arrow removed the woman's head from her shoulders with a splatter of rotted brains.

The other human forms were totally oblivious to the fight and the defeated woman crumbled to ash on the cavern floor without a sound. The legion continued its march, scattering the ashes as they went.

"They're zombies," Vorst muttered in disbelief. "Endless ranks of the dead." Both goblins shook their heads and wondered where they had come from. Vorst quickstepped through the river of corpses and retrieved her arrow from the ground, blowing the dust off the head before placing it back in her quiver.

"Should we continue on toward the necromancer that summoned this army? That is what Lady Scrapple wants. You of course are not bound by her will." Vorst playfully poked him in the stomach.

"We could march with them. If this cave system leads all the way to the city, it probably comes up inside the walls." The endless line of undead marched on, paying the goblins no heed. "Our quest is to take the city from the humans. It seems as if the alliance between necromancer and goblin has not been harmed. Yael and his troops are probably preparing the assault right now."

Vorst wrapped her sinewy arms around Gravlox's waist and held him close. "I don't want to fight anymore. Not against humans, not against anything. I just want to go home. I feel like I only found you moments ago, and now you talk of war. Is war against the humans what you really want, Gravlox?"

The naïve goblin foreman had never thought of that. Was there more to the goblin existence than bloody conquest? The goblins of Kanebullar Mountain were happy, content to live in the dark tunnels and passageways under the earth. They did not need a human city to live in, they already had a home. He returned her hug with all his strength, not willing to let her go.

A vicious tug in the center of Vorst's mind nearly toppled her. Lady Scrapple was telepathically commanding her minion, forcing her to fight. Gravlox watched in horror as her small hands took the sword away from him and leveled it against his neck.

"No..." Gravlox didn't know what to say. He had never felt the influence of the hive mind and therefore could not sympathize. "Vorst... Please," he begged, falling to his knees with the sword still resting against his neck.

Her eyes glazed over with pale fog and she pulled the sword back, gripping it tightly. Calm serenity danced about her soft features in the lightless cavern. The goblin's face betrayed no emotion. Vorst's arm swung, but her hand let go of the weapon and she collapsed to the floor. "I don't know how long I can resist it, Grav," she cried into his immediate embrace. "I'm not strong like you."

Gravlox held her tight against his chest. He had no words to comfort her. No inspirational speech came to him in a moment of clarity. The two lovers rocked back and forth on the cold cave floor and held each other for a long time as the horde of undead marched on.

TWO VERY DIFFERENT companions peered into the collapsed entrance of a cave shaft many feet above Gravlox and Vorst.

"You're sure they went down this passage?" Gideon asked, never allowing his hand to wander far from the throwing axes at his side.

"I am sure of it. I watched from a distance as the ground swallowed them. They did not expect it, nor did I," the demon hissed in response. Taurnil's acidic tongues tasted the air with urgency, guiding the lightless orbs of the vile beast down to the ground. "The female goblin went down on this side of the collapse." Taurnil spat a glob of acid onto the fallen leaves. "I can taste her in the air."

Gideon investigated the area but could not discern anything useful in the waning light. "If they are apart from each other, they should be easier to kill. The male goblin is the stronger of the two, by all accounts." The warrior brushed some leaves and broken sticks aside and tested the stability of the ground.

"I will rip his useless heart from his scrawny chest." Taurnil gnashed his broken teeth, biting the words as they came out.

"Is that what you said right before he forced you to retreat at Cobblestreet?" Gideon taunted, standing to his full height and easily towering over the demon.

Sinewy wings beat the air and dry leaves were tossed about the small clearing in a frenzy as Taurnil ascended. Without a word the beast dove for the ground, crashing into the rubble of the cavern entrance with a gracelessness bordering on reckless.

195

Not wasting any time, Gideon shook his head, dove feet-first into the stone chimney, and made the painful plummet down to the hard stone below. With a showy flourish, Taurnil's powerful wings brought him safely to the stone floor without a scratch or bruise.

Taurnil and Gideon stood in the lightless chamber and listened to the shuffling undead feet, unsure of their next move. "What is that noise?" Gideon asked.

"It is Reikall," Taurnil hissed in response. "The army marches through the lightless caves." Gideon closed his eyes against the darkness and pulled forth the energy within him, reawakening the strong bond with Vrysinoch that resided deep within his soul. When he opened his eyes, they glowed with white energy. Speaking the words to a simple cantrip, Gideon caused the rune on his back to flare to life. An ethereal eagle began to take form in the palm of his hand, illuminating the area.

Taurnil shielded his eyes from the piercing magical light and took a step back. The demon was visibly repulsed by the pure holy energy of Vrysinoch's paladin. Gideon smiled and tossed the small eagle into the air where it took flight, casting white light throughout the cavern.

VORST AND GRAVLOX, sitting on the stone around the corner from Gideon and Taurnil, saw the light and took cover. Gravlox scrambled to his feet, pulling Vorst behind him and the two goblins ran down the corridor in a hastened panic.

"Were you followed?" Vorst whispered once the two goblins were farther down the tunnel. Gravlox shook his head and stole a glance over his shoulder, unnerved by the sudden light.

We need to hide, he tapped on Vorst's arm. She looked around the underground complex nervously before finally spotting a cubby just large enough to conceal the two of them. Vorst and Gravlox darted into the cubby to wait, watching the glowing light from a distance.

"These men are dead." Gideon's tone was even and deadly serious. His deep voice echoed through the cavern, resounding around the mindless corpses that took no heed.

"Of course," Taurnil responded. "Hurry, I can taste the goblin scum in the air. They can't be far." Gideon didn't follow the demon.

"These men are dead," he repeated, staring at the endless river of zombies.

"Yes," the winged beast hissed, "and so are the women and children. What does it matter?" Taurnil turned to face the unmoving paladin. "Does the paladin fear these mindless undead?" he snickered.

"They are all *dead!*" he shouted so loudly that it rang in his ears. Gideon unhooked one of the throwing axes at his side and flexed, gripping the polished wood firmly. He felt the weight of the axe, the balance of its head at the end of his fingers. The luminescent eagle continued to circle around the cavern, casting magical light on Taurnil's pale skin.

Taurnil squared his shoulders to the man and flexed his wings. "What will you do, paladin? These corpses march toward Talonrend, something you have certainly deduced by now. My master controls them. With us, you will surely be spared. Keturah is well aware that you are a formidable warrior. It would be a shame to kill you now, underground, where no one will see you fall."

Gideon raised the axe up to his chest and inspected its razor edge in the gleaming light. "These corpses," he sneered, "are families. Sons march through these caves; daughters, husbands, wives, all of them loved by someone. You destroyed that."

Taurnil's sinewy wings shot out from his body and beat the air with strength. The throwing axe cut the air where the demon had been standing and clanged against the damp stone of the wall.

Another axe was in the paladin's strong hand before Taurnil's wings could beat a second time. The demon launched a glob of acid and spun, flying to the wall and finding an easy perch. The acid sizzled into the stone not far behind the ducking warrior, who exploded from the ground in a wild rush, sending an axe whirling end over end for Taurnil's chest. A sharp claw swiped the missile from the air and sent it to the stone below.

The slanted ceiling of the underground chamber wasn't high enough to afford Taurnil the room he needed to get out of the large paladin's reach. Gideon came on in a rush of steel, an axe in each hand. Taurnil's claws batted the axes out wide but the demon was clinging to the stone and leaving his back exposed. Drawing his wings in tight, the demon launched from the wall and collapsed on top of the paladin.

Gideon tried to pull his arms inside Taurnil's wings but wasn't quick enough. The demon wrapped the warrior in his strong embrace as they rolled on the stone floor. Taurnil used his superior position to pin Gideon's arms out wide where he dropped his axes. The beast brought his face down within inches of Gideon's mouth, snarling with his three writhing tongues. Acid dripped down onto the paladin's face, sizzling and boiling his skin.

"You cannot kill me," the demon hissed, spitting more acid with every word. The corrosive slime dug holes into the paladin's skin. The pain was excruciating. Gideon twisted and writhed, trying in vain to turn his face away from Taurnil's terrible maw.

Gideon thrashed violently and managed a weak headbutt. Taurnil barely noticed the blow. The sword on Gideon's back burned with holy fire. The magical eagle circling above the fight screeched in pain.

Vrysinoch heard that screech. The eagle dove down, tucking its wings against its sides and loosing another piercing scream. The sound cut the air and reverberated off the walls of the chamber, dazing Taurnil with its ferocity. Waves of divine magic emanated from the bird as it bit deeply into the demon's pale back.

Gideon scrambled, pushing the beast away and trying to scrape the remaining acid from his face. Taurnil whirled on the eagle, knocking it to the ground and dispelling the magic.

The two warriors stood in the cavern with just an arm's length separating them. The glow from Gideon's cantrip was gone but the cavern shined even brighter than before. Nevidal, Gideon's hand-and-a-half sword, glowed with fierce energy, bathing the walls in an eerie light. With grim determination, Gideon reached up and grasped the hilt of the mighty blade. In response, Nevidal surged with energy, flaring to life at the touch of the paladin's hand and nearly blinding the two warriors.

"I may not be able to defeat you," Gideon coughed through his scarred face, "but Vrysinoch is more powerful than both of us. You will die here."

Gideon drew his sword.

Thirteen

PRINCE HEROD STOOD tall atop the Talon-rend city walls. Herod wasn't sure if a man was supposed to feel more terror looking up at the wall from the ground or looking down upon the city from the top.

"Apollonius," the Prince called to the man as he reached the top of the winding staircase that connected the top of Terror's Lament with the base. "Has there been any news of Master Brenning? I have not seen him in some time." The obedient soldier shook his head and stooped over to catch his breath.

"Now you understand why I left my armor at the bottom of the wall with the other guards." The prince laughed and walked over to Apollonius. "I have faith that my friend will return to us in due time." He patted the heavily armored soldier on the back and directed his view out over the city.

"Tell me, Apollonius, when was the last time you stood upon this wall and gazed out upon the rooftops of Talonrend?" The prince had often done just that, but with his brother, King Lucius, at his side.

"Never, my liege. Only recently did I enlist to be a guardsman. Wall duty is assigned to the most veteran soldiers in the guard. I am not old enough to have earned that honor yet." The prince had never realized how young the soldier was. The man had a bit of a beard, but nothing uncommon for an average man of twenty years.

Herod nodded and turned around to face the north. "There isn't much out here, Apollonius," the prince lamented. "We have the farms and fields to the north and west, the villages along the Clawflow to the east, and Reikall somewhere to the south. This is truly a lonely and desolate land." The purple caps of distant mountains could be seen far to the north like the tiny silhouettes of children standing in a row.

"Do not forget Kanebullar Mountain, my liege, across the river," Apollonius was quick to point out.

The monolithic natural structure loomed on the horizon like a watchful overseer, poised to strike.

"And what is beyond that?" the prince asked. "In all of the histories of Talonrend, no one has ever ventured that far beyond the Clawflow. We are a young kingdom, compared to the Green City from which our ancestors came, but it surprises me that no one has ever gone out to map the rest of the world."

"Such is the fate of every frontier city," Apollonius replied. "I am sure that the leaders of the Green City looked out to the east, to where your castle stands strong today, and were filled with such trepidation." The young soldier sounded at ease with Talonrend's surroundings.

"Gather a group of volunteers for me, Apollonius. Get a patrol of five or six men together to travel to the north and another patrol to scout the east, beyond the Clawflow. I need to know what is out there if I am to be a good king." Prince Herod turned to make his way back down the winding staircase to the city.

"I will gladly lead such an expedition, sire." The soldier saluted but his eagerness was cut short as Herod grabbed him forcefully by the arm.

"No!" the prince shouted at him. "You need to stay in the city. I fear that the number of people I can trust within these walls is quickly diminishing. I need you by my side." Apollonius bowed. "You are my personal guard, remember that." The soldier bowed again much lower.

"I shall see to it that a patrol is organized at once for each area. A scribe and a cartographer shall accompany both groups." The soldier saluted and followed Herod back down to the city.

After the prince had donned his armor once more at the base of the wall he continued with Apollonius into the city proper. The two armored men walked down the wide avenues of Talonrend back to the castle without another word passing between them.

You will never be king. Herod was constantly reminded of his station in life by the nagging voice of his clawed god, Vrysinoch. The message echoed in the prince's head with every heavy crunch of his armored boot. Herod looked upon the castle, his brother's castle, and wondered what he was doing. Soldiers lined the parapet with crossbows and spears. Guards flanked the enchanted door and patrols of armored men could be seen moving beyond the moat in tight formations. *If I will never be king,* Herod responded to Vrysinoch in his head, *why do I do all of this? Why do I try to protect my brother's people? Why do I protect myself?*

Vrysinoch did not answer.

YAEL MOVED WITH his troops far to the north of Talonrend. The grassy fields and open plains provided little cover, but goblins are small. The soldier drones marched in coordinated blocks all at the behest of Lady Scrapple. The army of Kanebullar Mountain was comprised almost exclusively of these mindless drones. Each goblin soldier carried a spear, sword or mace, and had a small dagger tucked under its belt. The drones were never heavily armored, but the goblin at the head of each column carried a heavy metal shield on each arm and wore a thick helmet of shining iron plates.

Each column of drones had a captain, a goblin at the center of the group who was only partially enslaved by Lady Scrapple. The captains typically wielded javelins or throwing knives and wore light shirts of hardened animal hide. Tasked with singling out important targets for kills at range, the captains were afforded a measure more of freedom and discretion on the battlefield.

Yael was a commander in the goblin army. He, like Vorst, was almost fully autonomous. The goblins obeyed his orders but only because the Mistress of the Mountain forced them to obey. In a sense, Lady Scrapple was carrying out the will of Yael through the drones. The goblin commander often thought about that fact and what it might mean for him. With enough intelligence to understand that he was a slave, Yael frequently entertained the idea of ordering his troops to kill themselves just to see how Lady Scrapple would respond.

Yael's ranks were arrayed in the grassy field in perfectly straight lines. Each block consisted of ten rows of ten and Yael had been assigned to command three such blocks. Three hundred identical goblin soldiers stood before him on the plain. Their pale skin was beginning to take on a crimson luster as many of the goblins, being above ground for the first time in their lives, developed sunburn. The air was hot and thick about the army and smelled strongly of moist dirt and damp caves.

Engineers had dug a wide tunnel from the base of Kanebullar Mountain to the eastern bank of the Clawflow which allowed supplies to be carried half the distance to the army underground in fast carts moving along hastily assembled tracks. From the river, goblin teams waited until nightfall to transport the supply carts overland to the waiting army. Yael had ordered more construction materials, a shipment which he was still waiting to receive.

"We need hammers, nails, fasteners, metal braces; things with which to build. We can harvest all the lumber we could ever need from the forest but without tools, it is meaningless." Yael was one of the few goblins to have seen the human walls up close. The drone assistant attending to Yael nodded vigorously and the commander knew that Lady Scrapple had heard every word.

"Their walls are higher than our short arms can reach," he said to the drone with a shake of his head. "We must build siege towers, ladders, catapults, trebuchets! We must build great engines of war!" Yael had a way of working himself into to exhaustion over preparations. Even when conducting exercises within Kanebullar Mountain, the commander was relentless when it came to proper preparation. Yael assumed it was why he had been promoted to his position so early, which made him all the more angry that Lady Scrapple would not afford him the supplies he needed to build the siege engines.

With a wave of his scaly hand, Yael's troops dropped to their bellies on the field. The commander surveyed the army before him. Four other goblin commanders had been summoned to the field, each controlling three blocks of mindless soldiers. Another force of five blocks had been positioned on the eastern bank of the Clawflow as well, poised to overrun the human settlements to further add to the chaos of open warfare. Yael was smart enough to know that two thousand goblin soldiers would never be enough to take down the high walls of Talonrend, especially without proper siege equipment.

The commander ordered his soldiers to sit before returning to the comfort of his tent at the back of the army. Yael had met with the other leaders the day before but none of them seemed to share his concerns. Perhaps Yael didn't trust the hive mind enough, or perhaps his passion for preparedness had consumed him, but the goblin was thoroughly uncomfortable with the entire plan. "You hide something..." the goblin muttered as he splashed some water on his head and picked up a large parchment to use as a fan. "You would think that a proper general would tell her commanders the *entire* plan before deploying troops to the field."

Yael's joints locked into place and the parchment crumpled in his hand as Lady Scrapple invaded his body. Awkwardly overbalanced, the rigid goblin fell flat on his face in the dry dirt. Motionless, Yael remained on the floor of his tent for what felt like an eternity. He could feel the hive mind probing through his consciousness, investigating his memories, searching his being. Yael's eyes, filled with dirt and dust as they were, clouded over with a grey mist as Lady Scrapple searched every ounce of his body and mind.

A slow line of drool escaped Yael's open mouth and wet the dirt beneath his frozen face. The parchment was still clutched tightly in the goblin's right hand and the edges of the thick paper cut into the pale flesh of his side painfully. Droplets of blood began to mix with the dirt and spittle on the floor of the tent.

Suddenly, just as quickly as his creator had taken over his being, Lady Scrapple was gone. Yael gathered his wits and shook the dust from his clothes in silence. He attempted to stand, but the churning sensation in his gut knocked him back to the ground. Sitting on the hard soil, beneath a plain white canopy that served as his tent, Yael couldn't help but wonder if his entire company was being used as fodder. The possibility that his anger and questioning had turned him into fodder bothered him even more.

"If I am going to serve only as a distraction to provide cover for the actual attack," Yael said through gritted teeth, "I will die surrounded by human corpses."

Fourteen

H E COULD FEEL the muscles of his arms breaking down and knitting back together, growing stronger and threatening to rip out of his skin at any moment. Gideon's legs flexed and bulged with renewed life. His bones elongated, adding inches to his height and making his clothes seem like the garments of a child.

Loosing a primal roar at the top of his lungs, the paladin scraped his boots against the stone and charged.

Taurnil spread his arms wide and met the ferocious paladin head on, ducking his head at the last moment to avoid being rent in half by Nevidal's blinding overhand swing. The demon tried to use his natural agility to outmaneuver Gideon's hulking frame but the paladin matched him step for step with speed unnatural for his size.

Without an easy path to the side of the wildly swinging man, Taurnil had to quickly back step and use his sinewy wings to avoid the frenzy. Gideon's pursuit was inexorable. Swing after swing, Nevidal filled the damp cavern with blazing holy light. The sword was a blur, cutting the air with such speed that the retreating demon had no opportunity to parry.

If any emotion could be seen in the dark, soulless eyes of the winged Taurnil, fear would have shown itself in those lightless orbs. The demon tried to parry, tried to mount a counterattack, tried to stab out with his wings. Nevidal met every strike before it truly began.

Gritting his teeth and pressing forward, Gideon braced himself for the acid that he was sure would fly for his face. He had the evil creature back up against the wall, alternating high and low strokes to keep Taurnil's clawed feet planted firmly on the stone floor. A glob of sizzling acid broke through the glowing light of Nevidal's blade and divine magic flared to life around the paladin, encasing him in a fiery sphere of protection. The acid popped and crackled against the magical shield before falling to the ground harmlessly inert.

Fire engulfed the berserking paladin, swaying with his steps and surging forward with every lunge. Gideon could feel the intense heat of the cleansing flames but his skin did not burn. Smoke curled towards the ceiling of the cavern but its tendrils avoided the paladin's lungs as if the smoke itself were alive. The man's sweat ran off of his scalp and turned to mist in the flames at his feet.

Taurnil felt the cold stone against his back and knew he was trapped. Nevidal's brilliant light flashed before his eyes in a dazzling pattern the demon could never hope to discern. His claws flew about in front of him recklessly, trying desperately to keep the edge from his pale flesh.

Reaching within himself, Taurnil calmed his frantic mind and found his inner well of magic. The cord of ethereal servitude connecting master and slave thrummed with violent energy that begged for release. Keturah could feel the panic within her minion as keenly as the flailing demon felt the stone at his back.

Seated behind a massive oak desk in the grand study of the Artificer's Guild, the beautiful woman's eyes glazed over as the telepathic communion solidified. With whitened knuckles, Keturah's forearms bulged and her hands clenched the desk, digging lines into the polished wood.

Her sable tresses flew wildly about her face as the raw energy of her communion whirled around the study in a ghastly fog. Books flew from their shelves and pelted the walls in a maelstrom of fury as the powerful wizard pumped wave after wave of arcane strength into her puppet.

Taurnil's desperate parries began to hit their mark and Nevidal rang out violently against the demon's sharp claws. A jagged grin broke out on Taurnil's pale face. Overwhelming strength surged through the demon's body, hastening his blocks and turning the radiant weapon aside time after time.

Gideon could sense the energy flowing into his adversary. A song to Vrysinoch escaped his lips and the two mighty warriors found themselves on equal footing.

Keturah arched her back let loose a ghastly scream amplified by her two-tone ethereal voice. A bolt of lightning shot forth from the wizard, jettisoned through the incorporeal tunnel of magic, and found its way into her pet.

Flashes of purple lightning shattered the super-heated air all over the cavern, striking the stone with enough force to sunder it and send up a shower of rock and dirt. More than one of the arcane bolts collided with the divine shield surrounding the paladin's body. Gideon could feel his sacred protection waning and knew he had lost the upper hand.

With a growl that was more out of frustration than ferocity, the paladin hefted his mighty sword above his head, poising for a deadly overhand chop. Demonic claws reached high to stop the fatal blow. Nevidal surged brighter, a holy flare in the underground arena. Gideon stepped in close, exposing his left flank to the biting maw of the demon and shortening the angle of his sword to connect the hilt with the top of Taurnil's head. The winged beast bit down hard on the soft flesh above the paladin's meager armor a split-second before the heavy hilt of the hand-and-a-half sword cracked into his skull with resounding force.

Taurnil slumped against the stone and a lightning strike blasted apart the cavern floor between the dueling champions. Gideon flew backwards through the churning air and landed painfully on his back with the wet stone pressing up against his muscled flesh. Pain coursed through the man's shoulder, blurring his vision and scrambling his keen senses. Nevidal's enchanted might worked furiously to counter the necrotic poison eating the paladin's shoulder as he writhed on the blasted stone floor. Swiping frantically at the wound, Gideon grabbed onto the bleeding, wriggling tongue and ripped it free from his torn skin. The disembodied tongue had been severed by the lightning strike but it had done its work. Poison continued to pump out of the bloody tongue as it slithered aimlessly on the ground.

Gideon tried to stand but a thick gush of blood forced him back to his knees. With Nevidal still magically bound to his hands, all the paladin could hope to do was crawl inch by painful inch toward his crumpled adversary to finish the work.

Vrysinoch's restorative magic could only do so much. The vile poison sizzled within the warrior's veins and ate away at his flesh from the inside. The blood and muscle of his shoulder began to coagulate into a blackened ash of corrupted flesh.

The blazing sword flickered. Its glow faded with every pained shuffle of Gideon's weakened legs. Skin sloughed off his shoulder in fetid clumps like rotten apples falling from a dead tree. The holy magic imbued in Nevidal was still attempting to embolden the stubborn warrior, but the poison broke down tissue faster than the magic could knit it together.

Taurnil's wings twitched pathetically as they scraped against the stone. The once proud demon from the abyss lay nearly motionless. A stream of thick black blood meandered from his scalp and mouth to his ashen chest and pooled on the blasted rocks. The hard pommel of Nevidal had left a massive dent in the top of Taurnil's skull.

"You..." Gideon managed to cough past the blood in his throat. "You are dead, demon." The paladin tightened his grip on the large sword he used as a cane to pull himself along. "I will harvest..." A fit of coughing shuddered through Gideon's chest and sent more blood splattering out in front of him. "I will harvest your soul," he said with finality as he shakily stood before the fallen beast.

Gideon's heart raced at an uncontrollable pace. Adrenaline and Nevidal's enchantment combined in his body with the demon's poison in a virulent tempest of life and death. The sword hummed in his grip, eager for a kill. He knew that satisfying the blade would dispel the divine magic and allow the poison to consume him. The pain was so immense that Gideon started to smile at the thought of death.

Vrysinoch's champion loomed over the broken creature with a peaceful grin on his face. He mustered what was left of his resolve to raise his right hand up high. Nevidal gave off a faint bluish glow, barely enough light to reflect off the blood staining the ground, but the blade managed to release one last spark of energy as it swooped in for the kill.

Tears streamed down Keturah's face. The grand study of the Artificer's Guild was in ruins. Small fires smoldered in every corner. Priceless arcane tomes had been turned to powder in the fury of her spellcasting. The lightning storm had taken every ounce of magical energy the woman possessed. Her features were gaunt and emaciated. Her once lustrous hair hung limp at her shoulders. The flesh around her piercing eyes was dark and her cheeks sunk in, giving her a hollow and lifeless appearance. She used a sleeve of her beautiful gown to wipe a line of mucus from her inflamed nose and cracked lips.

With a whimper, Keturah mouthed the words to her final spell. Tendrils of oily smoke billowed up from her empty eye sockets. A gentle breeze made its way into the grand study from a shattered window set into the northern wall of the room. The soft whisper of the wind picked up the bone dry ashes of Keturah's corpse from under the folds of her elegant dress and scattered them around the room. Her dead hair snapped and blew away, but the spell was finished.

The final spark from Gideon's sword stole his vision long enough for the paladin to miss the wisp of smoke that curled around Taurnil's broken body. In the blink of an eye, the demon reverted back to his natural form. Nevidal clanged against the bloody stone with the sound of thunder and a small, jet black scorpion skittered away into the darkness unseen.

The momentum of the missed execution pulled him to the ground. His body was too weak to even gasp. Resigned to bitter agony, Gideon looked around the darkened cavern one last time. "A quiet place, but not..." his voice trailed off into a strained cough of blood.

Nevidal winked out and left the warrior in pitch black darkness.

Fifteen

"I HATE WALL patrol," Stratos grumbled. The soldier was a tall man, remarkably lanky and thin for his height, and he sported a thick, curly beard of brown hair. He pulled a strip of white cloth from under his tunic and used it to wipe the sweat from his forehead. His heavy metal boots clinked loudly against the polished stone of Terror's Lament as the newly recruited soldier walked.

Next to Stratos, Teysa tugged at the shining steel breastplate she wore and used a hand to keep the sun out of her eyes. She was Stratos' younger sister and bore a stark resemblance to her sibling's thin frame. The two had been inseparable from a very young age and had even joined the city guard

221

together. After being commissioned by Herod as Templars of Peace, Stratos and Teysa tried to take an extra measure of pride in their patrolling despite the punishing heat.

The deep green talon embossed on the templar's armor burned under the hot afternoon sun. Stratos pulled the chainmail coif back from his head. Sweat poured from his sunburned skin and sizzled on the stone walkway. The two soldiers stopped their patrol and sat down with their backs to the wall.

"Why do we have to walk in so much armor?" Teysa groaned. Their canteen had been empty for the past two hours but their patrol lasted another three.

"I know what you mean." Stratos' rag was soaked beyond use so he tossed it over the wall. All of the templars atop the high walls of Talonrend had recently been ordered to make their patrols with a full armament. Teysa slipped one of her scalloped steel gauntlets off and let it clang to the walkway.

"I'm not used to all this heavy armor. My hands are starting to blister. My feet feel like they are on fire." She began to unlace the straps on the back of her steel greaves. "I don't understand why we have to walk so many patrols."

Three other pairs of templars were slowly making their own rounds on different sections of the walls. They looked like shining stars, reflecting brilliantly against the pale landscape of the Talonrend countryside.

Teysa removed her heavy breastplate and set her greaves and gauntlets inside her chest piece's hollow shell. "Come on, let's keep moving. I'm going to stash my armor for the rest of the patrol." She stretched a hand down to lift Stratos off the stone. The supple leather and mail the guard wore under her steel breathed the gentle wind and cooled her body. The woman had only been patrolling the wall for a few weeks and hated every minute of it.

Stratos breathed heavily under the oppressive weight of his armor. The skinny man shrugged his shoulders and tried to adjust the fit as he walked. Nothing helped keep the heat at bay. "I don't understand why we need to have swords with us too." He thumbed the pommel of the blade on his hip and wondered if he would ever need to draw it. "What do we need swords for? Nothing can get up here and we certainly can't throw them with any effect."

Teysa hefted her crossbow up on her shoulder and looked over the edge of the wall. The two templars were on the northern face of Terror's Lament. "There isn't even anything out there..." The vast openness of the grassy plain was daunting, like an endless ocean filled with the unknown.

Stratos carried a similar crossbow across his shoulders. He set the large weapon down against the stone parapet and peered out into the vastness. "What is everyone afraid of out there? What are we protecting the kingdom against?" Stratos put a hand on Teysa's shoulder and pulled her back.

"No sane person living behind these high walls should be afraid of anything. Talonrend is impenetrable. No army has ever broken through Terror's Lament and no army ever will." Teysa shook her head against the heat of the day and ran a hand through her long blonde hair. She could see the redness under Stratos' curly beard and knew he must be burning.

"It isn't the people who are afraid," she continued. Teysa drew her sword and held it to the back of her head. With one tug of the blade, she cut the majority of her hair off and tossed it to the ground outside the city. "The bloody prince is the problem. Herod is afraid of his own shadow without his brother here to protect him."

Teysa offered the sword to Stratos, indicating that he should cut his thick beard from his chin to ease the heat. With a look of terror on his face, Stratos refused the sword and backed away. "Oh no, not my beard." He held his hands in a defensive posture in front of him. "Do you know how long it took me to grow this? I'm not crazy enough to cut it off just because of a little heat!"

Teysa shrugged and sheathed the sword. She walked past Stratos, continuing her patrol with her armor in hand.

The templar hesitated a moment before catching up to Teysa. Something caught his eye, something lurking just on the fringes of his peripheral vision. "Teysa! Did you see that?" He grabbed the crossbow and leveled it on the parapet, trying to discern what he had seen.

"Oh, settle down, Stratos. Nothing is out there." The confident woman kept walking and tugging at the leather jerkin for relief.

Stratos leaned over the edge with his crossbow and looked directly down the glistening wall. "Teysa, something moved down at the base of the wall. Look at it, I can't tell." The panic in his voice brought Teysa back. She knew he wasn't kidding.

Her leather and mail armor was much more flexible than Stratos' heavy plate and allowed her the necessary movement to more clearly see the base of the wall. "I don't see anything, Stratos. You have heat stroke. Let's find some water."

Teysa's soft armor certainly afforded her mobility but it did nothing to stop the flying goblin arrow that ripped through her chest.

"Teysa, no!" Stratos screamed, pulling her to the ground. He could see the blood-soaked feathers protruding less than an inch out of the woman's body. With his other hand around her back, Stratos felt the tip of the arrow scrape against his gauntlet.

Stratos slammed the visor of his helmet down over his eyes and breathed in heavily to calm his nerves. Offering a meager prayer to Vrysinoch, Stratos stole a glance over the parapet. Two goblins crouched at the foot of the wall, hidden in the tall grasses. One of them was holding a small wooden bow and grinning from ear to ear.

Stratos dropped back to the stone and drew his sword. The other guards on the wall were too far away to hear his call. He gripped his sword tightly and stood up. Teysa was lying motionless. There wasn't much blood, but he knew she was dead.

With a grunt of rage, Stratos gripped the parapet and launched himself over the wall. The terrified goblins below shrieked in fear and one of them managed to scramble out of the way before the flailing ball of living steel landed. The unfortunate goblin holding the bow was crushed in an instant.

226

YAEL PACED THE grounds in front of his soldiers. He had been waiting for the two scouts to return from the walls for hours. When Keegar, the surviving goblin from the scouting expedition, finally ran back into the camp, he was greeted with a harsh glare.

"Where is the other scout?" Yael yelled. He knew before Keegar spoke what had happened. The only reason for one goblin to return alone was the death of the second goblin. Keegar cowered before Yael. He fell to his knees before the commander and recounted the story of his scouting mission.

"The humans know that we are here. If any of the humans died, then we are no longer safe here. They will send their armies out against us. Thousands of humans will march into our camps! They will kill all of us!" Yael struck the scout and knocked him to the ground in his anger. Keegar's nose broke under the weight of the blow.

"She knew this would happen... She caused this to happen!" Yael wasn't a stupid goblin. His fears were confirmed. Lady Scrapple had full control of the scouting goblins. She wanted the human army to come out from behind their high walls. The hundreds of goblins arrayed in the field before their commander were going to be used as fodder. For his minor rebellion against the hive mind, Yael's forces had been condemned.

"Keegar!" the commander called to the bloodied goblin. "Come with me. We need to make plans." The scout fell into line behind Yael and followed him back to his tent.

"I've been thinking," Yael explained when the two were alone. "Our entire block of soldiers is going to be used as fodder."

Keegar nodded but did not quite understand. "The Lady does what is best for the mountain. We serve her."

"Of course..." Yael said. "Keegar," the commander shook his head, not knowing how to explain it all to the scout. "When you were at the wall... How did you get out of the way of the falling soldier?"

"I jumped. I saw him coming and I jumped..." Keegar spoke slowly. It was obvious that he was trying to piece things together.

"But your companion on the scouting mission, he did not have the same reaction?" Yael could feel the presence of Lady Scrapple invading his mind. She was like a slow poison tearing at his consciousness, taking more and more with every passing second.

"We are far from the mountain, Keegar, farther than any of us have gone before. And we are numerous. More goblins are outside of the mountain than Lady Scrapple can control." Yael gasped from the effort. Veins on his pale skull throbbed and pounded.

Clutching the center tent pole for support, Yael managed to speak once more before he collapsed: "Don't you see, Keegar? Our distance and numbers strain her abilities! We can be *free*! She can only control... us if we let her."

Keegar stood in front of the exhausted commander and was completely lost. A line of drool escaped his mouth and landed on Yael's face. The goblin scout ducked his head and exited the tent, unsure of where he should go.

Sixteen

FOUR GOBLIN EYES stared into the darkness of the cave. Nothing inside the cave moved. The soft trickle of water accompanied the endless scuffling of undead in the underground corridor.

"What happened?" Vorst whispered. "Is he dead?" The small goblin held a sword in her hand.

"I can't tell. I think he is." Gravlox was positioned just behind Vorst, using the smaller goblin as a shield against his mounting fears.

"He just collapsed though. I didn't see the winged one strike him. Maybe he's alive." Vorst's voice seemed far away in the damp cavern. The music that so often wove itself into her high-pitched timbre was gone. That comforting quality was replaced by fear, something Gravlox wasn't accustomed to hearing.

"I've seen it happen in the mines. When one of my miners has worked for a long time, sometimes they will just fall down and die. It only happens in the ones that have been in the mine for many, many years though. I don't know how to tell how old a human is." Somehow, Gravlox found the courage to take a step towards the slumped figure.

"I'm not positive, but this one doesn't look old enough to die like that. Maybe he decided to sleep." Vorst remained with her feet planted firmly on the ground as Gravlox continued his approach.

"I still don't understand why they do that," he muttered, never taking his eyes from Gideon's back.

"We should kill him, just to make sure he is dead," Vorst whispered. The man groaned then, but didn't move.

"He killed that winged thing we fought in the forest," Gravlox said. He glanced quickly over his shoulder and gave Vorst a smile. "Maybe this one is our friend."

Vorst shook her head but she knew that Gravlox couldn't see. The man let out another groan. It was weaker than the first, more of a whimper than anything.

The goblin foreman reached a hand out toward the fallen warrior and gently touched his shoulder. Gideon attempted to roll but only managed to cough and half turn his head. A thin line of blood made its way down Gideon's face and dripped onto the cavern floor.

Immediately, Gravlox could sense the immense energy radiating from the paladin. "He is powerful," the goblin said with astonishment, "but he is nearly dead."

Vorst was kneeling beside the paladin and inspecting his wounds. Her eyes darted all around the cavern. "Where is his left arm? Humans have two arms, just like us."

The foreman hadn't even noticed the brutal wound. Gideon's left arm ended in a short stump just inches from his shoulder. The skin was black like burnt ashes. Vorst picked up the sleeve of armor and set it down next to the paladin. The man attempted another groan but wasn't successful.

"Can you heal him, Grav?" Vorst was holding his hand and looking down at the battered man with sorrow in her eyes.

"I'm not sure how I even did that..." Gravlox gripped the man's ashen shoulder and closed his eyes. Not having any clue how to connect to the well of magic within himself, Gravlox concentrated on the feeling he got from accessing magic. Before he could enter into the clairvoyant state of spellcasting, Vorst kissed him and took him there herself.

Consumed by the whirling riptides of magic within his body, Gravlox could feel the malevolent poison in the man's body. The acid was eating through blood and flesh at an alarming rate. The foreman's primal magic wove itself into the regenerative force of Gideon's enchanted sword. Vrysinoch's soft voice whispered through the cavern and echoed off the walls.

The devilish poison fought back with wicked resolve. Gideon began to cough and wheeze, hacking up a stream of thick, black, congealed blood. The concerted efforts of Gravlox and Vrysinoch began to halt the progress of the poison and knit some of the broken tissue back together.

Coughing, the paladin crawled to his knees. Nevidal was still magically bound to his hand, making it awkward for the man to position himself. The paladin couldn't see in the dark like the two goblins but their eyes betrayed their presence. With all the strength he could muster, Gideon knocked the goblins aside and turned to face them.

"My god," the paladin stammered when he realized what had been touching him. With his back against the wall of the cave, Gideon swung Nevidal out in front of him. It was a feeble attack, one easily defeated by nothing more than Vorst's outstretched hand. She grabbed the blade and meant to disarm the man but despite his weakness, the paladin did not let the weapon go. She could see the man's fingers barely wrapped about the hilt of the hand-and-a-half sword. The sheer weight of the weapon alone should have dropped it to the stone but the stubborn blade didn't even waver.

With a high-pitched accent that grated against human ears and a halting knowledge of the human language, Vorst attempted to reason with the man. "Friend. We both friend." Vorst pointed to herself and then to Gravlox and said both of their names. "Both friend."

The paladin backed as far as he could against the wall. He could barely make out the images of the two 'friends' in the darkness. "Goblins…" The paladin's voice came out raspy and strained.

Vorst nodded her head vigorously, mistaking the anger in Gideon's voice for plain recognition. "Goblins!" she confirmed, pointing to her chest. "Gravlox," she patted the foreman on the back. "Gravlox is shaman. He heals you. Stay still. You hurt. Gravlox is shaman, heals you."

Gideon nodded slowly. Still clutching the sword he could not drop, he awkwardly pointed to himself and said his name. To the goblins, his voice was deep and mysterious, full of darkness and potential evil.

"My sword," Gideon said, growing stronger. The holy magic was still coursing into him and regenerating his body. The only way to halt the enchantment would be to feed a soul to Nevidal. The clever paladin realized at once that the shaman's magic had at least halted the devastating tide of poison within his blood. "I have to kill someone, to end the enchantment that makes me stronger."

Vorst understood the man's words but not the concepts he espoused. Defensively, the female goblin backed away and placed a hand over Gravlox's chest.

Gideon waved his hand in front of him as best he could to calm the goblins. He had no intentions of killing either of them. "His magic, I feel it," he said. He placed his hand over his heart and glanced down at the blackened stump where his left arm used to hang. "Thank you."

A long moment passed in the darkness between the trio. "You must kill..." Vorst responded. "Who must you kill?" She positioned herself in front of her goblin lover, not knowing what would happen.

"I didn't mean you," Gideon managed a smile. He could feel his body growing steadily stronger but he knew that he was a very long way from being whole again. "If I kill your shaman, his magic will leave me and I will die. I won't risk that." He winced as he spoke but didn't hold back. "Friends," he said, holding his sword over his chest and indicated with his chin toward Gravlox.

"Find someone for to kill," Vorst chuckled. She stood and pointed toward the corridor where endless ranks of the dead were marching toward Talonrend.

"I almost forgot..." Gideon used the length of his mighty sword to lift himself off the ground. Gravlox tentatively moved toward the massive warrior who stood closer to eight feet tall than seven due to the marvelous enchantment.

The three unlikely friends stood in the corridor and watched as entire families shambled down the tunnel. Some women even held little undead babies to their bosoms as they trudged onward. Gideon waited until an older man walked past and used his long sword to herd him into the larger cavern.

The zombie appeared to be about forty. He had a ragged, half-torn beard hanging from his chin and wore a thick leather apron over a white shirt and matching pants. He was covered in dirt and grime and his feet had worn through his boots to reveal bloody toes and blisters. The man had been walking for quite some time in the damp tunnels beneath the surface.

Completely mindless, the zombie flailed about in a meager attempt to scratch and bite the tall paladin. Gideon's heavy boot crashed into the man's maggot-ridden chest and caved it in. The zombie stumbled backward and landed on his back. With one quick swipe, the zombie's head rolled away from its shoulders. The mighty paladin's remaining shoulder bulged as layer upon layer of corded muscle reconstituted itself.

Frustration overcame the man and he loosed a roar that shook the earth. A dozen more brutal cuts had the decomposing corpse scattered into piles of fetid flesh all about the cavern. "His soul was not with his body." Gideon hung his head in defeat.

Vorst grabbed at the paladin's arm. "Poison still in flesh. You end enchantment, Gideon dies, yes?" The look in the man's eyes told her that such a fate would be welcomed.

"If I cannot cure the demon's poison, ending the enchantment will kill me. If the shaman dies, the poison will kill me. If the poison is cured before I can take a soul, the enchantment will kill me." Gideon kicked his discarded armor and spat on the ground. "I am condemned. The shaman's magic prevents the corruption from taking me now, but my sword's magic will overcome my body eventually. I can last for a few more days, a week at the most, before I cannot control it any longer. You should leave me here to die…"

Using the goblin language of finger taps, Vorst translated everything the human said for Gravlox. The shaman nodded his head solemnly.

"He is right, Vorst. We should abandon him. There are always more humans to take his place. One human is no loss." Gravlox picked up the armor sleeve and rolled it in his hands. It was far too large to fit his scrawny arms but he put it in his pack nonetheless.

"This man can help us, Grav! Look at the undead in that tunnel." She forcefully turned him back to the corridor. "With a powerful warrior like this one, we can do something about that. The army here marches for the human city. Look at how many there are! They will kill everyone in that city without mercy."

"Isn't that exactly why we came here?" Gravlox was cynical. "Yael ordered us to go to the necromancer who did this and salvage the goblin alliance with these monsters! Have you forgotten that, Vorst?"

Tears welled up in her eyes. "Gravlox.... Listen to yourself. You are an outcast, exiled from our mountain home. Have you forgotten *that?*" She shook Gravlox forcefully and took a step back in disgust. "If the human kingdom falls to Lady Scrapple, what do you think she will do? Will she let us go?"

Gravlox digested the words as he looked at Gideon's ashy shoulder. "She will hunt us relentlessly..." He knew it was true. "As long as Lady Scrapple is alive, we will never be safe."

Vorst nodded. "Exactly. We must help the humans now. If they can defeat the armies at their doorstep, maybe they will help us defeat Lady Scrapple. We have to try."

"Humans will never help us. Look at us, Vorst. We are goblins. They hate us. Even this one tried to kill you while I was saving it." He had doubt stamped all over his pale face. "I don't know... Even if we can turn back the army of our kin, what will happen to us? Do we live with the humans? Will they take us in behind their walls to walk among their children?" Downtrodden, he couldn't meet Vorst's intense gaze. His mind searched desperately for answers that he knew he didn't have.

"We can figure that out *after* we kill Lady Scrapple and free the rest of the goblins," Vorst said with a renewed strength in her melodic voice. "If we save this human, he will help us after it's done." The two goblins hugged each other for what felt like an eternity to Gideon, who was still standing awkwardly in the cavern. Vorst explained to the man what their plan was and he smiled to show his support.

Using the rope to guide Gideon through the lightless tunnels, Gravlox and Vorst ran past the zombie horde. They went against the flow of undead flesh, seeking the source of the rampant corruption. Reikall was only a day's run from the cavern where Taurnil fell but Gideon could not match the fevered pace of the goblins. His towering form was not fit for the cramped tunnels and he repeatedly bashed his head against the low hanging stone.

After an hour of running, the man was too tired to go on. The stink of the animated corpses was stifling. Being not far under the surface, it didn't take long for Gravlox to find a side passage that led to the surface. Gideon had to crawl on his chest, a difficult task with only one arm and sword in his right hand, but he made it. The three rested on the surface and were glad to be out of the horrid smell.

"I think I can track the passage from above, on the surface," Gideon told Vorst after he caught his breath. He gripped the hilt of his sword tightly and called upon the divine powers bestowed upon him as a paladin. A tiny ethereal eagle materialized on the tip of his sword and took flight. The small ball of sculpted magic landed softly on the man's shoulder and he whispered a gentle incantation to it. Without hesitation, the glowing eagle took wing and glided just inches above the ground.

"It worked," he said with a voice that indicated his surprise. "The bird will show us the way. It can sense the magic that animated the undead and can track them for us. We can stay on the surface for now." Gideon's powerful enchantment still coursed through his veins and enlarged his stature. He stood nearly ten feet tall and towered above the diminutive goblins like the walls of Talonrend hovering high over a beggar slumped against the base of the stone. "Let's go."

Seventeen

THE NEWLY COMMISSIONED Templars of Peace were arrayed outside of Terror's Lament. One thousand men, fully clad in steel plate, stood perfectly still in front of the massive eastern gate to the city. They had been organized into ten centuries and every single soldier was outfitted with masterwork equipment from Master Brenning's armory. Even though the grizzled old smith was nowhere to be seen in the city, his smiths had worked tirelessly for the past few days to outfit the new military campaign.

Supporting each century of soldiers was a unit of twenty-five mounted cavalry called an alaris. The cavalry were designed for maximum effectiveness on the open plains that surrounded the walls of

Talonrend. Some of the mounted soldiers carried lances but most of the warriors in each alaris wielded a heavy two-headed flail and a kite shield emblazoned with the symbol of Vrysinoch.

The Templars of Peace were supported by the common militia that was summoned from the outlying villages along the Clawflow and the city's own residents. Some of the men and women in the militia were volunteers but the majority of the force was comprised of draftees. Lacking the training required for vigorous melee combat in the open fields, the soldiers of the militia were typically taught how to fire a bow or crossbow as part of a volley. Primarily, the militia was used to man Terror's Lament, but pockets of draftees had been placed with crossbows all around the base of the wall. It was impossible to count every individual, but roughly three thousand villagers had answered the call to serve their prince. Most of the soldier's families had come as well, fearing that an attack would come from east of the Clawflow and destroy their homes. The city was packed with civilians. Even the royal audience hall had been set up as a shelter for the refugees. Fortunately, most of the families had also brought large stores of food and other essential goods with them so a siege upon the city wouldn't mean the death of the kingdom.

By the time the Templars of Peace had been outfitted with their equipment, little had remained in the royal armories for the militia to use. Farmers and other tradesmen had brought their own make-shift weapons from the villages. Everything from pitchforks to crude swords and simple brass knuckles could be seen among the commoners. The people not fortunate enough to have received a bow or crossbow were exclusively stationed as reserves, lying in wait just inside the first wall of Terror's Lament. If any section of the wall fell or if the gate itself was destroyed, the militia would be there to fill the hole and slow the encroaching army enough for an alaris or a century to be deployed to that area. Prince Herod understood that the militia behind the wall wouldn't last long if they were engaged, but that's exactly why they were stationed *behind* the wall.

The regal prince sat atop a magnificent war-horse in front of the gate. He was clad in golden armor fit for a god. The sun reflected so brightly off of his shield that even the horses in the nearest alaris turned their heads. Maelstrom and Regret were strapped to his hips and a heavy lance was suspended in a horizontal sheath just below his right stirrup. The golden shield was one that few soldiers recognized; until that morning, it had hung above the bed of King Lucius. Herod had the holy seal of Vrysinoch stripped from the metal and the whole device had been coated in solid gold. It was highly impractical, Herod knew, but he didn't intend to use it.

"Mighty soldiers of Talonrend! Defenders of civilization and peace!" Herod's voice boomed out over the army, amplified by the wall at his back. "The songs of war have brought you all here, but it is not a war we have chosen." The prince scanned the soldiers in front of him to gauge their reactions but none of them made a move. "We are engaged in a great defensive war, one that will be remembered for millennia! The high walls of Talonrend will be tested. The resolve of this army will be tested. The strength in our arms and the courage in our hearts will be tested. Talonrend will prevail!" A chorus of enthusiastic cheers rose up before him.

"We did not choose this war and we are not obligated to fight it. But keep this in mind: If you cast aside your weapons today, your families will be slaughtered tomorrow. If you grow tired of fighting and turn back, the men around you will die. We do not fight for any new lands or wealth or resources, we fight to hold onto everything we already have. A great army has amassed against us and our very lives are at stake." The soldiers pounded their weapons against the ground and sent a tremendous thunder into the air.

"The great walls of this city have never been breached!" More cheers erupted all around the soldiers but most of them were from the militia. The veteran soldiers knew the truth of the matter; the walls had never been breached because they had never been attacked. "These walls will not be breached today! They will not be breached tomorrow! They will stand for a thousand years as a testament to your courage!" Again, it was the drafted soldiers who celebrated with the most fervor.

"Some five hundred goblins have been seen in the north. A handful of goblins have been seen in the east, just past the Clawflow. They will need ten times that number if the filthy goblins expect to kill even a single citizen of Talonrend!" That was a claim the entire army could support. Vigorous cheers and salutations rang out through the city and sent adrenaline into the hearts of many.

"We do not know what else hides in the darkness of the forest, waiting to attack alongside the goblins like cowards." Images of fire breathing dragons soared through the prince's mind. "Whatever foes might show themselves on the field of battle will die on the field of battle!" Herod's warhorse reared up and kicked the air, bringing more shouts from the soldiers.Herod hefted the golden shield in both hands above his head and displayed it to the army. "As many of you know, my dear friend Master Brenning has gone missing. This shield used to belong to my brother." The soldiers were captivated by the golden relic and rendered silent by its magnificence. "Whoever has the good fortune to find Master Brenning or to bring me the head of his killer will claim this shield as their prize!" Roars broke the silence and forced Herod to give the army a minute to calm down before continuing. "My brother is dead. I accept that. His shield represents the monarchy, a prize waiting to be claimed by a hero. I have no children and have decided against producing any. Whoever claims this shield will be my heir and the heir to Talonrend!" The cheers that followed that proclamation were deafening. The army was hungry for glory and honor, things they had never had the chance to earn.

A FEW MILES to the north of the gathered army, Yael and Keegar strapped on their armor and prepared to move. The five hundred goblins formerly

under Yael's direction had been completely overcome by Lady Scrapple's will. The goblin commander had proved, to himself at least, that the Mistress of the Mountain was not omnipotent. Her
powers had a limit and with the distance at which
the goblins had been deployed, her limits were being reached.

Yael and Keegar watched helplessly as the five
hundred goblins on the plain readied themselves for
the incoming war. They were only lightly armed
and armored. Most of the goblins wore crude leather shirts and a few of them had small wooden buck-
lers attached to their forearms. To make up for their
short reach against the taller humans, almost all of
the goblins wielded spears or javelins.

The army began to march south in unison and
used the tall grasses to hide their movements as best
they could. The five blocks of drones waited at the
edge of the plain with their weapons drawn. With
such pale skin, the tall grasses north of Talonrend
concealed the army quite well. The sun glinting off
the human's armor made Terror's Lament appear on
fire.

THE CITY WAS calm and peaceful. Not a single person could be seen walking down the streets or standing among the smoldering ruins. A great fire had ravaged the once vibrant city and, judging by the heat still emanating from many of the collapsed buildings, Gideon could tell that the city had died recently. The three companions had made it to Reikall as the sun began to set a day after they left the caves. It was becoming painfully obvious that Nevidal's enchantment was going to kill the powerful man. By the time he looked upon the savagery of the ruined city, he was a giant. At almost twelve feet tall, the paladin had to stoop just to get through the city's front gate.

Everywhere they went nothing but death and suffering greeted them. It was a place devoid of not only life, but lacking hope as well. Gideon's astral bird still guided the group but it moved noticeably slower, as if Vrysinoch was saddened as well. Reikall was a city built from large squares of cut marble stacked on top of one another to form intimidating and beautiful structures. The sullen atmosphere didn't fit the architecture.

"This place is huge," Gravlox remarked, looking up at a colossal building that sported four white pillars and held what was left of the roof. One of the pillars had tumbled to the ground and huge chunks of soot-stained marble blocked the road. The incorporeal eagle floated gently through the fallen pillar with ease but the goblins were not even half as tall as the debris. Without as much as a grunt, Gideon wrapped his bulging right arm around the corner of the stone and pushed with his monstrous legs. The chunk of marble pillar moved as easily as if it had been a feather.

Vorst pointed to an area behind much smaller ruined building to the left of the road. "We could go around..." she said, but they were already following the bird unhindered once again. Gideon simply looked at her with sadness and shrugged.

They continued on through the smoldering ashes of Reikall until the bird glided to a stop on the edge of a moss-covered well at the center of a market square. Merchant stalls lined the border of the clearing and the whole place stank of death. Down a wide boulevard flanked by dead trees to the east of the market, one structure dominated everything. Reikall's royal castle was a larger building than anything the group had ever seen before. Turrets and spires wearing jewelry of stained glass clawed their way above the smoke and ashes to touch the sky. Only one small section of the keep had been destroyed. A square tower near the gatehouse and drawbridge had tumbled into the castle's moat. Like

Castle Talon, the land around the royal residence had been built up to give the castle an even better view. Where there had once been a gentle embankment of rolling green grass was nothing but black dirt. Not even weeds grew along the banks of the moats. Everything was dead.

The eagle chirped once and dove down the well before Gideon could get to it. "What do we do?" Vorst asked. She tapped out the question in the goblin language on Gravlox's hand so he could follow.

"I guess we go down too," Gideon said as he peered into the well.

"Will he fit?" Gravlox asked skeptically. The huge man's broad shoulders were at least six feet wide but he did only have a single arm to worry about. The paladin understood the concern before Vorst translated the question to him. He shook his head and walked to the other side of the market, toward the castle.

The trees that had once beautified the approach to Reikall's keep were tall and slender. Although their broad leaves had fallen to the ground and withered some time before Gideon ever laid eyes upon them, he still found the sight captivating. The paladin had lived his entire youth in a poor farming village where every structure and plant served a function. His adulthood was spent in the Talonrend arena and a smoky blacksmith's shop. Even Castle Talon, for all of its impressive size, was not particularly beautiful to the eye. Standing before the long boulevard and gazing up at the marble castle, Gideon wished he had been born in Reikall.

The giant leaned against one of the dead trees and let out a long sigh. The tower where the priests of Vrysinoch lived in Talonrend was aesthetically pleasing beyond question, but to Gideon, it represented a place of oppression. He had trained there for a decade alongside the other paladins, but he was never allowed to be an individual. All aspects of a paladin's life were meant to be for the good of the whole with no concern for the self. At first, it made sense to him. When fighting as a cohesive unit there was no room for personal issues or desires. That very oppression led Gideon to leave the tower at the end of his training. Somewhere deep inside his soul, the man wanted desperately to worry about just himself.

The slender trees and the wide open road gave him that. The boulevard and the castle were works of art meant to be admired. The paladin felt that he would love to live in a place like Reikall. Gideon could hear the small goblins shuffling about nervously behind him. He sighed, turned, and left his longing behind.

"What are we going to do?" Vorst asked. She had to strain her neck to look the giant in the eyes as she spoke. Gideon wrapped his arm, still tightly grasping Nevidal, around the tall tree he had been leaning against and ripped it from the earth. Sullenly, he marched to the well and bade the goblins grab the top of withered plant. With frightening ease, the paladin gently lowered Gravlox and Vorst to the bottom of the well where the glowing bird awaited them. The eagle was perched between two iron bars that were part of a larger grate set into the wall of the well. Without much effort, the skinny goblins slid through the bars into the passageway beyond.

The sewer channel was large enough to allow them both to stand and walk side by side. Letting loose an occasional screech, the bird continued to flap its silent wings and guide the pair along the underbelly of the city.

Vibrations from their footfalls caused chunks of rotting moss and other unidentifiable and fetid objects to fall from the crusted top of the sewer tunnels and onto the goblins as they moved. Eventually, Gravlox and Vorst came to a larger intersection of tunnels and sewers beneath the city.

The small, glowing cantrip guided the two goblins to a cramped passage that angled steeply downward. Without hesitation, Vorst jumped into the sewer tunnel and slid down the slick moss with Gravlox not far behind. Had the two goblins waited a moment between sliding, they wouldn't have collided so painfully at the bottom of the passage. Vorst's face was contorted against a set of three iron bars at the end of the slanted sewer. When her male companion slammed directly into her back, Vorst's contorted face became a clear image of pain and regret.

Master Brenning heard the clumsy creatures smack into the iron bars right next to his head. He recognized the screeching qualities in the two voices and knew that his visitors were not human. Mustering all the strength he could, Brenning got to his feet and brushed the dirt from his clothes.

"What in Vrysinoch's name?" Master Brenning jumped back a step when he noticed the incorporeal eagle casually gliding above his head. His sleep had denied him the frightful occasion of seeing the eagle enter the room.

The burly smith drew his sword and snarled. He had just enough light from the glow of the magical bird to tell that it was a pair of goblins who had found his sewer prison. "Have at me, then!" He yelled, slapping the flat of his blade against his hairy chest to summon his courage.

Within seconds, the stone around the edges of the iron bars exploded into a flurry of dirt and grime. Two tangled goblins dropped to the floor of the chamber right behind the loud iron bars. Fortunately for the goblins, the older man was too stunned from the blast to react with his sword before Gravlox and Vorst were on their feet.

"Friends," Vorst said, patting her hands in the air to calm Master Brenning. The softly glowing eagle landed on the smith's shoulder, pecked his face once with its ghostly beak, and dissipated in a burst of light that seemed to attach itself to the moss and continued to glow. Something about the peacefulness of the flitting bird eased the smith's mind and calmed his blood. He lowered the sword but did not sheath it.

"Both friends," she repeated and took another step closer. "Human with us. Work with humans." Her choppy command of the human language was unusual for a goblin and brought more questions than answers to the blacksmith.

Master Brenning's eyes kept darting back and forth from the goblin pair to the exploded sewer tunnel in the wall. It was hard to tell which surprised him more.

"Shaman," the amused female goblin stated as she patted Gravlox on the back. Brenning's face went pale in the darkness because he knew that attempting to defend himself would be fruitless. He sheathed his sword and took a confident step towards the goblins. Gravlox and Vorst had no idea what to make of the smith's outstretched hand so they simply let it hang awkwardly in the air.

After painfully slow introductions had been made, the three beings in the bottom of the sewer containment area sat down. The tunnel that Gravlox and Vorst had come down was far too narrow to allow the broad-shouldered smith to squeeze through. The walls of the circular chamber were far too smooth to attempt a climb and the smith had been trapped underground for days. He needed food and clean water. The man wasn't on the verge of death, but the sooner he was out of the dim underground, the better.

"Well," Gravlox asked. "How do we get out?"

Eighteen

THE FIRST GOBLIN wave came from the north, just as expected. About a hundred screaming goblins came rushing from the grass line waving weapons above their heads. The century stationed on the northern flank dug their heels in and waited for the charge to meet them. An alaris was stationed to the side of the century, ready to cut a diagonal swath of death through the measly charge.

"It must be a feint," Herod said to Apollonius from atop his warhorse. "Even if all of our soldiers were stationed *inside* the walls, not a single one of those filthy goblins would breach." Apollonius shook his head and looked to the east, expecting a second charge to compliment the first.

The goblins were halfway from the grass line to Terror's Lament when the alaris met their charge. Thundering hooves blasted through the weak charge. Goblin blood and bones flew through the air as dozens of the mindless drones were killed. As soon as the alaris had passed through the charge, a hail of arrows and crossbow bolts showered down upon what remained of the first attack. None of the first one hundred goblins ever made it to the steel clad soldiers of the century positioned on the north side of Talonrend.

Silence shrouded the bloody battlefield. The alaris trotted slowly back into place at the right flank of the century and waited for a second charge. The human army had survived the first minutes of war without a casualty. In their eagerness, the militia stationed atop Terror's Lament had fired nearly a dozen missiles for every target. Had they known how many goblins would face them that day, the soldiers would have thought twice about firing too many arrows.

Waiting for the next attack, the army was on edge. After an hour of standing in the bright sunlight, the soldiers were losing their focus. More and more of the militia on the walls lost the edge that adrenaline had given them. They sat down against the parapet and took off their roughshod helmets and hats. The sun was relentless.

Another hour of silence passed before Herod decided to act. "The alaris stationed on the southern flank, bring them up, Apollonius." The prince turned his warhorse toward the east and trotted out away from the wall. The eager soldier was riding a warhorse of his own taken from the prince's personal stables. The beast reared under his legs and took off.

In just a few minutes, twenty six mounted riders trotted up to the prince and saluted. "Good," Herod said as he met their approach. "I want you to execute a sortie. We know the goblins are camped out to the north. They sent a fifth of their number against us but even they aren't stupid enough to waste so many soldiers."

"Sir, with all due respect, why not?" The leader of the alaris wore a helmet fashioned with a large metal spike to designate his leadership and make him easier to spot. Curiously, the man also wore a set of throwing axes on his side like Gideon had.

"Why not?" Herod asked with venom in his voice. He had no patience for sarcasm.

"Why must the goblins be smarter than that? They send a bunch of goblins, wave after wave until they are all dead." The alaris captain used a mailed hand to shade his eyes from the sun.

"We can't afford to believe that, captain, even if it proves to be true. I am responsible for all of the lives here today. That includes the humans and the goblins. I want the goblins to die. If they will not come to us, we must go to them." Prince Herod indicated toward the man's throwing axes with a nod.

The alaris captain smiled and handed an axe to the prince. The handle was well worn and wrapped in supple leather strips. Curiously, the blade of the weapon was unscathed and pristine. "Throwing axes are not a very common sight in my army. I've seen things like these before. Actually, I've been attacked by very similar axes by a man named Gideon. Know him?" The prince handed the axe back to its owner.

"Gideon…. Yeah, I used to know him. We worked at the same armory together. We get to make these axes after we've been there for a few years." He tossed the weapon into the air and flipped it around before catching it again in his other hand.

"You have never used that axe. Have you ever been in a life or death situation, captain?"

"Just when I come home late to my wife," the man said with a chuckle.

"Perfect." Herod managed a grin despite the captain's relaxed attitude. "Go scout the goblin position. Kill as many of them as you can but don't risk your men. Figure out where they are hiding and how many more have joined their ranks. Then come back and report to me."

"Of course, my liege," the captain said with a stiff salute before he led his men away to the north.

Prince Herod watched his well-organized cavalry kick a cloud of dust into the air as they departed. "Where are the paladins? Where is Gideon?" The prince didn't dare let anyone near him catch a word of what he was saying. As far as the army knew, the paladins had been ordered to stay within the city walls and protect the people should a breach occur. In reality, the prince hadn't seen anyone from the Tower of Wings since he openly denied Vrysinoch. The paladins, assuming they still remained within the city, were cowering inside their tower. Herod only hoped that if the holy warriors were needed to fight back the gathering enemies, they would be ready and willing to do so.

YAEL AND KEEGAR crouched on the top of a slanted, thatched roof and watched the alaris gallop past. The solitary farm house was one of the few structures on the plain between Talonrend and the villages along the Clawflow. "Lady Scrapple!" Yael screamed at the younger Keegar. He knew that even though the hive mind was ignoring his consciousness, she could still be reached. "Lady Scrapple!" he yelled again into the frightened goblin's face. "They are sending heavy cavalry to the blocks positioned in the north! Those goblins need to get into anti-cavalry formations now!" Yael shook Keegar's body forcefully and knew by the mist in his eyes that Lady Scrapple had heard him.

The goblin blocks crouched in the high grasses moved immediately. They crawled along their bellies toward the incoming alaris and fanned out in a circular pattern. Just as expected, the human riders galloped onto the prepared battlefield. It took them a moment to realize they were surrounded. The captain clenched his hand into a fist in the air which ordered the riders to halt. The well prepared goblins never gave them a chance. A hundred diminutive drones swarmed the alaris with long spears that shined in the sunlight. Before the captain could even draw his sword, a spear head lodged itself under his horse's chin and sent the beast sprawling to the ground.

Two more spears bit into the horse's flank and silenced the animal's screams in a burst of blood. The alaris captain scrambled to his feet and tried to remove the blade at his side from its scabbard but it wouldn't budge. The horse's fall had bent the blade and locked it into the sheath.

A trio of goblins rushed the captain with spears and caused him to roll to his side to avoid being skewered. His armor was strong and the one spear head that did connect with his breastplate was easily deflected. Frustrated, the captain ripped the sheathed sword from his side and threw it at the nearest goblin which caused the beast to flinch. A throwing axe followed the sheathed blade and thudded into the goblin's lightly armored chest. The other two pale-skinned creatures pressing the alaris captain didn't notice their comrade's death. They poked and prodded with their longer weapons until the captain was pinned against his fallen horse's bloody corpse.

With a steel-bladed axe in his hand, the captain slashed side to side across his body to keep the deadly spear heads from finding their mark. The poorly constructed weapons splintered within moments so the two goblins threw the wooden shafts against the captain's armor and charged. With no room to dodge in the wicked melee, the alaris captain met the rush with his arms out wide and caught each goblin under the chin. Their pale skin crinkled and writhed as the muscular soldier hoisted the attackers off their feet. Holding the goblins at arm's length nearly three feet above the ground, the captain was defenseless against the third attacker he had knocked back with his thrown sword. No grin widened on the face of the ugly creature and it didn't let out a howl of victory. A blank stare bore into the alaris captain as he struggled to keep the flailing goblins tight in his clutches.

The free goblin picked up a stone and heaved it at the soldier, knocking a small dent in the man's strong armor. A broken spear shaft followed the rock but sank into the back of the goblin in the captain's right hand. The soldier banged the heads of his captives together with such force that both the creatures fell limp in his grasp. With a shield made of goblin flesh before him, the captain ran with all his strength at the third assailant and trampled the poor beast to the ground. Heavy steel boots crushed the soft goblin flesh and sent bits of bone flying among the grasses. Disgusted, the captain tossed aside the two dead goblins like chaff and drew another axe from his side.

Another line of goblins was nearly upon him by the time he loosed the missile. More goblins than the soldier had ever seen poured over him in a heartbeat. His thick armor was well built and prevented him from being quickly stomped into human mush but the immense weight of the armor made it impossible for the man to regain his feet. For a brief moment, the captain could see the sparse strands of wispy clouds that layered the sky. Soon, however, an ugly goblin face filled his vision, biting and spitting to chew at his face. The pile of goblins grew by the second as more of the stinking creatures leapt atop the fallen captain. Finally, after what felt like hours of being slowly crushed under all of that squirming weight, the captain succumbed to suffocation and died.

Yael and Keegar watched from a distance as the entire human cavalry unit disappeared into the maw of the waiting goblin ambush. "Her will must be getting weaker, Keegar," the pale-skinned leader remarked.

"Who is getting weaker?" Keegar wondered, still not comprehending Yael's discovery.

Yael backhanded his assistant out of frustration. It was a blow he truly wanted to deliver to Lady Scrapple herself. "The Mistress of the Mountain, Keegar. She is growing weaker every day trying to control so many goblins. We are too far from the mountain for her to fully control us. We are free out here, don't you feel it?"

The confused expression that followed showed Yael that Keegar did not fully understand his newly acquired mental freedom. "What did you do before you left the mountain for this campaign?" Yael asked, trying to make him think for the first time in his life.

"Back home? I lived with the soldiers and trained with them every day." Keegar scratched his wrinkled head as his tiny goblin brain worked furiously behind his beady eyes.

"What sorts of skills did you train?" the commander asked to lead his thinking in the right direction. Yael, as a high ranking member of the military, knew well the daily training regimens of the soldiers. The mindless drones rarely ever practiced anything but group attacks with spears or swords. A few goblins, those with more autonomy, were trained for specialized tasks such as scouting or stealth infiltration.

"I ran, I guess." Keegar was unsure of himself. He had never consciously experienced mental freedom before and the sensation was hitting him like a flood. "Every day I would train with the other goblins using my sword, and then I would run. Sometimes I would get to use a bow, but I was never very good at it."

Yael nodded. "How long would you run?" The wise goblin noted the thick leg muscles and dexterous frame of his companion with appreciation. It was obvious that Keegar had done nothing but athletic training for his entire life.

"I ran for as long as I had to…" His voice trailed off and his ugly features twisted into an expression of curiosity.

"Did you ever *want* to run, Keegar?" The commander smiled and knew he had succeeded.

"I…" Jagged teeth broke through the goblin's wide grin and he jumped up and down with excitement. "I always ran because I didn't know what else to do."

"Yes, you were being trained as a scout, Keegar! You were running so that one day, you could run faster than any of the other goblins and make reports. Lady Scrapple made you learn to shoot a bow so you could defend yourself while out alone. Scouts are the most valuable part of any army and the information you carried was worth more than your life. Our mother knew that if you were sent too far away, she wouldn't be able to control you and so you had to be fast enough to make it back alive."

Keegar jumped off the farmhouse roof and landed in a perfectly balanced roll. He began to run circles around the dilapidated building. "I *want* to run now!" he shouted back to Yael with glee.

"Lady Scrapple knew that there was a possibility that she could lose control..." Yael whispered under his breath. "She knew...." Looking over his shoulder at the dark silhouette of the massive mountain, Yael couldn't help but wonder what that meant. "If she knew, why would she send so many of us? What is so important about this human city that she would risk losing her control?" Yael climbed slowly down from the rooftop to join the elated scout in his celebration of freedom.

With the alaris thoroughly destroyed, the battlefield was quiet again. The towering walls of Talonrend reached to the bright summer sky to the west. Behind the goblin pair, Kanebullar Mountain loomed like the mighty shadow of a god poised to fly from the stars.

Nineteen

STALE WATER TRICKLED down from somewhere above and played beautifully in the
reflecting light of the magically luminescent
moss. All around them, soft colors darted about like
a torch tossed into a room full of gemstones. "Can
the shaman get us out?" Master Brenning asked. He
pointed to Gravlox and then pointed up to the dripping water overhead. "Grav... lox?" The man tried
to pronounce the name the best he could but the
high-pitched goblin language was far too complex
for the smith to control. The foreign word came out
as a bit of an embarrassing squeal that left his cheeks
flushed.

Gravlox and Vorst both laughed at the attempt
and tried to imitate the unusual sound. The barrel-

chested smith's strained falsetto was still much deeper than any sounds the goblins knew how to make. "Gravlox," the foreman repeated, pointing to his chest and smiling. Vorst tapped a translation of Brenning's question against the stone.

The shaman didn't know what to do. He wasn't familiar enough with his innate magical abilities to command the energy much beyond short bursts like the one that had destroyed the small tunnel opening in the sewer wall. "I can try," Gravlox said, more to himself than anyone else.

Calming his mind to concentrate, Gravlox closed his eyes and placed both of his hands against the stone. He remembered the feeling of energy he commanded in the clearing against the human soldiers.. The magic within his small body swirled and made him nauseous. Gasping for breath against the swell of energy, Gravlox let it go. Tiny cracks shot forth from his hands and split the stone where he was kneeling. Tendrils of black smoke curled up from his hands. "There is too much magic," he whispered. "I can't control it."

Vorst and Master Brenning moved away from the shaman and watched him in silence as the cracks along the stone slowly spread. They weren't deep, violent fissures, just a small sign of the unpredictability of shamanistic power.

Try again, Vorst tapped against the stone floor, although she wasn't sure if Gravlox would even notice.

Gravlox put his hands against the damp floor of the sewer and sought out the unstable source of magic within his soul that connected him to everything. His pale hands trembled with energy and the air around his fingertips crackled. More black smoke curled away into the stagnant air and a profound shudder rocked Gravlox's body. He could sense the immense river of natural magic coursing just beneath the edge of his consciousness. The shaman could see the glowing river like a fire on the horizon, blurred by a distant setting sun. With a hesitant mind, Gravlox reached toward that fire and brushed it with his fingertips. The jolt was unlike anything he had ever felt before. Pure white magic shot through his body and brought him to the ground. With a violent convulsion that nearly broke his spine, Gravlox retreated his consciousness from the source of magic.

Approaching the fire more slowly, he called out to it. No words accompanied the message, just a magical sensation of peacefulness. The burning image of magic revolted against the telepathic communication and raged with blind fury. A great heat swelled up in the stone chamber, sizzling the moist water droplets and causing the moss to wilt.

Fire was surrounding Gravlox in the mysterious realm of magical connections. He had not tried to approach and manipulate the essence but somehow it surrounded him, burning his mind and tearing away at the walls of his sanity. A voice behind the fire pushed out like the blast from a massive furnace and tore through the air. "Get out!" it yelled. The disembodied voice was full of anger and restlessness that betrayed underlying fear.

Gravlox did not waver. His magical being held firm against the torrent of ethereal flames that continued to assault his mind. Without thinking, Gravlox stepped forward through the fiery wall and saw a face on the other side. His features were strained, tortured even, and Gravlox could make out thick white ropes binding the face and holding it above the flames. Gravlox tried to reach out to the face with calming energy but the fires lashed out at him before he got near.

The sewer around the three beings shimmered in unseen heat. Vorst and Master Brenning both feared that they might be blown apart by the release of energy when Gravlox's trance subsided.

With fire licking all around and igniting the world, the face turned to snarl and spit at Gravlox's intrusion. The shaman recognized the face at once and nearly lost his concentration. Gravlox sent another magical wave of energy toward the burning face. The message was delivered like a barrage with fleeting images of pain, fear, darkness, and suffering. As if the face understood the communication perfectly, the fires subsided and died to smoldering embers. The face struggled against the white ropes, tossing and turning in every possible direction.

Gravlox could feel his strength deteriorating and knew that his willpower was about to break. The shaman sent one final message flying forth from his mind, a message of urgency and a clear mental picture of the sewer where he was trapped.

Fully exhausted and moments from his mental breaking point, Gravlox collapsed into a heap on the floor. The stones of the sewer were hot to the touch and steamed where his pale skin trapped water against them. Vorst rushed to his side, thankful that her beloved had survived and equally thankful that Gravlox had not destroyed the entire city.

"The magic wasn't mine," Gravlox managed to say. He rolled to his side and coughed. The air of the sewer was too hot and too stagnant to offer any relief. "Gideon, it was his. Everything I felt was coming from him. He could set the whole world on fire, but he is coming to help us." Vorst cradled him in her arms and held his head close to her chest.

"Human friend comes and rescues us," Vorst said without taking her eyes from Gravlox.

Master Brenning breathed a sigh of relief for the first time in many days. "I'm very interested in meeting this friend of yours," he muttered, but knew the goblins weren't listening.

Within a few short minutes, a thunderous sound shook the sewer and knocked moss from the walls. The shimmering magical light wavered in the air and more water started to drip down from above. A second report followed the first and a large stone fell to the ground beside Vorst. More and more hits rocked the chamber until a large shaft of natural light suddenly appeared. The three shielded their eyes against the brilliant sunlight as one more strike turned the top of the sewer system into rubble.

A massive tree was lowered into the sewer, temporarily blocking the harsh sunlight. Gravlox and Vorst, knowing the trick well, grabbed onto the tree limbs and held on tightly. Master Brenning, not knowing what to expect, shook his head and wrapped his arms around the tree next to Vorst. One great heave had all three of them sprawled out in the sunlight behind the Castle of Reikall.

Master Brenning recognized Nevidal before he made the connection between the massive man and the apprentice he had once trained. The two men didn't say much but rather nodded their appreciation to one another in a solemn moment of silence. The old smith stroked his beard as he walked around Gideon's tree-like legs and inspected the tight cords of muscle breaking out all over his body. There was no question that the paladin was nearly consumed by his sword's enchantment. Gravlox's healing magic had staved off the demonic poison well enough to stabilize the mixture of magic working within the paladin but the enchantment could not be stopped. Without the remnants of the poison slowing Nevidal's consumption, Gideon would surely be dead.

"There isn't much time," Master Brenning said while Vorst acted as a translator for Gravlox. "We need to return to Talonrend before it suffers the same fate as this once-fair city." The four companions stood behind a castle they had previously thought beautiful. From a distance, they couldn't see the charred streaks of ash around the shattered windows and the dried patches of splattered blood that dotted the stones. Reikall had undergone great terror and had not survived.

"You need food," Vorst replied. They had none with them and the city was so consumed by blight that anything they might salvage from the ruins was sure to be rotten.

"I can get food along the way, but we have to move, now," Gideon said definitively. Gravlox, Vorst, and Master Brenning climbed atop the giant's shoulders and hooked themselves into the leather straps of his armor. The metal sleeve, tucked away in Vorst's pack, had remained unchanged by Nevidal's magic, but the rest of Gideon's armament had grown with him. The paladin's braided black beard was well over the average height of a normal human and swayed calmly back and forth with every step like a great pendulum.

Speed and endurance were two things of which Gideon's enchanted body had a great deal. He bounded into the forest, leaping streams and fallen trees as though they were puddles and broken sticks. It didn't take the paladin long to spot a deer and deftly cleave it in half with his sword. A flare of holy radiance from Nevidal cooked the meat of the animal almost instantly. Able to make fantastic speed, the group could see Terror's Lament shining high against the sun before nightfall.

"The goblins will come from the east, from the river," Vorst said, pointing at the imposing shadow of Kanebullar Mountain far in the distance.

"We should return to the city at once and warn them of the incoming horde of undead!" Master Brenning shouted. He beat his fists into Gideon's back but the huge man remained silent.

"Your people will kill both of us." Vorst knew it was true. She would never be accepted into Talon-rend, even to help fight a war. She pulled Gravlox down from the harness and led him by the hand in the direction of the river. "If we can just tell them that there is more to life than war and conquest..."

Gravlox stopped and brought Vorst tight against his side. "Are you alright?" he asked in the high-pitched goblin language. The concern in his voice did little to mask his fear.

"I can feel her again. In the dead city, it was like I was free. I felt like you. We are closer to her again. Lady Scrapple knows I am here. I sense her presence like a painful splinter in my back that I cannot reach. I know she is there and can see me. I'm scared, Gravlox." Vorst buried her head in his chest and fought back tears.

The two humans didn't know what to make of Vorst's sudden and emotional outburst. Until very recently, Gideon and Master Brenning had never imagined that the short, pale-skinned creatures were capable of any emotions at all, much less love and fear.

"If we don't return to the city at once, we will be branded as traitors and exiled!" Master Brenning's bearded cheeks flushed a deep red as he yelled. Few people who had known the revered smith had ever seen him so torn. Before anyone else could speak, Brenning started trudging through the open plain toward Talonrend.

"Do we just leave them here, then?" Gideon called after his former teacher. "These two goblins saved both of our lives. We have a debt to them." With one massive stride, Gideon was able to put a hand firmly on Brenning's back and turn him around. "We cannot leave them until we know that they are safe."

"The goblin army is camped out there by the river," Vorst said, pointing east. "If we return, they kill us, both of us." She stood hand in hand with Gravlox, looking Master Brenning in the eyes.

The smith ruffled a hand through his beard. "We have to prove your worth, then, to the folk of Talonrend. If you were spies," Brenning spit as though the very taste of the word disgusted him, "you wouldn't have dragged me out of that hole. I owe you that much."

"We should make ourselves useful then," Gideon said. "Master Brenning, go back to the city and tell them I rescued you. Don't mention the goblins, but we need to warn them of the reanimated corpses approaching the city." The paladin smiled and the sword in his hands flared to life. "I will stay with these two brave warriors and see if we can't go and stop this invasion before I die."

"Yes, there is also the matter of that sword…" Master Brenning thought back on how many years it had taken him to craft it. The project had nearly bankrupted his forge, but it was his life's work, whether Gideon knew it or not. "You do recall how to stop that enchantment, right?"

The humor of Brenning's jest was lost upon the giant paladin. "I have to kill someone. The abominations in the caves didn't have souls."

"And as far as I know, no offense to you two, goblins do not have souls either. At least, goblins do not have any souls that would please Nevidal." Master Brenning thought to his long hours of study in the library at the Artificer's Guild that had led up to the forging of Nevidal. He had lived in that library for what felt like a lifetime.

"You may want to try a graveyard," he said wistfully, entranced by the soft magical glow of the weapon. "Souls are said to linger there. All sorts of aspiring magic users and artificers visit graveyards at night to see if they can't capture the wandering souls and harness their energy. Most of the time, the dark energies of a captured soul will turn against the wizard and either kill him or corrupt him. Poor fellows..." The smith, despite loathing the amount of time he had spent away from his beloved forge, had truly enjoyed his time of study in the library and remembered almost everything he had read.

"If I find any souls wandering a graveyard, I will be sure to tell you." Gideon managed a half smile as he hefted the wicked blade in his strong grip.

Brenning's unruly beard jostled as he laughed. "If I remember correctly, a few of the famous necromancers throughout magical history have recorded finding flowers that bloom atop gravestones in the dead of night. The ghost flowers, as they are called, are rumored to be born out of the combined souls of everyone buried at the site. Pluck me one, will you?" Master Brenning turned to make his way back to Talonrend before Vorst furiously burst into action.

"What's wrong?" Gravlox asked with a fearful voice.

Vorst ripped through her pack and withdrew the lantern she had stolen from the necromancer the two had killed. Lifting the lantern above her body like a warrior who had just decapitated a dragon, Vorst was too excited to even speak. Gideon and Brenning stared at her in wonder, looking all around and worried that the small goblin's actions might be a prelude to danger.

"This… This, metal torch," goblins didn't use lanterns or oil lamps so Vorst had no idea what the word might be in the human language, "This has soul. Take soul!" she said, jumping up and down.

"What are you talking about?" Master Brenning said, his tone suddenly serious. "That beat up lantern has a soul locked inside?"

Mimicking the motions of the necromancer at the graveyard, Vorst tried her best to explain that the man had captured ghost flowers within the object before she had stolen it. "We try and find necromancer dust for poison, got metal torch full of glowing flowers from graveyard!"

Stunned into silence, the humans stood slack-jawed and stared at the elated goblin female until she finally threw it at Master Brenning and yelled. He caught the lantern and peered through the glass, seeing the swirling mist of captured souls up close for the first time.

"Not yet," Gideon said as he took the lantern from Master Brenning. It was awkward to hold the item with the handle of Nevidal still firmly attached to his palm. "The enchantment will end, yes, but if I am going into a war against soulless goblins, I will need my sword." He patted the throwing axes dangling from his side. The deadly projectiles looked like tiny playthings against the giant's tree-like legs. "I will keep this with me and use it when the time comes. The enchantment won't kill me just yet."

"So you think," Brenning scoffed. The burly smith shook his head, unsure of how much time Gideon had left before the holy magic consumed him. Using the rope from Vorst's pack, Gideon tied the lantern around his neck.

"Go now, warn the city, and get them ready for our two goblin guests." The giant shrugged to adjust the rope that felt like an unwanted collar of oppression. Knowing that a captured soul was lingering inside the magical metal lantern made the paladin uneasy.

Without another word, Gideon, Gravlox, and Vorst watched as the man they rescued from Reikall disappeared into the horizon toward the towering stone walls. The paladin felt a renewed vigor for battle with the lantern swinging awkwardly around his huge neck. Using his massive fingers and making sure not to let Nevidal accidentally touch anyone, Gideon hoisted the two goblins onto his back and began striding toward the Clawflow.

Yael and Keegar saw the fast approaching giant and fled back to their own lines. The hand-and-a-half sword pulsed and thrummed with every powerful step the man took, sending fear into every goblin who managed to see him. "We will need more than a cavalry defense for that behemoth," Yael whispered to himself. Images of a sprawling goblin army flitted through his head, mental communications from Lady Scrapple. "Yes, it is time," he said with more confidence. "We must strike now. If every human is as large as that one, we are doomed." Keegar's thickly muscled legs propelled him much faster ahead of Yael, who struggled to keep the scout in his sight. A foreign emotion, something between nausea and curiosity, crept up from the depths of Yael's mind and made him stop. He knew that Lady Scrapple was inside his mind and he keenly felt her presence like a tangible object resting in the back of his skull. She was suggesting that Yael go and meet the main bulk of her forces. It wasn't a command. Lady Scrapple was *asking* Yael for obedience. The pale-skinned goblin readily complied and turned his course for the river.

The sheer number of goblins arrayed on the eastern bank of the Clawflow River took Yael's breath away. The army stretched for miles to either side and seemed to extend all the way back to Kanebullar Mountain. Spear tips and arrowheads glinted in the waning sunlight as the rigid drones swayed slowly in the breeze. "Oh, Mistress..." Yael couldn't believe what he was seeing. "This is why you can't control us all... There are so many..." Lady Scrapple sent telepathic emotions of peace and silence to the commander as he surveyed the army.

This is what you were bred for, Yael. The voice was strangely soothing, coming from the back of Yael's consciousness. It felt almost like a thought, except that it wasn't in Yael's own voice. *They will listen to you, Yael. You are their commander. Start the invasion. I will move when the time is right and destroy the human walls.* Yael sucked in a deep breath and tried to steady himself. *There will be more soldiers, always more soldiers. Do not concern yourself with their safety. Victory is the only path now, Yael. Make the mountain proud.*

Lady Scrapple's departure was even more shocking than her speech. In an instant, faster than he could respond or even think, the Mistress of the Mountain was gone. It was then that Yael realized she had always been there. Her sudden disappearance left a gaping void in the outer reaches of Yael's mind. It was a chasm he did not know how to fill.

"Are there any left in the mountain?" he finally managed to say after he regained his composure. None of the goblins responded. "They are mindless, totally vacant," Yael reminded himself.

"Soldiers of Kanebullar Mountain!" Yael shouted. At once, the thousands of empty goblin eyes locked onto their commander. He stood on the bank opposite the army and looked slowly from one flank to the other as he spoke. "We take the human city this night!" Yael would have continued, but he realized that inspiration was meaningless to soldiers lacking the capacity to understand it. "To me," he commanded and the response was overwhelming. Goblins splashed through the river without hesitation. The once clear current of the Clawflow turned into a muddy morass of goblin soldiers as wave after wave of the drones swam across. They assembled themselves into the blocks as quickly as they could and Yael was forced all the way back to an abandoned farm house in order to make room for the army.

Catapults, trebuchets, and all manner of siege equipment floated across the river alongside the endless army. Platoons of goblins all wearing leather vests stained with red hauled massive baskets and long lengths of animal hide that Yael had never seen before. He couldn't begin to imagine what their purpose was so the commander shrugged and continued to watch the assembly. Finally, after the goblin horde had filled in the entire area of farmland between the rickety house and the river, Yael had to order a charge. There was simply nowhere else for the drones to continue their muster.

A wicked and toothy smile broke out on the commander's pale face.

Twenty

"**G**OBLINS FROM THE north!" The shout rang out from the parapet and all eyes turned to see a thin line of dark creatures running toward the city. "Push north! Defend the walls!" Herod called back with fervor. The horsemen and foot soldiers inched toward the northern walls, eager to spill goblin blood. There had been a lull in the action in the quiet hours since the alaris had galloped out, never to return. Master Brenning sat tall in his saddle next to the prince. His horse was barded in silver and gold armor that glowed in the soft light of the dying day. The burly smith wore plates of steel that he had crafted himself. They fit tightly over his chest and served as a painful reminder of how young and thin he had been when he made the armor.

"It's just a feint," Master Brenning scoffed. He watched the soldiers moving away from the eastern gate and shook his head. "These goblins are much smarter than you think, my liege."

Herod turned his warhorse to face his most trusted advisor. "You presume to know much about our enemies, Master Brenning."

"I told you already, Gideon was working with two goblins. They saved me. The goblins were rogues who had left the army. You cannot afford to underestimate their cunning!" Brenning had told the prince a hundred times. No matter how much he told everyone, not a single person believed his story.

"For the last time, Brenning, I will believe you when I meet these goblins myself! Why is it so hard for you to understand that these goblins we fight today are just as stupid as they look and act? We have scouted out their location, we know they will come from the north. Our walls are well defended from every single approach. We can hold off a million of the stinking creatures if we have to. Why should we not push out to meet their attack and crush them under our feet?" Herod's horse whinnied and stamped the ground as a crudely-made goblin arrow struck near the animal's feet.

"What did I tell you?" Brenning screamed. He moved his powerful horse closer to the wall and looked up to the archers. "How many?" he called up to the lookouts.

"None, sir, I can't see a single goblin!" The lookout was leaning far over the wall and squinting against the darkness of dusk.

Herod ordered the soldiers to crowd back against the gatehouse and called for the portcullis to be raised. "Where did that arrow come from?" he barked. None of the men could see anything other than darkness on the horizon.

"The better question would be to ask why no others have followed it. The goblins test their range." Brenning didn't mean for the prince to hear his remark but he had said it louder than he thought.

"Clever bastards..." Herod muttered. "One volley, flaming arrows, light up the sky!" he shouted to the wall. Within seconds the archers sent brilliant streaks of fire soaring out over the soldiers to litter the battlefield.

"Get the men back into the city. We need to move behind the walls to hold our advantage as long as possible." Master Brenning had his horse turned in an instant and galloped for the gate. The portcullis was slowly creaking upwards on its metal chains and offered just enough room for the soldiers to start pouring through on hands and knees.

Remembering the river of undead men and women walking the dark tunnels from Reikall to Talonrend, Brenning realized the goblin plan. "They want us to cower behind our walls..." he said to himself. "We have no place left to run and nowhere to turn for help."

What the men had mistaken for empty darkness in the fields beyond the walls was actually an unimaginable sea of living creatures. The goblins were packed together so tightly that their dark leather armor had created the illusion of empty space. At the sight of the blazing flares, the goblin army charged.

High-pitched wails and screams filled the night air for miles around the city. Herod commanded two of his best runners to order the retreat of his army from the north but, in the panic, it was impossible to know which orders had effect and which died before they reached their destinations. The alaris trying to push through the gatehouse was causing so much commotion that Herod ordered the unit of horsemen to sacrifice themselves in order to slow the goblins. Untrained militia soldiers stationed behind the walls only added to the quagmire of men attempting to run to safety. Herod was still outside the gate when the first line of goblins fell upon the retreat.

"Brenning! I need you!" the prince called. The smith realized that in the tight quarters between the walls his horse was too frightened to be of any use. He dismounted the unruly beast and pushed his way out from the horde of soldiers back to Herod's side. "Close the gate!" Herod yelled, even though only half of the soldiers had made their way back to safety. With a resounding crash, the heavy steel portcullis thundered into the dirt and sealed the city.

"Rally around the prince!" Brenning waved his sword above his head to organize the remaining troops. The first line of the human defenses held well despite the confusion and panic behind them. Goblin corpses started to pile up around the gatehouse and each human that fell took at least 10 of the noisy creatures with them. The press of enemies was relentless. Pale-skinned goblins came in at every angle and with all manner of weapons.

The archers overhead rained death upon the field, firing as fast as they could into the goblin tide. Dozens of goblins died with every volley but their numbers were simply too great for it to matter. Arrows, hammers, javelins, and even rocks answered the human volley with devastating effect. The goblins were completely unorganized in their attacks but fought with such numbers that they quickly broke through the initial human defense.

Brenning leapt into the fight with reckless abandon. He wore a shield strapped onto his back and picked up a well-balanced mace to wield in his left hand. The burly man spun his way through the goblin ranks and used his short sword and mace combination to blast any foe unlucky enough to get in his path. The shield on his back rang out with hit after hit and many goblins got close enough to ding his chest plate just before they died.

YAEL'S EYES GREW wide with amazement as he watched the onslaught. He had only intended to let a few thousand goblins die in the first real attack but the beauty of the carnage mesmerized him. The commander was drunk with power. He had never felt so alive in his life. When he gave an order, the telepathic relays of Lady Scrapple's consciousness delivered the order instantaneously to the corresponding drones. Scrapple's mental connections spread throughout the entire army, a sensation that felt awkwardly comforting to Yael. The goblin matriarch was helping Yael, but not directly controlling him or watching his thoughts.

The goblin troops in red had cleared out a large area of the field and used it to light fires under their makeshift balloons. In groups of four the goblins piled into their wicker baskets and floated up into the air. Long ropes were passed along the ground through the goblin army and pulled the hot air balloons towards the towering walls. Yael couldn't help but smile as he saw nearly a hundred such balloons dotting the battlefield.

RAGE AND ADRENALINE coursed through Brenning's blood, turning him into a senseless killing machine. Countless spear heads and arrow tips ricocheted off his polished armor every minute, but still the man fought on. His sword and his looted mace were so slick with goblin blood that they nearly flew from his hands as he executed a vicious two-handed swing that blasted a tiny goblin to pieces. All around the courageous smith, the humans at the gate rallied. Cheers floated through the air to mingle with the deadly missiles flying to and from the wall.

Covered in blood and missing a hand, one of Herod's runners collapsed at the prince's feet with a message. "Goblins...in the north..." the man gasped.

"Yes, I know there are goblins in the north! What is it?" The soldiers outside the gate had formed a semi-circle around their commander with their backs to the wall and no goblin had yet tried to attack the regal man atop his warhorse.

"Sir, the goblins in the north... they have been turned back! Our cavalry overran them, they are fleeing!" the winded runner used the shield of the nearest soldier for support as he delivered his message.

"Good!" the prince bellowed. "Stay back behind the shield wall and try not to get in the way."

"Yes sir," the man nodded before falling to the ground. The battle raged on all around the sheltered prince and his remaining soldiers.

Herod looked to his last remaining runner. The man was young, maybe 20 years old, and wore a scrappy beard on his chin. His arms were scrawny and lanky, but the soldier's legs were huge with muscle. "Get to the officers in the north," the prince bade the runner. "Have them move every alaris in sight to our aid. Tell them to leave the archers and the militia where they are, but every other man is to relieve our position immediately! Return to me as soon as you have delivered the message. Go!" Herod watched the young runner depart through the shield wall toward the north.

"My liege, on the horizon!" Herod's gut churned as he imagined a mighty dragon swooping down from the clouds to lay waste to his precious city. He turned his head in the direction of the soldier's pointing arm but saw no dragon.

"What are they?" the prince asked but the men around him could only shrug. "Illuminating volley!" he called to the archers on the wall who fired a line of flaming arrows into the sky a moment later.

"Flying machines, sir!" one of the soldiers guarding the prince shouted. "They are coming toward us, higher than the walls!"

A fresh wave of panic filled the air. Herod stood with his back against Terror's Lament and contemplated death. The balloon brigades made slow and steady progress toward Talonrend. An occasional arrow would fly from the basket of a nearing balloon but no real attack was ever mounted until the first line of balloons neared the wall.

An alaris came thundering down upon the goblin flank from the north just in time to kill the few drones that had been holding the guide ropes to the flying machines. The balloons continued to drift lazily toward the high city walls as the alaris reached the main bulk of soldiers still fighting in front of the gate.

A surge of morale propelled the soldiers at the front line into a killing frenzy. Horses shattered goblin skulls like a child stepping on insects. The relatively tiny creatures were no match for armored hooves and swinging flails that rained down upon them from impossibly high angles. Human warriors charged into the wake of the cavalry, eager to kill any survivors. After two devastating passes of the alaris, not enough of the riders were left alive to press their advantage again.

For a brief moment, the tide of goblins seemed to slow. The humans reformed their barricade around the prince and more soldiers came from the northern flank to support them. Then, with precision that only comes from a hive mind entity, the goblins began their siege.

Drone warriors fell back to get out of the way of the plethora of flying projectiles that bombarded the human position. Catapults and trebuchets sent huge boulders slamming into the thick stone walls of Talonrend at an alarming rate. Goblin archers unleashed a hailstorm of arrows accompanied by a shower of smaller rocks from soldiers wielding slings.

Ingenious goblin miners and alchemists ensured that every payload of rock that slammed into the human knights and walls was laced with high levels of rich magnesium. The jagged shards of metal coated the battlefield in what the goblins frequently called "flare stone".

Goblins in red leather vests stood up on the edges of their floating baskets and leapt toward the gatehouse. Their outfits were coated in a volatile magical substance used in the mines of Kanebullar Mountain to blast through tough deposits of ore. On impact with the ground, the magically imbued oil turned the unfortunate bombardier into a highly explosive mess of goblin gore. Fires from the exploding oil quickly spread to the chunks of magnesium littering the battlefield and turned the ground into a blazing inferno.

Steel-clad human knights were cooked alive in their armor and fell to the ground without a chance.

"Open the damned portcullis!" Herod screamed. The prince scrambled out of his saddle as his horse's mane caught fire. A sliver of shrapnel from one of the trebuchet blasts had punctured his fine armor and subsequently ignited. Herod clawed at the burning piece of metal but, with his bulky gloves, he couldn't get the stubborn debris loose. He could feel the flesh over his ribs on his left side start to bubble and ooze as the fire took hold. Thinking to smother the ember, Herod clamped his gauntlet over the puncture, but the magically induced burn would not be extinguished so easily.

Reeling from the agony and screaming at the top of his lungs, Herod pushed his way toward the opening portcullis. The heavy metal bars of the gate were slow to rise amidst the tumult of war. Soldiers scrambled all around the wounded prince to make it to the safety of the walls as the fires burned. Men fell flat on their chests to shimmy their way through to the other side where more soldiers waited to try to beat the fires from their armor and skin.

A thoroughly blood-soaked hand ripped the prince from the burning ground and forcefully shoved him through the opening in the gate where a host of healthy warriors immediately attended to his many wounds. Master Brenning grinned at the prince and turned back to direct the flow of wounded soldiers through the gate. His sword and mace were long gone and the shield strapped to his back had taken so many hits that it was reduced to splintered bits of kindling and leather.

Handfuls of mindless goblin drones rushed through the portcullis on the heels of the retreating men but were cut down almost immediately by the awaiting militia. Firebombs and boulders continued to hammer the walls and great chunks of stone began to fall from the parapets. The outer wall of Terror's Lament was crumbling.

More payloads of rock and magnesium flew over the walls and through the gaps in the portcullis bars, causing more panic and spreading flames among the militia and wounded. Through the smoke of chaos, Brenning spotted a group of five goblins rushing the gatehouse in unison. Each goblin wore a backpack filled with volatile ore attached to a red leather vest. The seasoned blacksmith beat his fists against his armored chest and grabbed the nearest healthy soldier by the wrist. "What's your name, son?" he shouted into the knight's face.

"Nef," the panicked soldier replied. "My friends call me Nef." Master Brenning shook the knight violently by the arm in an effort to knock the confusion from his mind.

"Build a pair of statues for us, Herod! Nef and Brenning are about to save Talonrend!" The smith smiled wildly as he shoved Nef through the portcullis and back into the licking flames. Master Brenning stood beside the young knight and patted him on the back. Nef drew his weapon, a curved scimitar that looked more like a mantle ornament than a tool designed to take life.

"For Talonrend and King Lucius!" Brenning cried as the two poorly-armed warriors rushed through the smoke and fire toward the red vested goblins that dripped with volatile oil.

The massive portcullis slammed shut just before the explosion.

Twenty-One

"**W**HAT DO WE do?" Vorst whispered into the night. The two goblins crouched down behind the tall grasses of the plain as the massive army of their kin marched to the city walls. Gideon knelt beside them and Nevidal glowed faintly in his hand.

"We need to attack, to keep the humans from being overrun." Gideon's deep voice rustled the amber stalks like a ghost. Fires burned around the base of Terror's Lament and threatened to spread throughout the plains.

"If we attack now, we die. We must wait. There are too many goblins for us to be effective." Vorst tapped everything she said into the palm of Gravlox's hand, translating the conversation as she went.

"As long as the walls don't come down, the humans can survive." The shaking tone of her voice betrayed her fear.

Gravlox gently kissed the back of Vorst's hand. "If we can find Yael, we might be able to stop the invasion before they break through the walls. It might work."

After Vorst translated the message into the human language, the three agreed on their plan. They would find the goblin field commander, kill him, and hope that the war would end. If the death of Yael didn't end the carnage, the three agreed that only Lady Scrapple's demise would bring peace.

As the blindingly bright fires continued to burn, there came a lull in the combat. The goblin balloons continued their aerial assault over Terror's Lament but the bulk of the goblin forces held back. A broken stretch of thirty yards separated the battered stone walls from the sea of pale-faced creatures swarming about as far as the eye could see.

Catapults and trebuchets continued to deliver their devastating cargo into the walls with great, thunderous reports. Thick plumes of smoke choked the air for miles around and the heat at the top of the walls was nearly unbearable. Archers covered their mouths with anything they could find and fired arrow after arrow into the tough leather of the hovering balloons. Many of the flying machines went down, but not before spreading more fire and devastation throughout the human ranks.

"We can't wait for their next move," Gideon growled, and the three companions took off toward the back of the goblin lines. The paladin's great braided beard swung furiously from side to side as the giant ran. His throwing axes, unaffected by Nevidal's divine enchantment, looked like tiny toys attached to a belt so thick it could have served as rigging for a ship.

Imbued with godlike strength and speed, the two goblins watched from a distance as their hulking giant friend crashed into the back of Lady Scrapple's army. With one foot planted firmly in the Clawflow River, Gideon swatted goblins away as if they were nothing but tiny flies buzzing about his meal.

Swords and spears alike were shattered into rubble with every pass of Nevidal, the wickedly sharp sword the size of a tree. Holy fire flew off the blade in great balls as big as boulders. The giant paladin fought with fury. He swung the mighty sword with his remaining arm as quickly as he could. A song in praise of Vrysinoch found his lips and escaped, the tune bringing a strange sense of peace to the wanton death all around him.

Not being able to run nearly as fast as the giant, Gravlox and Vorst could only watch as hundreds of their kin were lifted through the air or rent to pieces by the brutal sword. Gideon's boots snuffed the life from dozens of goblins at a time. The paladin's inexorable march was accented by the piercing screams of dying goblins and the sizzling of blood off the flames of his sword. From the wall, the surviving humans could see the great arcs of fire dancing through the smoke of the battle but had no way of discerning the man's giant form.

The two rogue goblins stopped not far from the destructive giant and scanned the army for any sign of Yael. "Look," Gravlox pointed to the lone farmhouse standing amidst the sea of their kin. With vision perfected in the lightless mines of Kanebullar Mountain, Gravlox could easily discern the form of a lone goblin standing atop the human structure. "That must be him," the shaman said with determination.

Without a moment of hesitation, the two sprinted through the mess of goblins. The mindless drones didn't even possess enough autonomy to get out of the way as Gravlox stormed through them. Lacking enough will to think for themselves, the horde of warriors let the unrecognized goblins pass without incident.

Before long, Gravlox and Vorst stood below the battered farmhouse and locked eyes with Yael. "You may be a powerful shaman," the goblin commander called out to the pair from his perch, "but I am the Mountain!" He spread his arms out wide and surveyed the sea of his minions. "This is my destiny!" he shouted with spit flying from his mouth. "Everything you see is under my command. I am Lady Scrapple's chosen! Her commander!" The goblin drones surrounding the two at the base of the building all turned at once and leveled their weapons.

"They listen to *me*, now!" Yael howled into the night. The nearest soldiers charged in at Gravlox and Vorst with flawless unison. The shaman gripped his short sword tightly in both hands and Vorst wasted no time putting her deadly bow to work. Four goblins struggled for life and clawed at the arrow shafts buried in their flesh by the time the first drone engaged Gravlox's sword.

The shaman met the charging spearhead with a sidelong swipe of his sword that pushed the thrust wide to his left. The stone and mortar of the farmhouse at his back reminded him of his days beneath the mountain. The mines were full of such rough textures and Gravlox had grown to love them. With a slash aimed for Gravlox's neck, the spearhead came whirring back in and again the shaman beat the attack with a well-timed parry.

A second goblin stood next to the spear-wielding drone and brandished a mean looking jagged mace. The warrior executed a powerful overhand chop with the crude weapon that forced Gravlox to roll to his side and into the thrusting metal of the spear. The shaman caught the longer weapon's shaft with his sword hilt just before the pointed tip would have opened his chest. He turned the spear aside with a rotation of his wrist and continued the motion into a downward swing that pinned the spear against the ground. The second goblin drone bore down on Gravlox with his mace but the shaman was quicker and able to sidestep the blow. In the same motion, Gravlox's pale foot snapped through the weapon's wooden shaft and buried the deadly point in the dirt.

Mimicking Gideon's style of combat, Gravlox threw his sword the short distance into the chest of the second goblin drone. The pale creature dropped his mace to the ground and fell down dead. The shaman scrambled to the fallen mace and snatched it from the ground as the first goblin, now clutching a large rock in his hands, leapt at Gravlox and attempted to overpower him. The spiked mace ripped through the pale creature's innards and halted his body mid-flight. Gravlox pounded his attacker's corpse a second time with the vicious weapon, caving in his skull with ease.

Vorst held back the tide with her bow well enough, but her quiver was nearly depleted. A bloody ring of dead goblins surrounded the two lovers like an ancient rune of death etched into the dirt. Yael made the soldiers hesitate a moment to regroup and then unleashed them in a full wave meant to overrun the two rogues.

The shaman felt his pale skin pressed against the cool stone of the farmhouse and willed his consciousness into the bricks. He could sense an energy in the building; not a source of magic, but a sensation of readiness, like the elements of the stones and mortar waiting to be used. As a mine foreman, Gravlox had witnessed gifted miners using shamanistic magic to blast through rock and extract difficult ore with ease. Closing his eyes and remembering scenes from his previous life, Gravlox willed the stone wall of the farmhouse to life.

The grey stones of the inanimate building absorbed the energy as fast as Gravlox could deliver it. As the second screaming wave of goblin drones cleared the bloody ground to the shaman and reared their weapons back for the kill, the stone wall exploded. The conical blast was directed against the oncoming creatures and, miraculously, the two rogues were spared. Chips of stone flew through the goblins ranks like daggers and large chunks of hard mortar shattered their bones.

The farmhouse trembled and rocked from the force of the explosion, lingering only a moment before the entire building collapsed to the ground. Yael roared as he went down in the heap of rubble and dust.

Gravlox, Vorst, and the enemy commander removed themselves from the debris of the farmhouse in seconds, ready to fight. Yael held a sword similar to the one in Gravlox's hand. Vorst loosed her last arrow at the commander but the shot ricocheted off a fallen section of the farmhouse's roof and went wide of its mark by inches. She dropped her bow to the ground and pulled a small dagger from her belt with a snarl.

Yael tossed his blade from hand to hand as the three goblins circled in the debris. Drone soldiers all around the fallen farmhouse made a wall of spears and other weapons that prevented any of the combatants from fleeing. Gravlox positioned himself with his back to the city; he could see the dark outline of the giant paladin wading through scores of goblins off in the distance. His great fiery sword sent marvelous gouts of light sailing over the battle-field, briefly illuminating random parts of the plain.

The goblin army looked limitless.

Vorst kept herself well to the side of the sham-an but close enough that she could leap to him if the need arose.

"Look around you, Gravlox," Yael said with a sneer. "The mountain has come to fight. You cannot stop us all. Even if you kill ten thousand of us, you will die." The commander glanced over his shoulder at the destruction wrought by Gideon and his divine enchantment. His estimation of the goblin casualties seemed accurate. "Unless you have a hundred more giants with you, this city will fall. You cannot stop that."

Gravlox continued to circle in the rubble. Bro-ken wooden beams and crumbled stone made his footing unstable. "Have you ever dreamed of great-er things than being a slave?" he called out. He spoke loudly enough for the nearby drones to hear him but, if they comprehended anything he was saying, they didn't show it. "There is more to life than slavery! We can be free, *all* of us. Don't you feel it, Yael?"

The commander stopped circling for just a moment, mulling over Gravlox's statements in light of his own recent revelations. He could feel the consciousness of Lady Scrapple in the back of his mind, stirring and growing restless. Lady Scrapple took interest in the situation, but did not take control. Whether the Mistress of the Mountain chose not to overcome Yael's consciousness or her lack of dominance was merely a result of her waning power, Yael could not tell. There was an awkward level of disconnect between the pathways of his own mind and the intricate relays of the collective. Images of fire and brimstone flashed through his mind from matriarch. He saw telepathic images of Terror's Lament surrounded by fire and cheering goblins as it tumbled down.

"Yael," he heard, but the voice was somewhere in the distance, too far away for him to recognize. A thousand different scenes flashed through the commander's mind in an instant. He saw himself sitting atop a throne made from the piled bodies of dead humans. Yael saw an entire world devoid of human life where the goblin race was free to walk amongst the trees and spread throughout the entire land. The final image imparted to him was of his own short sword piercing Gravlox's heart. Yael enjoyed what he saw.

"I have more power than you could ever imagine, traitor," Yael said. He inched forward through the cluttered rubble and ordered the drones to begin closing the circle with their spear tips out in front of them. "You, Gravlox, are the enemy. You have chosen to ally with the filthy human scum, and for what?"

"For love," Vorst whispered, but no one could hear her soft plea.

"If you are so bent on helping these pathetic surface dwellers," Yael continued, "then you will die like one." The goblin commander planted a foot on a large black kettle that had been overturned in the tumult. He launched himself through the air, howling like a banshee, with his sword aimed right for the shaman's chest.

Gravlox had plenty of time to anticipate the jump and waited until the last possible second. He sidestepped the leap and tried to use his own sword to disarm the flying goblin but missed. Yael retracted his arm before he hit the ground and Gravlox's sword cut through nothing but air. Vorst slashed at the commander from his side with her dagger aimed low and was met by a deft parry that turned her blade well before its mark.

Gravlox wasted no time and attacked with his own weapon, executing a slicing chop that Yael easily ducked. The commander brought his sword up and in to his chest as he spun, deflecting another strike from Vorst's dagger before extending his arm and snapping his wrist. Gravlox had to stumble backward to avoid losing his nose. The movement was too fast for the untrained foreman to follow.

After being well trained by the Ministry of Assassinations, Vorst was well versed in combat, although she was used to killing targets that were completely unaware of her presence. With Yael spinning his body between her and Gravlox, she couldn't find an opening to go for a kill. She had to settle for smaller nicks and cuts scored on the commander's back.

Yael was pressing Gravlox with a furious attack combination. He used the tip of his sword to force Gravlox to parry again and again, each time striking just a little closer to the shaman's shoulder. After four such attacks, Gravlox blocked the swing with his hilt and Yael turned the blade sideways as he punched with his sword hand. Blood splattered from Gravlox's mouth and nose.

The commander turned just in time to use his free hand to clamp down on Vorst's wrist and turn her attack aside. Gravlox tripped over backward on the broken remnants of a table and his sword flew from his hand.

Yael seized the opportunity and slashed out with his blade against Vorst. Still locked tightly in his grip, she was forced to turn her body sideways to avoid being skewered. Vorst kicked out with her leg and slammed her foot into Yael's knee. The commander buckled but did not let go. He slashed again with his sword and drew a thin line of blood down Vorst's side. The female goblin yelped and clenched her teeth against the pain.

The ground was too uneven for Gravlox to quickly get to his feet, so he snatched Vorst's bow from the ground and pulled himself to Yael's feet. Using the bow as club, Gravlox swung the weapon hard into the back of the commander's legs. He attacked furiously, hitting him again and again until Yael finally fell to the rubble. Vorst was quick to bear down on the fallen foe with her dagger leading the way.

The tip of her blade bit into the soft, pale flesh of Yael's gut and a spurt of blood wet her hands. Yael had both of his arms in front of him, holding the blade back and using all of his strength to keep it from sinking in to the hilt.

Gravlox was on his feet. He found his sword in the wreckage and scampered back to where Yael slowly bled. His sword glimmered in the dancing firelight of the war as he lifted it above his head for the killing blow. Vorst rolled to her side, withdrawing her dagger and covering her face. Yael used one hand to clutch his wound and his other offered a meager defense that both of them knew was useless. Gravlox's sword whistled through the air with deadly precision.

With the blade just inches from the commander's face, a powerful, sinewy wing sent Gravlox flying over the ruined farmhouse. He landed painfully on a collection of fallen stones that cut into his back, but managed to keep hold of his sword. Taurnil bellowed a deep, throaty laugh that sent shivers down Gravlox's spine.

"I've already seen you die once, beast," Gravlox muttered through the pain. "How many lives do you have?" Swirling tendrils of acrid smoke wafted up from the ground and mingled with the smoke already choking the night sky. With the flickering light of Nevidal's holy magic at his back, Taurnil was truly frightening. Yael managed to sit up against a piece of rubble and clutch his side to stem the bleeding.

"Gideon!" Vorst called out but she knew the paladin was too far away to hear her. Gravlox used his innate shamanistic connection to the vast realms of magic to navigate the swirl of goblins and find Gideon on the battlefield. Like before, his magical essence raged like a towering inferno of hatred and violence. Gideon felt the magical plea for help in his soul and the fires of his hatred licked the heavens.

Twenty-Two

INSIDE THE HIGH walls of Talonrend, the city was quiet. Herod had ordered the militia and all the remaining soldiers inside the city during the respite. The prince's eyes darted nervously from building to building, expecting *something*, but he wasn't sure what. There was tension in the air hanging like a thick curtain. Soldiers stood nervously in the streets and paced back and forth. The occasional boulder smashed into the walls and shook the ground under their feet.

Archers maintained their posts on the tops of Terror's Lament but it had been hours since any goblin soldiers had come within bow range. Herod looked up at the Tower of Wings with a frown. The doors at the base of the tower were locked and the building was eerily silent. The soft glow of fire outside the city illuminated the highest reaches of the magnificent tower, making the wings dance and flicker. Another siege engine made the ground shake. Herod wondered how long the triple-layered walls would hold.

The prince gripped the soft leather handles of his swords as he paced back and forth in one of the city's marketplaces. Empty vendor stalls loomed high above him like sinister giants waiting to come to life. Even late into the night, there should always be merchants trying to turn a profit. The whorehouses that lined the busiest streets in the city had extinguished their lamps and boarded up their windows. The whole of Talonrend was prepared for war. Herod knew that if Terror's Lament fell, every single person inside the city would surely die. The roiling tide of goblins waiting just beyond his doorstep was overwhelming.

"What do we do now, sire?" someone wearing a fine set of silken clothing asked quietly in the darkness. Herod turned to see the man, one of his advisors, but he couldn't remember his name. The monarchy of Talonrend had always been counseled by a small advisory group, but Herod had rarely concerned himself with such things. After all, he was never the king. With Brenning dead, the prince was in dire need of good counsel.

"I do not know, good sir," Herod responded. The earth beneath his feet shook again as another blast ripped chunks of smooth stone from the walls. The prince paused for a moment, reflecting. "That last blast," he mused, "I felt it before I heard it, right?" he asked the advisor.

"Sometimes, when things happen far away, it takes time for their sounds to reach your ears, my liege." The advisor was old, perhaps older than sixty, and spoke with a steady voice despite the fear brought on by the war. Another shockwave vibrated the stones and dirt of the marketplace and again, a loud blast followed almost immediately.

The calm and steady voice of the advisor gave way to fear in an instant. "No, sir, I fear you are correct. That blast at the wall was *not* the origin of vibration." The man moved away, staring at the ground. Slight tremors shook through the dirt floor of the marketplace faster and faster. The soldiers standing nearby readied their weapons but did not know what to do.

Herod moved his back closer to a building and shut the visor on his helmet. Panic was spreading throughout the ranks and crept its way into the prince's resolve. A large grey moth flitted through the night air, going to and from the various merchant stalls as if inspecting some hidden wares that none of the men could see. Herod thought back to his favorite afternoons he spent leaning against the parapet of Castle Talon while ducks playfully swam in the moat. The moth, a simple creature like the ducks, would never know the cruelties of war. It might be caught unaware under the vicious blast of a goblin trebuchet, but the little grey animal would not suffer. The ducks in the moat would never be tormented by the nagging worries of a siege. The moth lifted up from a wooden railing and disappeared over a rooftop, oblivious to the horror that surrounded it.

Another tremor rippled out from the center of the marketplace. The army held its breath. Prince Herod drew Maelstrom and Regret from their sheaths and steadied the rise and fall of his chest.

Herod's advisor shrieked and leapt back into the morass of gathered soldiers as the ground of the empty marketplace sank. A gaping, cavernous hole opened up and swallowed the empty wooden stalls in an instant. Shouts of panic rose up throughout the army, indicating that many such holes had appeared all over Talonrend. The prince peered into the oily darkness of the cave. He could hear movement but saw nothing. "What is it?" he heard an eager soldier call out.

"It's like..." Herod pondered, "shuffling feet? Thousands of shuffling feet..." He knew that if goblins were about to pour forth from the holes their charge would be accented by a host of battle cries. "Everyone at the ready!" he shouted and soldiers throughout the city unsheathed their weapons. A chorus of unhallowed screams rose up from the streets as the entire population of Reikall shambled up from the caves on dead legs.

"I WILL SEND you back to hell where you came from!" the giant's voice washed over the battlefield. It was late into the night and Gideon stood just a few feet taller than Terror's Lament. The small metal lantern roped around his neck was lost in the thick tangle of his braided beard. One monstrous arm pumped furiously through the horde of goblins, smashing them to pulp by the dozen. The paladin had fallen within himself to the tune of his song and the swing of his sword. Nevidal burned with a furious light, blinding all those it cut down in a plume of ragged smoke.

With two surreal leaps, Gideon cleared the distance from the rear of the goblin army to the ruined farmhouse where Taurnil stood cackling like a fiend. Using his powerful wings, Taurnil took off into the air and narrowly avoided being stomped to powder. Gideon smiled as he sang out to his god and the demon trembled. Everything trembled.

Taurnil knew that he could not stand against such a towering foe. Nevidal swept through the air like a guard tower being thrown by Vrysinoch himself. The sword, sixty feet of enchanted steel, whirled back and forth in front of the paladin, taunting Taurnil to advance.

At the command of Yael, the goblin drones stopped trying to bring down the raging behemoth and simply fled from his devastating footfalls. Tens of thousands of goblin soldiers were scattered in pieces across the battlefield for their efforts trying to stop him. For as many as he left dead in his wake, Gideon could not discern where the sea of pale faced creatures ended. Yael continued to order the retreat and save as many goblin lives as he could.

Lady Scrapple's consciousness fought to turn her siege weapons upon the giant as quickly as she could. The catapults and trebuchets loaded the largest boulders they had and fired upon Gideon. The paladin's exposed skin took hit after hit from the boulders, forcing him to block the shots with Nevidal.

Using the boulders for a distraction, Taurnil heaved glob after sticky glob of acid at the giant, but it only sizzled and evaporated from the heat of Nevidal's holy fire.

DEEP IN THE catacombs under the Artificer's Guild, Jan peered into an enchanted crystal ball. The battle was going perfectly. A smile creased the man's face as he watched his undead army destroying Talonrend from the inside. Soldiers ran through the streets in total chaos as the shambling zombies clawed at them and pulled them to the ground with overwhelming numbers. Only two sections of the battle were not going as planned.

Jan rotated the crystal scrying device and spoke a short incantation. The magical fluid locked inside the clear ball swirled and reacted, taking Jan through the battlefield and outside the massive stone walls. He looked on through the mists as Gideon, missing an arm, deflected boulders with his sword. Taurnil darted around the paladin's head and spat caustic acid everywhere he could.

"Damned demon doesn't stand a chance," Jan muttered. He didn't care about Taurnil. The abyssal monster was his sister's pet, not his. Jan swiveled the crystal ball again to get a better view of the surrounding goblins. He could see Gravlox and Vorst scampering off behind the farmhouse ruins but did not recognize them. The goblin commander was coordinating a partial retreat, moving the drone soldiers out of Nevidal's fiery reach.

Taurnil stretched his claws out wide and timed a diving strike with a shower of boulders from a goblin trebuchet stationed along the western bank of the Clawflow. The winged demon collided with the paladin seconds after spinning chunks of stone struck the man squarely in the back. Razor-sharp claws tore into the vulnerable flesh surrounding Gideon's charred stump where his left arm used to be. The demon planted his hooked talons firmly in the giant's side and scythed back and forth as quickly as he could.

Jan watched the scene with growing excitement, eager to see the holy warrior fall. With a whispered arcane phrase, he opened a tiny sliver in the night sky several yards from the giant and let a controlled portion of his magic flow through the gateway. Taurnil's lean frame bulged from the surge of potent energy and the demon's strikes became faster by the second.

With a howl of pain and anger, Nevidal came rushing in for Taurnil's body, but a well-aimed catapult shot sent a spray of sharp debris into Gideon's eyes. With only one arm, the paladin was defenseless against the stinging rocks. Another large chunk exploded against the hilt of the sword and the man stumbled. Blood flowed freely from the ragged cuts on his shoulder and side.

Jan laughed as he watched the paladin start to fall. Gideon's knees hit the ground with the force of thunder and another boulder sailed just inches above his head. Taurnil's virulent tongues twisted their way from the demon's maw and latched into the paladin's skin just below his burnt stump. Deadly poison pumped into the holy warrior and a flying stone the size of a horse crashed into his legs, nearly throwing Taurnil to the ground. The missile broke apart upon impact and spinning chunks of shattered rock tore through the unfortunate goblins nearby.

"Just kill him, finally," Jan said through a sinister grin. "I want to see him suffer and die." Jan's darkly colored robes shimmered with the sound of his voice and the necromantic runes attached to the cloth pulsed with power.

Gideon was determined not to let the evil demon have his victory. Ignoring the pain in his entire body and the deadly missiles flying through the air, Gideon slammed the heavy, flaming edge of his sword through his own side. The blade didn't cut deeply but cleaved away enough of his skin to dislodge Taurnil and send the monster haphazardly careening through the air.

"No," Jan shook his head in disbelief. "He cannot prevail!" the man shouted into his crystal ball. He pumped more of his magical energy into the winged demon and willed it to recover. Disoriented from the blow, Taurnil flapped his wings and beat the air furiously. For all of his effort and the magical augmentation from Jan, Taurnil could not right himself enough to fly.

Gideon grunted and hefted Nevidal high over his head. Jan gasped in the darkness of the catacombs under the Artificer's Guild. Yael looked on with horror as the demon was torn asunder in mid air.

An explosion of blood and necrotic magic leapt from Taurnil's smoldering corpse. Jan reached with his soul through the crystal ball. His magical essence screamed through the ethereal corridors of space and ripped open the seam Jan had created. The shimmering robes of darkness he wore pulsed with malevolence to herald the arrival of the powerful necromancer on the field of combat.

With his shining black boots pointed toward the ground, Jan descended slowly through the air, laughing all the while.

A bolt of purple magic arced from his fingertips. The magical projectile sped toward Yael and mingled with the goblin commander's being. Just as quickly as it had appeared, the magical bolt shot through the stupefied creature's mouth and into his consciousness.

The entire battlefield calmed. The drone soldiers stopped moving. They continued to breathe, but their lungs were filled by shallow, raspy breaths. Yael was alive and relatively unharmed, but his capacity to think and make decisions was rendered useless. The necromancer cackled as he felt the telepathic connections between the thousands of drones and their hive mind. The battlefield was vibrantly alive; he could practically taste the life around him. Life sickened Jan.

Gideon's huge arm flexed. He was kneeling, which placed his head somewhere around thirty feet above the ground. The two goblin rogues cowered behind a piece of fallen roof that smoldered with a remnant of Nevidal's holy energy.

Everything was eerily quiet. Nothing remained of Taurnil. After his body was rent, it disintegrated as if he had never existed at all.

The paladin's masterful sword glowed in his hand; it was hungry for the blood of evil. Jan lifted a hand casually into the air and spoke the words to an ancient incantation of beckoning. The slightest trace of dismay crossed Jan's face but he immediately suppressed the emotion. Gideon remained calm, staring into the eyes of darkness.

"I will have your soul, holy warrior," Jan spoke in an even tone. His eyes were statuesque, pitiless orbs of contempt. He repeated the words of the spell, a powerful utterance that was supposed to rip the soul from his target.

The paladin remained motionless. Gideon gazed into Jan's wicked eyes and saw no mercy there, no humanity. Jan had given himself fully to the dark magic of necromancy; the undead spells had consumed him.

Gravlox held Vorst's hand tightly as he watched the scene unfold. "I can feel his power," the shaman spoke in a hushed tone. "He is death."

"Your soul, paladin," Jan shouted with a voice of command that brought fear to everyone in earshot. "Surrender your soul!"

The small metal lantern resting underneath Gideon's immense beard slowly creaked open. Small wisps of white smoke escaped from the lantern. The ghostly flower trapped within the magical device curled through the air in front of Gideon and slowly drifted toward Jan's outstretched hand. The paladin, somewhat familiar with such powerful spells, recognized a moment of opportunity.

Gideon collapsed to his side, feigning instant death, and willed his sword to extinguish itself. The night sky swallowed the battlefield without Nevidal's flames holding the darkness at bay. Gideon landed on his left side, keeping his wide open eyes locked on the necromancer. Jan pulled the soul in with bolts of lightning and blighted pulses of energy.

The captive soul within reach, Jan closed his eyes and let out a howl of glee. Gideon didn't waste the opportunity. He lashed out with speed unexpected for his gigantic size. Nevidal cut through the air and sliced the floating soul in half. The sword drank the air and pulled the shattered soul into its steel. In an instant, Gideon returned to his normal height and build.

The transformation happened so quickly that Jan assumed the man had teleported. Outraged, Jan struck the ground with his fist and released a wave of death upon everything around him. A wall of black ash emanated from the epicenter, immersing everything in sorrow and decay.

"Hold on," Gravlox shouted, grabbing Vorst by the arm. He didn't have time to think or even breathe. The shaman reached into the realms of magic and summoned a countering wave of healing. Thick green roots erupted from the broken ground and formed a cocoon surrounding Gravlox and Vorst that protected them from Jan's torrent of death. A similar case of roots rose up to protect and heal Gideon. Seconds later, when the roots receded back into the ground, Gideon flexed his powerful left arm. Taurnil's poison had left his regenerated body. Gravlox collapsed to the ground exhausted. The shaman's vision blurred and he struggled to regain his breath. The magical effort was more taxing than anything he had ever done before.

It was Gideon's turn to laugh. Jan's wave of necrotic death slaughtered thousands of unprotected goblins for nearly a mile in every direction. The magic turned their pale skin to blackened husks, as though the goblin corpses had been rotting in the fields for weeks. Yael's decomposing skeleton stood with his rusting sword tip buried in the ground. The goblin army was broken.

Twenty-Three

MAELSTROM WOVE A beautiful song of destruction through the clawing ranks of undead.

Talonrend was in disarray, with soldiers and citizens alike dying in every street. The zombies were entirely unarmed but they felt no pain and wanted only to taste warm flesh. Families barred their doors and nailed boards over their windows, but still the horde was able to kill thousands. The sheer number of animated corpses was able to collapse whole walls and tear families apart with their disease-ridden hands.

Sweat dripped from Herod's head to mingle with the blood and flesh staining his regal armor. Soldiers had leapt to the defense of the prince as soon as the undead had appeared but it took them only moments to realize that Herod was far beyond their abilities. The shambling monsters fell to pieces as the dark tendrils of Maelstrom cut them down. Brenning's masterwork creation whistled through the air with every swipe.

"My prince!" a sentry called to Herod from across a street. The templar was wearing a set of heavy mail that showed dozens of holes and blood-stains. He clutched a battered crossbow to his chest and his eyes darted around the city as he spoke. "Men on the wall report that the zombies are being contained, but there have been heavy losses!" the man yelled. A wall next to the man began to crumble into the street. Bricks and mortar fell onto the cobblestones and three undead rushed the templar. The man lifted his broken crossbow high above his head and smashed it down on the nearest zombie's rotting skull. Decrepit bones and fetid skin flew all over the man's armor. The second zombie raked its gnarled fist against the soldier's helmet and lunged in with its remaining teeth barred.

Herod jerked his sword up and shot two thick tendrils of magic from Maelstrom's blade that ripped through the zombies and cut them to ribbons. The soldier's expression as his undead assailants broke apart was enough to make the prince laugh aloud.

"Thank you..." the startled man stuttered. "Thank you, my liege."

"Have you heard any news from the gate-house? What of Master Brenning?" Herod sprinted across the broken street to meet the soldier. "What news of the goblins?" he shouted into the man's face.

The soldier straightened and dropped his crossbow down by his side. "The goblins have pulled back. The market sector is ruined, they over-ran it, sir."

"I know, son, I know." Herod patted a hand on the young man's shoulder. "I was in the market when it happened. Has there been any news of Mas-ter Brenning?" he asked again.

The soldier hesitated, giving Herod all the an-swer he needed. "We haven't heard anything yet, sir." Both of their heads hung low.

"You've done well," the prince said, trying to repair the man's confidence. "There must be another attack coming. Spread the word to regroup at the gatehouse, inside the walls."

"Yes sir," the soldier replied.

"For Talonrend!" Herod shouted as he took off down the street.

The area around the gate was consumed by chaos. Fires still smoldered everywhere the prince looked. Bloody parts of men and zombies alike were scattered all over the cobblestone and one particularly garish bloodstain on the stone wall made the man shudder. A hole the size of a small house had opened up almost directly in front of the gatehouse. Few soldiers remained near the site and they were all leaning against the walls clutching at various wounds. Three men in fine armor lay dead, riddled with infected cuts and bite marks.

Herod could see a face peering over the top of the wall in his direction. "What of the goblins?" the prince shouted up to him.

"It seems that we have won the night, sir," the man called back in a hoarse voice. He had been shouting commands and relaying information all night.

"I need to see it," the prince said. He made his way past the line of wounded soldiers to the nearest door that would take him inside Terror's Lament. After the long trek up the spiral staircase to the top, the prince was winded. His regal armor was made from solid steel plates emblazoned with the emblems of the city. The plates were certainly effective, but also restrictively heavy. Herod clutched at the burn on his side, a painful reminder of the moment when his armor had failed him.

"You're hurt, my liege," was the first thing Herod heard when he reached the cool air of the top.

Standing up as straight as he could manage, Herod waved off the observation. "It's nothing, trust me," he said. "Now, show me this retreat."

The soldier was a burly man, young but well-muscled, and sporting a healthy beard under his helmet's chinstrap. There was a small shield strapped to his back. The man turned to lead the prince to a tower at the corner of Terror's Lament. Herod noticed a crude goblin arrow lodged between the iron banding of the soldier's shield. The prince nodded his appreciation of the man's mettle and followed him to the tower.

A telescope was mounted next to a large ballista inside the square tower. Half a dozen archers stood inside the tower, scanning the dark horizon for any signs of attack. "There used to be some sort of light out there, but we could never tell what it was," one of the archers said.

Herod peered through the lens of the brass telescope. "Bah, it's too dark. This is useless." He moved away from the scope frustrated.

"Light up the sky for your prince, men," the guard with the shield barked. Herod put his eye back to the lens with a smile. A series of twelve flaming arrows, fired two at a time, lit up the night sky brilliantly.

Herod was breathless. He shook his head and used his thumb to wipe the lens before placing his eye against it again. "Fire another round," he said softly.

More fiery arrows arced through the air and cast light all over the battlefield. "Everything is dead..." the prince muttered in disbelief. "They are all just... dead."

"Yes, my prince," the guard responded. "We don't know what happened, but some of the goblins have retreated back across the river, and the rest of them have simply fallen over dead." He scratched his beard ponderously.

"Fire one more round," Herod said to the guard. More arrows illuminated the night as the prince gazed through the telescope. "There, a clearing, something is happening there." He pointed to the spot on the battlefield but the soldiers inside the tower couldn't see. "Gideon!" Herod shouted with excitement. He could just barely see the champion's form in the flickering light. His excitement quickly turned to dismay. "Jan," his voice dripped with malice.

The prince pounded his fist into the stone of the tower and spun. "Lift the portcullis," he commanded. Without another word, the prince ripped open the door to the spiral staircase and flew down the steps.

The steel portcullis creaked slowly up on heavy chains. Breathing heavily, Herod darted under the portcullis and shouted back to the tower for it to be closed. The prince leaned over his knees to catch his breath. He unstrapped the leather bindings of his greaves and let them drop to the ground. His breastplate and gloves followed. Herod kept his helmet seated firmly upon his head and took off again toward the clearing in the battlefield.

GIDEON ROSE FROM his crouch on the ground and stood to his normal height. He lifted his sword in his hand and smiled as he slid it into the leather sheath on his back. His hand released from the hilt for the first time in days.

Gravlox and Vorst climbed out from behind their place among the rubble to stand next to the paladin. Jan took a few hesitant steps backward, unsure of how to strike against them. Apart from his sister Keturah, he had never met another spell caster able to withstand his magic. The goblin shaman not only surprised him with his power, Gravlox inspired fear in the empty space where Jan's heart should have been.

The necromancer spread his arms out in front of him and pulled at the magical tendrils of the corpses scattered in the grass. Bones broke through the rotted skin and floated through the air to hover about Jan's body. With a flick of his wrist, the bones jolted and spun, forming a whirling barrier of pale bone around him.

Gravlox reached down and plucked a small shard of magnesium from the dirt. It was a sharp piece of metal and rock that had shattered against Gideon's back. He held the rock in his hands and beckoned to it with his natural, magical spirit. The magnesium responded, alive with energy.

Gravlox hurled the shard toward the spinning bone armor surrounding the necromancer and willed it to ignite. A spark flew from Gravlox's outstretched hand and struck the magnesium shard just as it hit the bones and burst into flame.

Jan responded quickly, jumping back and dousing the armor in a thick fog of black magic. Jan felt the heat from the explosion singe his skin but quickly dissipate. He could sense that Gravlox was only testing him. Jan thrust his hands forward, blasting the smothering fog toward the shaman and his companions.

Gideon stepped forward and the holy symbol etched into his back flared with life. He arched his neck and screeched, sending a bright splash of holy magic into the air that quickly dissolved the evil fog.

At an impasse, Gravlox and Vorst stood beside the paladin and measured Jan. His black robes shimmered in the dancing firelight that dotted the scene.

"Be gone!" Jan shouted, twirling and sending forth a purple skull from his chest. The magical cantrip cackled as it flew toward the three. Small slivers of lightning bounced around the skull, sizzling the air.

"We have to run," Vorst said, clearly panicked. She turned on her heels to retreat but Gravlox caught her arm.

"It isn't real," he growled to her, trying not to break his mental concentration.

The magical skull was followed immediately by a beam of dark energy filled with sharp fragments of bone. Gideon knocked the goblins to the ground and the beam passed harmlessly over their heads.

The paladin grabbed a throwing axe from his belt and looked to Gravlox. "Time the attack," he whispered, and Vorst tapped the message's translation. The paladin rushed over the rubble of the farmhouse, ducking and dodging bolts of necrotic magic the whole way.

Vorst scampered parallel to Gideon, making her way through the debris. Jan pumped his arms furiously, covering the area with suppressive fire. The bones continued to swirl around his black robes. Gravlox dropped to the ground and pushed his hands through the dirt and stone. He could feel the depletion of his energy but knew he had to press on. A thick pillar of jagged earth sprang up under the necromancer, threatening to impale him.

Without a moment of hesitation, Jan summoned a magical gust of wind that lifted him above the pillar and out of harm's reach. Gideon launched his axe perfectly. The weapon spun end over end directly for Jan's head. Vorst launched herself up at the necromancer's feet at the same moment.

Jan pushed himself higher and the bone wall protected him, morphing into a rounded sphere that easily deflected the axe. Vorst landed a hit on the top of Jan's black boot and her tiny dagger bit through the soft leather easily and protruded out the bottom of Jan's boot. A fast-moving bone knocked her in the head as Jan continued to levitate higher. Vorst had to let go of her blade in order to avoid being dragged too high into the air. She tucked and hit the ground hard, but was altogether unharmed.

"Get back!" Gravlox shouted through his weariness. With his flawless vision he could see the outline of Herod charging into the fight. Like a taskmaster whipping his slave, Herod slashed with Maelstrom. The dark tendrils broke through Jan's bone wall as easily as if the barrier were made of thin paper. Jan yelped, feeling the sting of the black tendrils wrapping around his waist. Unable to understand Gravlox's warning, Gideon assumed that the black tendrils connecting Jan and the prince were some form of evil instigated by the necromancer. He snatched another axe from his belt and chopped down on the ethereal bands as hard as he could. Gideon stole a glance over his shoulder and saw Herod but did not understand.

The prince growled in frustration as Maelstrom's tendrils evaporated into dust.

Jan laughed hysterically. The magical swirl of wind carried Jan higher and higher into the smoke-filled air. "So," he bellowed, "the fearless leader has come out from his castle to play!"

Herod grasped the hilt of Maelstrom firmly, watching the necromancer ascend. He lashed out with the blade again and again, tearing chunks of Jan's bone armor from the sky. The blood-red blade pulsed with every swing, drinking in the violence and loving each drop. Jan responded to the repeated attacks by sending forth a ripple of decaying magic. The spell crashed into Herod's unarmored chest and sent him sprawling to the ground. He frantically clutched and scraped at the wound in his side. The cut he suffered earlier was starting to rot and fester. Necromantic energy coursed through his body and filled his blood with disease.

With a great sigh filled with pain and acrimony, the prince returned Maelstrom to its sheath on his hip and slowly moved his hand over his other sword's hilt. His eyes clouded over when he drew Regret. The blade, forged by Master Brenning in the renowned Blood Foundry, reflected the shimmering fires of the battlefield off its translucent edge. Regret had a deep blue hue, like a crystal with flecks of gold suspended in its matrix.

The sword was weightless. Had Herod released his fingers from the hilt, the blade would not have fallen an inch. "Brenning," the prince murmured to the sword, "if only you were here…" Herod moved the weapon slowly through the air, watching the myriad array of colors scattering over the ground. The hilt was made from the same crystalline material as the blade; the entire weapon had been crafted from the same piece of wondrous material.

When the blade moved, even slowly, it was nearly impossible to track. Gravlox watched the prince testing Regret and was mesmerized. The sword seemed to disappear when it was in motion but reappeared instantly when it was still.

"You should see this, Brenning," Herod spoke to the night. "Truly, you have outdone even your high standards." The prince locked eyes with Jan, his former servant and trusted friend, and found his strength.

He gritted his teeth and charged. Jan, still hovering high above the ruined field, rained down a shower of sulfuric fire that engulfed the entire area. Evil winds blew through the rotted corpses and tossed bones into the air. Gideon had to brace himself to keep from being blown over. Vorst held onto Gravlox tightly and the pair ducked into a crater to avoid being picked up by the storm.

If the swirling torrent of death had any effect on the stalwart prince, he did not show it. Running at a fast pace, Herod swung Regret downward as he neared the hovering necromancer. Some unseen force vaulted the prince high into the air, higher than Jan, and held him there for a breath. The deep blue sword reappeared in his hand and throbbed with energy. Blue and gold sparks flew in every direction from the blade to join the magical storm.

Gideon tried to watch the action far above his head but the violent winds made his eyes water and obscured his vision. Impossibly fast, Herod vanished with his blade and reappeared behind the necromancer. In the blink of an eye, the prince materialized a dozen times at various angles all around Jan's form. Before Gideon had the time to bring a hand up to his face to shield himself from the storm, the winds stopped. Everything stopped.

Dull black robes drifted lazily to the ground. Herod stood up in the midst of the rubble as though he had been crouching there forever. Maelstrom and Regret were both secured within their sheaths. The prince stretched his back and yawned, physically exhausted.

"It is time that we return to Talonrend, Gideon." Herod said calmly to the holy warrior who stared at him slack-jawed.

"My liege, Master Brenning said he would return to the city when the fighting first started. Where is he?" Gideon's voice trembled. The carnage all around him was a grim omen of what he would find on the other side of the high walls.

Herod shook his head. He couldn't look Gideon in the eyes or speak past the lump in his throat.

"He was a good man," Gideon said softly. He pointed to the location where Gravlox and Vorst were hiding. "Those two goblins saved his life. Actually, they saved my life as well." The paladin walked toward the crater and helped the two goblins climb out.

Horribly mispronouncing their names, Gideon attempted to introduce Gravlox and Vorst to Herod. "We both friends," Vorst said as she held Gravlox's hand and giggled. "We both friends of humans."

Herod shook his head, not knowing what to believe. He had seen enough in the last few hours to open his mind to any possibilities.

"Gravlox is shaman," she said happily in her high pitched goblin voice. "Both friends."

Looking to Gideon for some kind of explanation, Herod could only guess the answers to his questions. "You are telling me that these two *goblins* saved your life and saved Master Brenning?"

The paladin nodded. "I'm sure we will have plenty of time to go over the details once everything is back to normal." His eyes surveyed the battlefield and the heavily damaged walls. "Well," he continued, "once everything is normal enough."

Herod thought back to the golden shield and the promise he had made to his army concerning the revered smith. *You will never be king*, Vrysinoch gently echoed in the back of his mind. *You will never sit upon your brother's throne.*

Epilogue

CROWS CAME FROM miles around. Thousands upon thousands of goblin skeletons covered the fields from Talonrend to the banks of the Clawflow. To the north of Terror's Lament, a large plot of land had been cleared and excavated and now served as a mass grave for all of the human dead. After the first plot had been filled with corpses, a pyre had been constructed to burn the rest of the bodies.

The city behind the walls was eerily quiet. A heavy shroud of death clung to the shattered houses and storefronts. Loads of stone and dirt were being carted into Talonrend to fill the gaping holes that dotted the streets.

The royal bedchamber inside Castle Talon was draped with thin wisps of silken cloth and windows had been cut in the stone walls. Servants stood beside the windows with fans, moving fresh air through the room to cool the prince. Herod's wound festered.

The prince wasn't weak and frail like a dying man should have been. His heart was strong and his stubborn spirit was stronger. Still, the disease spread through his body. His skin radiated heat like a blazing forge.

Gideon kneeled at the prince's side and prayed to Vrysinoch for healing. He could feel the intricate web of magic connecting the world around him, but no matter where he searched, he could not find even the slightest shred of mercy.

"Sir," the paladin said softly, "the shaman, Gravlox...." Gideon pulled the sheet back slowly from the prince's side and looked at the garish burn. The necromancer's spell had ravaged the open wound. Rags were piled beneath the weeping cut to catch the putrid ooze.

"I will not have a *goblin* walking freely in my city!" Herod shouted. His voice was full of life that contradicted his body's decay.

"Herod, look at yourself! You will die if you stay like this." He hung his head in frustration. "He can heal you. The paladins have tried to save you; I have tried to save you, Gravlox... Just let him try." He beat his hands into the white sheets of the bed.

"It is only your word, Gideon, which has spared those two goblins from the end of a noose. They will rot in the dungeon for eternity before I let either of them put their filthy hands on me!" Spittle flew from the prince's mouth. His vivid animation sent a fresh wave of puss and blood out of his side to splatter the sheets.

The paladin closed his eyes and thought about the dungeon beneath Castle Talon. Although no one besides official templars were permitted to visit the underground cells, Gideon had done so unchallenged. With Herod in no condition to physically stop him, Gideon's reputation afforded him many privileges that his lack of rank otherwise denied him. *Gravlox could easily escape that cell*, Gideon thought to himself. *He has power far beyond anything I have ever seen.*

Gideon rose up from his knees slowly and shook the memory of Gravlox's cell from his head. "Then it will be your death," he said to the prince. Gideon pushed through the white silk and exited the room without so much as glancing over his shoulder.

DEEP INSIDE THE dark labyrinth of Kanebullar Mountain, Lady Scrapple's rage consumed her. Goblin servants entered her chambers timidly. More than half of them ended as a red stain on the stone walls. Her thick, root-like appendages flailed wildly, splattering anything unfortunate enough to get caught in their path.

Dozens of pulsating arms spread through the mountain, rapidly replenishing the goblin army. She was evolving and adapting, lengthening the gestation period of her spawn to create taller and more muscular underlings.

Lady Scrapple's vast consciousness flew over the miles from Kanebullar Mountain to Talonrend. She prodded, searching the emptiness of space for any shred of Vorst's mind that she could latch onto and devour. The edges of Vorst's mind appeared like bright tongues of flame in a world of darkness. Lady Scrapple could feel the goblin and pushed her mental powers to their limits. Vorst's vibrant fire fought back against the intrusion with such solidarity that the Mistress of the Mountain was forced to retreat. She seethed in her mountain lair and vowed a thousand times to kill Vorst. The matriarch managed a grim smile as she imagined tearing Vorst limb by limb and feeding her to a pack of wild dogs.

WIND HOWLED OVER the opening to a solitary cave nestled just below the snow line of an unnamed mountain north of Talonrend. The icy waters of a gentle stream trickled from an elevated lake before meandering to the plains and joining the Clawflow. A tall creature with thick fur covering his well-built torso drank from the stream before returning to his cave.

The minotaur sat just inside the cave opening, basking in the soothing heat of the fire behind him. His black, beady eyes watched with great interest as a clan of orcs steadily marched through a valley not far from his cave. They carried a great banner ahead of them, draped in furs and painted with blood.

"The Wolf Jaw clan," the minotaur growled with a raspy voice. He knew the orcs well. "The whole Wolf Jaw clan…" Several hundred of the cruel orcs, the entirety of the clan, marched south.

On a normal day, the minotaur would have pounded his fists into the cave wall to summon his own clan and slaughter the orcs. The horned beast hated everything that didn't belong to his own clan. But this was not a normal day. With a shake of his heavy head, the minotaur turned back into the cave. Oil dripped from the goblin slowly rotating on a spit above the flames. Goblin meat didn't taste particularly good, but the minotaur was hungry and nothing wandered into his cave without suffering repercussions.

There was an open scroll held to the ground with rocks sitting in front of the roasting creature. The various tribes and clans of the snowy mountains rarely welcomed visitors and never entertained emissaries. Minotaurs spoke a gruff language that was seldom written, but the runes inscribed on the scroll were clear. For what felt like the hundredth time since the goblin had wandered into his cave that morning, the minotaur read the scroll. *Gather your clan. Talonrend will fall.*

THE ADVENTURE CONTINUES IN
PART TWO OF
THE GOBLIN WARS,

DEATH OF A KING

AVAILABLE NOW.

ABOUT THE AUTHOR

Born and raised in Cincinnati, Ohio, Stuart Thaman graduated from Hillsdale College with degrees in politics and German, and has since sworn off life in the cold north. Now comfortably settled in Kentucky, he lives with his lovely wife, a rambunctious Boston terrier named Yoda, and two cats who probably hate him. When not writing, he enjoys smoking cigars, acquiring bruises in mosh pits, and preparing for the end of the world.

Interested in contact?
Please direct all emails to
stuartthaman@gmail.com

Want to stay current with all the latest news?
Check out www.stuartthamanbooks.com